THE ART OF REDEMPTION THE

THE ART OF REDEMPTION

Also by Bob Truluck

Street Level (2000)
Saw Red (2003)

HAHAHAHA

THE ART OF REDEMPTION

A Novel

Bob Truluck

Dennis McMillan Publications
2007

The Art of Redemption by Robert O. Truluck,
copyright © 2007. All rights reserved.

Disclaimer

FIRST EDITION
Published July 2007

Dustjacket and interior artwork by
Michael Kellner.

ISBN 978-0-939767-56-4

Dennis McMillan Publications
4460 N. Hacienda del Sol, Guest House
Tucson, Arizona 85718 Tel. (520)-529-6636
email: dennismcmillan@aol.com
website: http://www.dennismcmillan.com

*This one's for my peeps. You make it more
than it is. Thanks for hanging in there, keeping
the faith, digging eloquent profanity.*

If God were omnipotent and omniscient in any literal sense, he wouldn't have bothered to make the universe at all. There is no success where there is no possibility of failure, no art without the resistance of the medium.

—— from *Playback* by Raymond Chandler

Well, you know I need a steam shovel, mama,
        to keep away the dead.
Need a dump truck, baby,
        to unload my head.

—— from "From a Buick 6," by Bob Dylan

[1]

The Mexican pilot wasn't bad. He dropped the big Boeing on the wet tarmac like it was something he did all the time.

Jimmy Cotton made some vague hand jive at the boss sky waitress. She nodded.

The seat belt light was still on, the plane still moving, but slowly. The attendant says, in Spanish, over the speaker, how everyone needed to stay seated until notified.

Some grumbles. Jimmy got up, grabbed his bag, grabbed a stuffed monkey. The plane jolted to a stop.

Anna was asleep on her seat. Jimmy collected her and she roused.

"Where's Mama, Crazy Jimmy?"

Seven. Impressionable. Only pretty much everyone in Cuba she saw said Jimmy was crazy. *Loco Norte Americano.* Walked in, demanded the girl.

Got her. Got her quick. Got her home quick—looked like.

"End of the walkway, peanut. Hang on."

Anna buried her head in Jimmy's neck, maybe crying. Said: "Hurry, Crazy Jimmy."

Jimmy hurried. Bum rushed the family. Hug mama. Hug some *tías,* shake some *tíos'* hands.

He said bye. His father lay ill and dying. Had to run. So sorry.

It was a lie. His father was thirty-five years dead.

1

[2]

Hospitals seem to keep it waiting at the door to remind you where you are. Death and dying, the septic stench of sickness. Jimmy moved through the unencouraging atmosphere to a room with an open door.

Joe Ready lay on his back on a bed. Sheet to chest, arms folded, tubes lying around. He looked a little like some forgotten marionette.

Jimmy found a metal chair no one had wasted many non-utilitarian issues on, slid it over, and sat.

The silence megaphoned Joe's steady breath. Jimmy could hear his own.

He sat back, put an ankle on a knee, watched the old man.

Eyelids fluttered, and cool ageless blue eyes took in some ceiling.

"What's up, Joe?"

A deep breath like dry corn husks rustling. "How you doing, kid?"

"Better'n you, *viejo.*"

"Yeah. You and everybody else still breathing." Pause to breathe. "Looks like I lied about making that century."

Jimmy nodded. "Yeah. I was just thinking about that."

The fatalism in the words jumped up and shouted.

"Who knows, Joe?"

The silence was dainty like dancing elephants are dainty.

"Nah, kid, this is it. I feel it inside. I still got the juice to do it; my body don't, though."

More elephant silence.

"You find the kid?"

"Yeah." Jimmy watched the side of Joe's face. He was old.

"She okay?"

"Yeah. She was in Cuba with her pop."

"The one everyone kept insisting was dead?"

"You called it."

"Yeah, well that don't exactly make me Jean Dixon, baby." A small silence. "It was good, wasn't it, kid?"

"What's that, Joe?"

"The run. Me and you."

"Great. I'm glad I threw in with you." Joe's term. One from the old days.

He'd mentioned something about how they'd thrown in together back in the seventies. Truth was Jimmy'd thrown in with Joe Ready.

The dry chuckle. "I got you, didn't I? The first time? Got you good, huh?"

"Yeah you did, Joe. Took me to school." Jimmy grinned at the memory. He could grin now. When it happened, it wasn't funny a little.

"You been set up since?"

"No." Not even close to that.

Joe turned his head a bit. He still couldn't see Jimmy.

"Tell me about it, kid. And, for God's sake, put this fucking bed up; bring your chair around so's I can see you. Goddam, lemme die with a little dignity."

Jimmy moved his chair, pushed some buttons on a plastic box to bring Joe more upright, and sat.

Joe Ready's eyes looked at him and smiled. They were the same eyes that smiled at him thirty-odd back when Jimmy met him.

"Where you want me to start? Woodstock?" Jimmy was being funny.

The Art of Redemption

Joe moved a parchment hand. "Fuck Woodstock. Start some-where just before I came in. Set me up here. Okay—start with your lucky number, Kent State, that shit."

Jimmy nodded. Joe closed his eyes, a hand palsied, and he could have been asleep.

Jimmy spoke slowly and directly at Joe. He watched Joe, watched Joe's temple pulse under the parchment skin.

[3]

Lucky break—a three hundred fifty-three outta three sixty-six; Jimmy's roomie pulls a three. The guy was good as gone. Could even get drafted into the freaking Marines. The roomie started talking options: Air Force, Navy, reserves—the six-year dodge. Only psychos *joined* the Marines, right? Canada? Europe? Mexico? The guy skied out for Amsterdam and Jimmy never saw him again.

Winter session, 1969. A cold fucking December in Ohio, the wind whipping off that godforsaken lake. The draft lottery was all there was right then. Luck up, luck down, too close to call. Depended on your number. The number was everything.

Then March and some gunfire, Jimmy right there in it. People going down. Screams, panic. Jimmy ran. Kept running. Up the stairs to his apartment, packed his shit, put it in his car. On the road.

Twenty-one, unencumbered and just about clueless.

Went to his sister's in Atlanta. Her husband was an officer in the Guard there. He and Jimmy didn't share many warm moments, Jimmy sure the guy'd change his tune his guard unit got called active.

The second Atlanta Pop Festival was going on down the road, a place an exit sign called Byron. Jimmy drifted down, did some real good acid and some real bad acid, lost his car for three days.

Got to see Hendrix do Star Spangled Banner ten months before he croaked in London. Man played the song with his dick. Turned the fucking guitar around and strummed it with his dick.

Jimmy found his car, flushed out the road trash that had commandeered it—two guys and a girl.

They asked for a ride. Jimmy asked which way they were going. They must have seen his Kent State sticker—one of them said *Cincinnati.*

South it was. He put the fried, untidy trio in his rearview. Did some more I-75 south.

A bit of Daytona, a bit of Lauderdale, and his last two bucks worth of gas put Jimmy at his mom's condo in West Palm Beach. Oceanside, ground floor. Old fucks. Boredom. Masturbation. No drugs.

Then he met some kids at the park, got laid, stoned, and connected in an afternoon. Life was at least tolerable again. But for the boredom. Big, unhandy pieces of the stuff.

Jimmy tried a couple of times to explain it to his mom, why he was done with school for awhile. She'd look bewildered, reminding Jimmy how his father had expressly stated that Jimmy should finish school. Jimmy'd remind his mom how his dad had died and really wasn't around to discuss it, was he?

"I feel like your father's still very much around."

"Mom, that's creepy. Dad's dead. Gone. Finis."

Which would get him the mom-stare. Usually, it got him an additional: "Why are you so angry, Jimmy? Your father didn't choose to die."

That's where she'd lose Jimmy. He'd walk out the slider, close it behind him, and fire up a big doobie. Then, usually, Jimmy would hear the glass door move on its rollers and a conversation would ensue like:

"Jimmy, I'd rather you did that in your bedroom than out here." "Why's that, Mom?" "Someone might call the police." "For smoking a joint?" "You don't know my neighbors."

Yeah, Jimmy did know her neighbors. He thought.

• • •

Similar and recurring episode number whatever, Mom closed the slider; Jimmy relaxed into the metal chair, as much as anyone can relax into a metal chair, and watched the sun bounce off the ocean. He'd nabbed an ounce of Jamaican collie, pulled out the few buds one actually got in those days of leaf-and-stem marijuana merchandising. Rolled the seeds out on a Stones' album cover—*Beggars' Banquet*—twisted a joint, a big fat-bellied number that looked like a guppy. He took a good healthy pull, exhaled into the muggy morning.

A few tokes into the doob a voice in the hedge separating the patios said: "You don't bring that over here and share it, *I'll* be the one calls the cops on you."

Jimmy locked up mid-toke. He blew smoke out silently.

"Kid, I know you can hear me. I can hear you moving around over there. Want I should call the cops?"

Jimmy grinned, puffed the joint back to life. "No, not really."

He got up, carried the guppy joint around the hedge. Finally unbored, grinning about it.

Around the hedge was a mirror image of his mom's place. A cast-iron patio set distantly related to his mom's was scattered loosely here and there where hers sat at ordered ready—Mom's chairs tucked in neatly, her sandbag ashtrays clean.

A couple of cushioned wicker chairs were at this table. The plastic cushions were a tangle of jungle-life and not too un-tacky. The sun wasn't being any more kind to the chairs than anything else in Florida—they were becoming pale versions of the original.

In one of the chairs a man sat, elbows on the enameled tin top of the table. He could have been fifty or seventy. Jimmy couldn't tell.

He looked like he'd been around but his crisp blue eyes went ageless on you. He was in good shape; strong legs coming from

7

big Bermuda shorts; tan, strong arms coming from one of those four pocket Cuban shirts, this one pale blue. High cheekbones, well-drawn schnozz, a smiling mouth with thin lips—the smile telling you nothing.

A pork-pie hat, one of the cheap ones you could get at the straw market in the Bahamas, sat high on his head. The hair, what the hat left for display, was fine and gray and cropped close to the guy's head.

On the table lay a newspaper, a large sandbag ashtray with a plaid base. A big green cigar as long as an arm smoldered in the ashtray. Two well-rolled joints lay beside another unburned cigar.

Jimmy babied the joint, passed it to the pork-pie hat. The hat knew what to do with it, did it. Puffed the cigar to life and blew the smoke after the reefer cloud.

"You need to learn to smoke cigars, kid." The guy nibbled at the joint again, chased it with cigar smoke. Passed it back to Jimmy.

Jimmy took his turn; his eyes drifting to the two hand-mades on the table.

"You roll your own cigarettes?"

"Not usually." The guy was enjoying this. Maybe he was more bored than Jimmy was.

Jimmy nodded, passed the joint back. "That reefer?" A point to the joints.

"Yeah." The guy worked the doob, readjusted his pinch on it, toked, passed. Exhale, then, "Joe Joseph." No attempted handshake.

"Jimmy Cotton."

"Yours smelled better'n mine."

"What?"

"Your herb. Smells better'n mine. You were wondering why I got two reefers laying here but I still call you over—yours smells better."

Jimmy inspected the joint-now-roach, took a last puff, lips

8

dainty and fretful that close to the ember. Dropped the roach in the ashtray, said, "It's bud. All bud," through tight lips holding onto that last toke.

Joseph nodded. "You know, you use a little leaf, a little bud, you're smoking decent shit longer?"

Jimmy shrugged. "How come I never smelled you over here burning one? The cigar?" Jimmy recalled sometimes smelling cigar smoke in the mornings.

"Yeah. And I smoke when you do. Anybody matters snoops around, takes a whiff, there your young ass is, I'm home free." The grin.

Jimmy gave him back one, spiced it with a little head wag.

"So my moving in was a lucky break for you."

Joseph shrugged out some dunno. "We'll see, kid." He picked up a joint from the table, inspected it, used a gold Zippo one handed to fire it off.

Joseph's nose wrinkled. "Tastes like shit after your tops."

It wasn't as pungent as the select stuff Jimmy brought to the party, but it was righteous. They shared it silently, Joe Joseph pouring Cuban tobacco smoke after the reefer smoke.

The new joint went brown then died. It was discarded next to the earlier version of Jimmy's; Joseph said, "What you doing with your life besides bugging your mom?"

Jimmy shrugged.

"You dumping school for good?"

Jimmy looked at Joseph. "You put a glass to the wall, listen in?"

Joseph grinned, jerked a thumb. "Thin hedges, big ears. What can I say?"

Jimmy got okay, shrugged out, "Right now, yeah."

That floated around. The dependable wind off the Atlantic didn't want it. Nothing wanted it.

"Everybody's gotta have something they do, baby."

"My something got kinda screwed up. I was gonna get my degree, move to Africa, save the world."

More silence.

"So what happened, kid?"

Jimmy figured Joseph knew already, but tossed out one more shrug, said, "Africa's going to hell."

"And you're not sure the rest of the world ain't right behind it. Right?"

"Right on."

Quiet.

"How'd that shit up at Kent State make you feel?"

Jimmy got funny eyebrows.

"Your mom's prouder of you than you think. She talks about you."

Funny—Jimmy had never heard any mention of his mom knowing this guy

And no one else had asked how it felt. "A kid not four feet away took one in the head. It sounded like you slapped a pumpkin with a baseball bat. The kid fell over and blood spurted out like nothing I'd ever seen, like a water fountain or something." Saying it out loud felt funny, maybe felt good.

"What were you thinking? At the time?"

Another odd question.

"I was glad as hell I wasn't standing four feet in his direction."

This seemed to satisfy Joseph on the subject.

"You retired, Mr. Joseph?"

"It's Joe, and sorta kinda." No more to add.

"What was your something, Joe? When you weren't kinda sorta retired."

Joseph had the blue eyes pointed at the sea, but Jimmy didn't think he was seeing it.

"Different shit, kid. Mostly I found people who got stolen."

"You were a cop?" A grin and the tone to say Jimmy didn't believe it.

"No. Well—yeah, a long time ago. Forty years ago."

Jimmy didn't know where to go with that.

Joseph said: "That whole school up there, there was nothing interested you? I mean besides booze and pussy?"

Jimmy grinned. The old guy was a trip. "Declared journalism this year."

"You gonna pursue it?"

The shrug. "Whadda I got to write about? I'm twenty-one years old, live off my mom. I'd just be another dumb sounding hack. Another vicarious tough-guy doesn't know what the shit he's talking about."

"Never stopped Hemingway."

"Nor Steinbeck either."

Swapped grins.

"Tell you what, kid, lemme think about something. Maybe I got a story or two you could use. You want a little something to get you on beyond vicarious—" a head bobble, "—maybe I got something could get you there."

[4]

Jimmy left all smiles. He'd cruised through some of his mom's drinkie-poo parties, heard the old wrinkle-sacks bullshitting the ladies. They were worse than junior high kids, the lives and lies they built from rarefied air. This guy was more of the same— full of shit.

Yeah, he had an extra spark, but still: interesting people don't live in West Palm Beach. The guy must have been a hell of a salesman at one time.

• • •

A few days, Jimmy had all but forgotten the meet. Through the hedge: "Hey, kid, you over there?"

"Yeah."

"Whatcha burning? The garbage?"

Jimmy had scored a matchbox of some pretty nasty reefer. It smelled like fish but tasted more like chicken shit when you scorched it. He'd be smoking better but the fifty bucks his mom had fronted him was thinning.

"You got better?"

"You know I do."

Jimmy went over and Joe proved it.

"Where you get stuff like this?"

Joe looked at the perfect joint like the country of origin could be written on the wrapper. "A guy I know up the asphalt a ways." Joe adjusted the hat of the day, a flat crowned straw so frail the wind would bend the wide brim occasionally.

"Where?"

"Savannah."

"What's in Savannah?"

Joe killed the roach against the aluminum side of the ashtray, hit the stogie a couple of deep ones. "Shipyards." A glance, a puff. "You don't know shit, do you, kid?"

Jimmy could feel the blood gushing up his neck, his ears popping. He caught the anger. Credited it to residuals from last night.

He'd scored four Mexican Quaaludes at the park yesterday. Mexican 'ludes being cheap imitations of Rohrers—worn-out presses with blurred stampings. Half the kick of the original version, but four of them and a bottle of Annie Greensprings would knock the right angles off a Mondrian. "No. I don't know shit."

"That what makes you so mad? Not knowing shit? Don't know what to do with your life. Don't know where to cop decent reefer. Didn't even know where your mom's condo was last night for a few minutes. What *do* you know, Jimmy Cotton?"

"I know just because my old man's dead, I don't necessarily need a new daddy figure. But, hey, man, thanks for the offer. I need advice, I'll know where to come."

Jimmy was standing, shoving the wicker chair back; Joe was saying: "Sit the fuck down—stop acting silly."

Joe's eyes went pale. He didn't look old. He looked like he'd kick your ass. Jimmy sat.

Joe composed himself. The smile didn't return; the eyes stayed pale. "No offer was being made. I ain't looking for a kid to raise. You stumble around, acting like a dumb ass, embarrassing your mom in front a her peers. Hanging out at that fucking park

13

with the other riff-raff hangs out there. Fuck, kiddo, no wonder nobody feels sorry for you. You get in their way doing it yourself. I point out how you're being stupid and you get all red about it. Makes me think you ain't so happy about it." Pause. "How am I doing?"

Silence, then: "Pretty good." Silence, then: "My mom's embarrassed?"

"Yeah. In an amused, kids-these-days sorta way. I didn't say she was ashamed of you, which is what you're thinking. There's a difference."

"Yeah. Sure there is."

Joe laughed. "Boo-fucking-hoo. Whadda you expect? You cutting up like you are, she's gonna be proud?"

Jimmy made a sound like a moan. Or a groan. His head wobbled in a few wide, erratic arcs. "You're a trip, old man."

"Yeah? And what's Jimmy Cotton?"

"Nobody knows."

The eyes were sparkling again. "Time somebody found out. You wanna hear some stories?"

Jimmy shrugged. Why not? "Sure. What kinda stories we listening to?"

"I'll start you off on one you heard some about. I got the skinny though, baby."

[5]

George Kelly—or Barnes, whichever you prefer—had horrible sinuses. Allergies so bad his wife Kathryn couldn't wear even the mildest cologne.

Shame, too. A woman as good looking as Kathryn Kelly should have smelled like Paris. She damn sure looked like Paris.

I'd met them both, George and Kathryn, at a poker table in Kansas City. Was looking for someone else at the time and was impressed by neither the man nor the novelty surrounding him. The woman I was.

Could have bedded her, I guess.

George was making goo-goo at the chippie I was using for cover, Kathryn steaming. She bailed the poker game and went out on the hotel's balcony.

I took a stretch and a piss, ambled out to mess up the night's air with a ready-roll. Kathryn was still out there, still fuming.

She had a few choice items to unload about the quality of my companion. I told her I couldn't agree more—I was a private dick outta LA doing some snooping, needed a foil. The chippie I'd hired was what a sawbuck got you in KC.

I got a Betty Grable, then a Bette Davis.

"Not after me and Machine Gun I hope."

"No, dear. I'd not have told you anything if I was. I'da had you. I'm chasing a kike name a Pearlie Friedman. Know him?"

15

"What's it worth?"

I shrugged. "The man who wants him wants him so bad he's leaking dollar signs."

She laughed. "I've seen him around some, but we don't mix with that crowd much."

"Who do you mix with, sweetheart?" Got the laugh. It wasn't a bad laugh.

She told me I wasn't hard to look at, drifted inside, giving me the coy smile, doing Grable again before she disappeared.

Before I stubbed the butt, Kelly wandered out, led by a cigar barely bigger than a dachshund.

The paperboys had him tough. I had him soft—a doughboy. Decent size on him but lacking the essential for a bonafide red hot—the eyes. Kathryn had those.

Kelly said, "You play decent poker, buddy, damn decent. You outta Nevada?"

"No, baby, I'm no pro. Outta LA. Do it as a hobby when I got the roll to bank it."

"I hear you. Hey, your girl, Luanna? You lookin' to marry 'er?"

I laughed, pulled another Benson and Hedges from my breast pocket, lit it with the first. "I'm just passing through, baby. She's not. You hear me?" This was going to the interesting side.

"I hear. Listen, you seen my old lady. She looks all right."

"Yeah, she looks just fine." Like a double-scoop ice-cream cone looks all right in August.

"You wanna trade out for the night?"

I didn't take it well. I'm sure it showed.

All I had was: "You serious?"

He was serious.

I told him lemme think about it.

I had already thought about it. I thought I'd just as soon sleep with Lizzi Borden as Kathryn Kelly.

That was then.

[6]

A couple of years later I'm tethering a hot Auburn and an adjusted agenda at the curb outside a club called Many Ha-Ha's in Memphis. I'd picked up the Auburn at a dinge juke joint two-three cuts off Beale.

An old friend of mine named Johnny Chaplain had rounded it up for me. Johnny also rounded up something else—street talk.

Word on the street was somebody needed a fast ride quick. Johnny said this certain party was hanging around this white juke club, Many Ha-Ha's. But the party was offering two for one on bills that needed some time to age and no one had taken them up on the barter. Ransom dough can be red hot for years—no takers in Memphis.

The situation left the Kellys stalled here, sitting on a mountain of marked bills from a kidnap. Like I told Kathryn that time before: *If I was looking for you, I'da had you.* I had 'em. Maybe.

Many Ha-Ha's didn't live up. Square joint, no style, no ha-has. Tables and chairs from a home cooking place. Primitive bar. Plumbing pipe for a foot rail. If the dive had been painted since Lincoln's inaugural, it fooled me. Plain wood floor. Spittoons. All but the chickens, baby, and the end of Prohibition was still young.

I eased up to the bar, tossed a buck down, leaned against the rail being careful about splinters.

"Whatever's coldest."

A moke, door height, made of sticks slid up. He'd wasted some Lucky Tiger on the hair.

"All the same, partner."

"For a buck you could surprise me."

"Sure, mister."

Long tall shoved off, went down a hall off the bar.

Not long, he wobbled back, popped the cap on a tall brown bottle. I didn't recognize the brand but I did recognize ice cold.

The barkeep put a finger to his lips. "There's only so much ice for a nickel beer."

I saluted him; he tossed a towel down.

Low: "Keep it wiped down, okey?"

I told him sure; enjoyed my dollar beer.

Why not? I was on a rich man's expense account and the rich man didn't care shit about his two hundred great ones in ransom. Screw money. This guy wanted pounds of flesh from people's asses. Trust me on this: odd behavior for a rich man.

The gent's name was Charles F. Urschel. I didn't know what the F was hiding but I had a clue. Urschel had the opportunity to spend a few days with some of George and Kathryn's kinfolk down in Texas. Only Kelly and his running buddy Al Bates used Thompson .45's as an invitation. Then charged this Urschel fellow two hundred gees for the lodging.

Had I gotten out of that tight spot with nothing but my life and my drawers, I'd have felt blessed. Not Urschel. His version: the Feds weren't fast enough; the Feds weren't smart enough; the Feds were chasing the money, catching the small fry who were passing off the dough—where the hell was Machine Gun Kelly?

Wasn't too hard. I found him in Memphis second rock I flipped over.

The beer was cool; the air in the bar wasn't. When I was done, I went out, sat on a wood bench in a park across the street. Some regular folks strolled by.

Some irregular folks with pilots' sunglasses, sideburns and pointed shoes went up a long stair beside a house two numbers north of the bar, disappeared through a screen door.

A bit later, another irregular climbed the stair.

Not long, all three irregulars plus Kelly and Kathryn came down the stair.

She was stunning even on the lam. Hennaed hair, tall pumps on her feet, a dress so diaphanous it had to be a dark color or you could have seen her garters.

The crew went in the bar behind Kathryn.

I ate a few cigarettes, got up strolled over, bellied at the bar again.

"I'll do scotch this go. A dollar's worth again."

"Sure, mister. I'll be back." The same hall. Maybe there was a decent bar back there somewhere.

Kelly and company had hemmed in a table at the back end of the room.

Me, them—that was the customer list in its sad entirety at the moment.

I put my spine to the rail, tilted my hat off my forehead. I looked at them, smiled like I wasn't a cop. They looked—the whole table looked. I read them.

Kelly didn't recall me. Kathryn knew me, maybe even knew why I was there.

My dollar pop came back. Nice—a highball glass full, one dissipating ice cube bouncing around in there.

I took it over to the table, sipped on the trip. Nice scotch. Another sip, I fronted across the table from Kelly, looked down.

"'Lo, George."

"I know you?" Kelly drank to it. Up close he didn't look so good. Rough, tense, shadow line on his jaw. His eyes had been drunk for several days.

Kathryn pointed. "Poker game, Kansas City, I believe." A smile to make a moke wanna use a .45 caliber Thompson on another moke.

"You got a good memory, ma'am. Seven stud, nothing wild."

"You were the big loser, weren't you?" Razzing me for not taking Kelly up on the playmate swap in Kansas City those two years back.

I caught her drift, played with her some. "I walked out with three grand and change I didn't bring in."

"Yeah, I recall now, buddy. You cleaned up." Kelly thumbed at me. "Guy's holding four queens, I gotta solid flush, Kewpie Darrow's got a damn boat, kings over sevens."

"Kings over sixes, baby."

Kelly grinned. "Man, what a hand. Stakes went to nearly six gees. You won. Why come you only took three home?"

"I was down so far the bottom of the well was tapping my feet when I hit the homer. How you and the lady been?"

"Been good." He didn't sound like he believed it.

Kathryn said, "I still think you were the big loser that night." Coming back to it, looking at me but making it about Kelly, how he was too dumb to get it.

"Pull out a chair, buddy." Kelly pointed with a spare finger.

I pulled, sat.

"What's payin' the bills? The queens?"

I wagged my head. "Nah. Strictly a hobby. I got a piece of this, a piece of that. Know what I'm saying?"

"I hear you. Why Memphis?" Being a cagey bastard for a simpleton.

"A dinge I know off Beale picks up highbrow motor cars. I fly out from the coast, drive one back. I swing south of the border at Laredo. Time I'm back in LA, the car's clean as new—foreign registration."

Kelly clued up, sniffed at the bait. He liked.

Kathryn watched—I could feel it on the side of my face like

sunshine. I don't know what face she was wearing. If I looked at her, I'd give it away.

"What you pickin' up this trip, buddy? What was your name again? Tom?"

Kathryn: "Joe."

I nodded, still wouldn't look at her. "Got it already. A thirty-two Auburn. Super charged, a hundred-sixty horsepower. Not much'll touch her on a flat road."

Kelly nodded. "Get somethin' to drink, for God sake, how 'bout it, somebody?"

The guys with the Kellys were southern slickers. Pompadours, pegged pants, two-tone sport shirts, two-toned shoes with the pointed toes. Big hayseed grins and unruly side-whiskers.

Low-on-the-pole got up, went to the rail.

"Whatchu get on somethin' like that Auburn automobile it was in California?"

I shrugged. "I can put it in the newspaper out there, get retail."

"Bullshit."

I shrugged some concession. "Close to retail."

"What's retail?"

I was getting ready to set the hook; I could feel it.

Kathryn watched me pull him in.

"Two, two and a half grand." I lied. Legal it was worth maybe a grand. I'd paid four C's for it.

"I'll give you a grand." Kelly emphasized with a fist, one finger out, banging on the table, the one finger pointed at me.

"I'll drive it home for the other grand."

"Fifteen, buddy, and you ain't got no troubles. Pick you up another high-ride in nigger town, make who knows what kinda dough." Slinging his jowls around. "What'd you pay for it, a grand?"

Yeah, sure, sweetheart. "Eighteen, it's yours."

"Seventeen."

Sold to the stupid guy in the stained straw hat and the five o'clock shadow.

I looked at the key in my hand, tossed it at Kelly.

He said, "I gotta get the cash. It's down the street."

"There a poker table down there?"

Kelly grinned. "What, you giving me a chance to win back my sixteen hundred?"

"Seventeen. Yeah, you're lucky you can. Anybody else here gamble?"

Kathryn said she did.

I said I'd noticed.

[7]

A man without a car in modern society is nothing short of pedestrian.

I walked my travel bag a few blocks from Kelly's crib. Pure Oil gas station, there was a sign in the window of a two-year-old Buick ragtop with good tires and most all the dinguses available. Tan with red leather interior. Two eighty-five I drove it off.

Drove it back to the house. Did a set of stairs that could have used some attention.

A big Stetson answered the silly knock Kelly gave me. The man said he was J.C. and I said I was Joe. We left it there on names.

He asked was I the poker player.

I said I guessed I could be—I'd played some here and there.

I elbowed the screen door open more, a bottle in each hand.

"Wha's that, fella?"

"Greek moonshine, J.C. Make your socks roll up and down."

"I might try me some a that."

"I hope you do."

J.C. said, "In the dining room. Down the hall, second door to your left. Come on."

Led me along to the second left. No door—a pass-through to the dining room.

"Hey, buddy. You get wheels?" Kelly in the beat, stained white straw and an undershirt.

23

"Yeah. This town's full of 'em. Whose deal?"

No pompadours. Kelly, Kathryn, a guy introduced as Lang. I didn't know if it was first or last. Didn't really care. He could've been the local version of upper-crust hooligan. Looked slick till he lost the suit coat and showed me some jaundiced shirt underarms.

J.C. and his big hat sat with us. Five hands present but another someone was due any minute.

Then Kathryn decided she didn't want to play.

We bought chips, and a portly man with fat, deft hands and no name joined us. He had a bowler hat that he didn't remove.

The table drew for deal. The fat man won. My jaw didn't bounce off the floor.

I watched him shuffle. Almost prissy hands, small and fast.

He wore a loud, plaid suit which, along with the impertinent bowler, gave him a bumpkin air. His hands weren't bumpkin— hands straight from up-town.

I was in for a fleecing. Kelly had a dealer and his two spoilers— J.C. and Lang—who would be in on the fix, knew the ever-so -subtle signals. A rub at a chin. A hand through the hair. Even a nose pick if need be. High man stays on me, everyone else folds.

I'd brought Kelly's marked bills, another two grand of a rich guy's retainer and two bottles of ouzo. I'd bought the exotic hootch in Florida—Tarpon Springs. It was the real toy. I'd been saving it for a special occasion. Here it was—special occasion.

They let me win a hand here and there, no biggies though. I took a few at the end and blamed it on the ouzo. J.C. had gotten into the stuff and was passing out shots. Everyone but Kathryn and me'd had four of five. I was down a little over two grand and full of two short ones.

We got another eight hundred out of me but it wasn't easy. I had to fold aces and jacks, a winning rack. Kathryn stood behind me, watched me taking falls.

The ouzo had the room a little funny for me—everything a few

24

degrees left or north of something—but I was thinking it was a fog for everyone else.

I went all in on a king high, got cleaned out.

J.C was telling Kelly it was *Greece* whiskey, slurring it out. Kelly tried to focus on the bottle, took a slug instead, did it from the neck.

"Whooey. That's some liquor, buddy. Where you goin'?"

"I gotta get a room before it gets too late." I had a room.

"Come back. Drink a few with us. Bring more money next time."

"Sure, baby. I'll bring a wheelbarrow full. See you boys next time."

Kathryn appeared on cue in the hall.

"What're you driving?"

"A tan Buick canvas top."

"Give me five minutes."

A pretty good kiss came with it. She pressed into my body, wrapped me in her womanness, showed me how well it fit.

I stumbled out to the Buick, took a couple shots of rum to chase the ouzo away. The rum did okay, but I'd planted a couple of snootfuls of coke over the passenger visor to counter the opium in the ouzo. I put the coke in my nose.

Two minutes, she opened the door and slid in. I watched the windshield. The coke kicked in, caressed the rum.

It was raining the day I was born. It was raining now.

• • •

Four in the morning, Kathryn and I were back, sitting at the curb in the tan Buick. She was on my end of the red leather seat.

Six of the best hours I'd ever lived had come to an end.

I kissed her. Was the last good kiss I ever had.

She said, "You've got us, don't you, Joe?"

"Yeah, baby."

"Whadda you say to a break for the lady? I could corner a few grand. I'm sure you're not shatting on uppers. South America's cheap."

"Whadda we waiting on?"

She reached over, touched my face. "My family depends on me, Joe. I'm all they've got between them and the soup-line. I just can't right now. Let's go to Texas."

The damned green eyes. Diamonds—they were that hard.

"I'll call my guy, cut my deal in half if he'll let you slide."

"What if he says no, Joe?"

I knew; I couldn't say.

"Smoke this while I make a phone call."

I handed her a reefer.

The phone booth in front of the bar was dirty but had service.

I called a guy in Oklahoma named Urschel. He was in bed like any sane person, but he took my call after a long wait.

"The hell are you?"

"Memphis."

"Tennessee?"

"There's another?"

"Don't get cute, young fella."

"I'm not cute, Mr. Urschel. I'm not young tonight and full of no sleep and no coffee. Please just listen."

I got done and we spent a few nickels on some silence.

"So let me get this straight. You've set them up—Kelly and his wife—but you've fallen for the wife and want to give back half my money and nail only Kelly?"

"Yes, sir."

More wasted nickels.

"I believe I hired you to put the both in jail, mister."

"Yes, sir, you did."

"Then, that's what I expect for my money. Nothing more, nothing less."

"Screw you, Mr. Urschel. Hope you rot in hell."

I dumped the connect while he begged hell out of my pardon.

Kathryn was dreamy when I got back to the Buick, dreamy in near red hair. Skin like raw milk. Eyes on fire.

She put out a hand, caressed my face again. "If I'd have met you five years back, we'd be wealthy and retired." Off in Neverland.

"Baby, you got two choices. South America's cheap. We could light out—I got the dough and the Spanish to carry us like royalty for ten-fifteen years. We can't come back though, ever—you say you can't do that so it's not a choice."

"What's my other choice, Joe?"

"You know, Kathryn. You've got the one choice—the cophouse. Right now."

She shifted around, leaned against her door. "No can do, Joe. Oh, I'm so tired. So, so tired. We've been running since September, Joe—two months. I gotta see my old ma, give her some money for lawyers—the G-men have her locked up. I'll need a lawyer myself."

Yes, she would. "Kat, you don't have time for that. You got time to go save yourself. Worse rap, you do a couple a years. Cut a good deal today, give them Kelly, give them the dough."

"Take me to Texas, Joe. I need to see my old ma first. I'd rather be in jail in Texas." She lay her head back.

One way or another, Kathryn was going to see a rough night.

"Come on, baby. Let's go see the cops."

"Let's go to Texas."

"Let's go to Chile."

She laughed, popped the door. "I don't even know where Chile's at. Sounds cold. Joe, please call tomorrow. Let's work this out."

"Baby, don't go. Let's get past this right now."

27

"Not tonight, Joe, sweetie." Out of the car she was unencumbered by my charm. "No cops before coffee."

Ten feet, maybe twelve, I said: "It could have been good, sweetheart. I'da run away with you."

She never turned. Over a shoulder, she waved, said, "You'll call me tomorrow. We'll talk about it."

• • •

It took me twenty minutes before I didn't feel mule-kicked in the gut. I got out of the car, moved slowly. I hurt, physically hurt.

Loosened up, I walked across to the phone booth, got a sleepy operator.

"Hey, toots, you wanna get your name in the paper?"

"You said what?"

"You wanna be famous for a few days?"

"What's the joke, buster?"

"No joke, doll. Listen up. There's some guys from D.C. got the whole top floor a the old Peabody, the nice rooms. Get one of them on the line, tell him Machine Gun Kelly and some a his boys are at a very green house two numbers north of a bar called Many Ha-Ha's. You got that, sugar?"

Some quiet.

"Who're you?"

"Just a guy knows where Machine Gun Kelly is. This is straight dope, sweetie. You want I say it again, you write it down this time?"

The rain became serious, beat me from booth to car, came in sheets to the city limit sign.

Maybe a mile—maybe twenty, maybe fifty—outside Memphis the sky cleared and poured a beautiful sunrise over a damn sad morning.

I'd rather it had rained all day, washed away my sin.

[8]

You think I died on you or something?"

Joe had been quiet for sometime. Who knows how long—time in a hospital is time made of lead and sand.

"No. You croak, your machines flat-line I hear. I just finished the story is all."

"Nah. You couldn't have. It's not done yet. Hey, kid, what'd you think when I told you that story about Kelly?"

Jimmy said, "I thought you were full of shit, Joe."

"Yeah, you did. What'd you learn, baby?"

"Don't piss away the listening time by thinking too much."

"Focus too close and the shit in your peripheral is doing all sorts a stuff you don't know anything about. Watch the pea; don't watch the cups. That's what you learned, Jimmy, baby." A few quiet seconds, then: "Pick it up from the party at your mom's condo, West Palm, the time I busted your coke cherry." A laugh like it was pretty funny.

• • •

Jimmy left all grins. This Joe Joseph dude. Cat. The guy was a cat.

Full of shit like all the other wrinkled sacks hanging around West Palm. Jew canoes and Lincolns full of them. Double-knit leisure suits in Easter egg colors, pastel plaids. Seriously sad comb-overs. Suspicious teeth.

Who'd have thought people were horny acting at fifty and sixty, even seventy. Gross stuff. Schoolyard stuff but old people doing it. Jeez—maybe they were doing *it*. Maybe they were balling. Man.

Inside the slider, Jimmy told his mom he'd met Joe.

Mom asked, *Joe next door?* Mom wasn't that dumb.

"Yeah. How many *Joes* you know, Mom?"

"Several. I'm having a cocktail party tomorrow. Maybe I'll invite Joe."

"He a man about the complex?" Jimmy nabbing an olive off whatever Dot was making.

"Oh, no. No, Joe doesn't mix. Very mysterious. Very exclusive—never does mixers. But cute."

"Oh, Mom, please."

"What did you and Joe talk about?"

Why not. "Joe's got some outlandish stories he wants to tell me so I can write them."

Mom's brows went up. "What sort of stories?"

"You wouldn't believe, Mom. The guy says he was like a private eye or something. Told me about him setting up Machine Gun Kelly. Doing Kelly's wife."

"Watch your mouth. *Machine Gun Kelly?*" Like it was a sack full of used kitty litter.

"Yeah. He's full of shit. . ."–Mom: *Watch you language*–". . .but very entertaining. Cool old guy. Wears a hat well for a white dude."

Jimmy thought it could be funny telling his mom about Joseph and his reefer habit but would never. Joseph *was* cool for an old guy.

• • •

Next night, half a real Quaalude and a bottle of Bali Hai, Jimmy stumbled onto his mom's patio.

30

Whoa. Double whoa. Party. Cocktail party.

Okay—get it together. Okay. Now. Hey, Joe should be there. A peek through the slider. Lots of really unhip people. No Joe Joseph through the glass slider.

"Hey, kid."

"Goddam, old dude. Quit doing that." Slug of Bali Hai.

"What?"

"Talking through the shrubs."

"Croton are more an herb than a shrub. I thought you meant quit surprising you when you were fucked up on downers."

No noise.

Joe: "You *are* fucked up on downers, right?"

Jimmy: "Some. And wine. Cheap shit a class guy like you couldn't handle."

Joe: "You have a couple a cups a Cuban joe with me I'll go to your mom's party, hold your hand." Said it like Jimmy wasn't being an ass-hole.

Jimmy stumbled around. Sobering up off 'ludes and cheap wine and making mom's party could be interesting, you looked at it from the right angle. Not a ninety-degree right angle—the correct angle. Whoa, he was zipped.

The coffee did the trick.

He and Joseph did a couple of shots of some sort of brandy, smoked a nice reefer from Joe's new batch. Gave Jimmy a Baggie full, no charge. Killer shit. Righteous shit. Nearly holy shit. Real Oaxacan buds, seeds the size of marbles, buds two, three feet long.

"You clear enough to see your mom's friends?"

Jimmy caught a snag on a sharp edge. Gave Joe some attitude, trying to focus on him.

Joe read it: "You gotta nasty chip on your shoulder, kiddo. The sooner you lose it, the better you and the world both are gonna feel."

It's hard to say *go dick yourself* to a dude just gave you an ounce of pure bud. Jimmy let it dissipate.

31

Did some more shots, smoked another doob, felt pretty damn good. Lost the wobbles.

"Come on, Joe. Let's go do this party thing, get it over with."

"Nah. I'll tell you, kid. . . ."

"Fuck you. I'm going in there, then so are you. Come on."

Jimmy went in thinking the coffee and the reefer and the brandy had knocked the spines off the 'lude high.

So wrong.

Too much noise, too hot, too busy for his mom's small place. Too much sensory assault all the sudden.

Joe pushed Jimmy in the ribs, said, "Be cool."

Jimmy nodded, said a quick, *Hi*, to Mom, went to his room and puked in the trashcan.

Breathe deep, count five—Jimmy's out the bedroom door, ready to jam into the bathroom. His mom and Joe are in the hall. Jimmy tried to grin, mumbled some about the bathroom. His mom's eyebrows got funny. Joe grinned like the whole deal was funny. Jimmy shut the door on them.

A few gulps of cool water, some on the face, a good piss and Jimmy was nearly human. He felt so good he brushed his teeth, washed his face with some soap his mom had that smelled like Hai Karate.

Whooo. Way better. He could handle the room of people now. Get out there, sell some charm.

Open the door. Mom was still there, eyebrows under control.

"I'm so glad you made it, honey. Come meet." The last involved a tug on his arm.

Colonel and Francis Something, Judge Whoosit, Doctor Thumbnail. *Hi, hello, how are you? Well—I'm doin' fine.*

Jimmy's eyes caught Joe. Poor old Joe, he looked like a coyote in a jaw trap. The man was about to gnaw something off. Maybe the heads of the two color-adjusted brunettes who'd cornered him between the wall and the end of the folding table full of refreshments: nuts, Chex-mix, dips and chips, this and that salads,

32

Swedish meatballs Jimmy personally knew tasted like sweetened dung, then some bottles and cocktail mixes.

Bailing Joe out was no problem—some BS about needing a private congress with the gentleman. The brunettes didn't have a clue what a congress was, but they gave Joe a nice aloha with giddy smiles, eyes of promise.

• • •

Jimmy's room—

"Jesus, kid, regular folks are nuts. . . ." Stop.

He came back someone else. "Fuck it. Kid, you ever do any cocaine?"

Jimmy said not yet.

Joe said, *watch your cherry,* pulled out a piece of tinfoil. "Gimme something glass. Smells like somebody puked in here."

Jimmy got a picture of some ducks off the wall, used his shirttail to wipe the dust off. He laid it on a desk thing his mom had put in his room in case he went back to school. University of Miami was getting to be a pretty good school according to her.

Joe dumped the tinfoil, thumped it, said, "Lock the door, kid."

Jimmy locked.

Joe had his license out chopping the coke. He made four lines maybe an inch and a half long, found a hundred, rolled it up, tried to pass it to Jimmy.

Jimmy said, "You first."

"Want me to take you to school, huh?" Grinning like it meant something else to him.

Joe made his two lines disappear. He did some nose patting and upper lip stretching.

Jimmy jumped in the deep end, hundred-dollar bill in hand. Yes. He saw the need for the nose wiggle. Bit of a sting but the sting dying fast.

Nothing—then, man. His face warmed up. Oh fucking man. This shit made amphetamines look like a cheap high. Euphoria.

None of the greasy regret you get from speed. Sky's-the-limit buzz.

Joe said, "Greatest social lubricant ever invented. Let's go do a quarter-hour social responsibility, sneak off to my place, watch Carson."

Jimmy, being funny: "What you got for watching Carson? Some of that ouzo?"

"Nah. Too hard to get the real thing nowdays. But I do got anise liqueur and some opium; you're looking to experience the high, separate but together."

"You're shitting me."

"About the high?"

"No. The opium."

"Why would I shit you about that, kid? I fucking live right next door. Let's party. And give me my hundred."

• • •

The Colonel cornered Jimmy pretty quick into party time. Had Jimmy thought about the army? Yeah, all the time till the draft lottery and a high number. Well, if Jimmy decided to go serve as cannon fodder, let him know. He could grease some wheels, get Jimmy in OCS. Right—a fresh lieutenant's life span on the ground in Nam was like twenty minutes right now. Thanks. Jimmy'd think about it.

Next a guy named Saul got him. Hi, he was blah-blah, did blah-blah before he died and came to West Palm. What was Jimmy doing with himself? Jimmy needed some guidance in the employment world Saul was here for him, come over. Jimmy says, *I will*. Meaning it in a I-probably-won't sort of way.

The guy was a study in polyester and insincerity.

Saul says he heard Jimmy's writing a book. What's it about?

Jimmy said, "Some stuff Mr. Joseph's telling me."

Saul said, "How kind of him. Nice meeting you. See you around sometime."

The guy made for a chubby platinum blonde in red spike heels.

Jimmy looked for Joe. Across the room, watching the crowd. Something seemed to almost make Joe smile.

He looked over at Jimmy, smiled for real. Smiled like they shared a secret, something beyond reefer and cocaine. The smile ran a cold finger up Jimmy's back.

A tall woman who squinted and wore decidedly un-Florida clothing—a coarse knit brown skirt, a turtle-neck sweater—turned on cue from her conversation with another tall woman, as Saul left. She reminded Jimmy her name was Eleanor, and they had met briefly at his mom's place. Did Jimmy know she was published? No, he didn't, but felt sure he was about to get filled in. It was a book of poetry and had sold well throughout New England. According to Eleanor New York didn't get it, the work too cerebral for the coarse, mercantile mind-set of Manhattan. But if Jimmy needed any advice, any help on that last line, let her know. She could also refer him to her agent, a nice Jewish fellow working from his home in Ann Arbor. He'd gotten her a great deal on her book—only cost her three thousand to get a hundred nicely bound copies. Jimmy said he'd surely be in touch—nice seeing you—bye.

The coke helped him work his way around to his mom in ten-fifteen minutes. She was with Joe again, talking like they were old pals.

"Thanks, Mom. Everyone thinks I'm going for the Pulitzer. You know Joe?"

"We've met; we talk here and there."

"We're neighbors, kid, you hadn't noticed."

Jimmy had a zinger but one of the hungry brunettes came up talking.

She had a voice like a man, a laugh like an air-raid siren. She smelled like she knew Coco Channel personally and had eyes she stole from a mounted swordfish.

Jimmy asked Joe: "You ready for your interview?"

Joe nodded, a deferential nod. "Sure, kid. Excuse us, ladies. Literature awaits."

The brunette stretched the eyes till they were scary. "Oh. What are we discussing this evening?" She put an *e* between *eve* and *ning.*

Joe said, "Coleridge. His sins, his religion, his genius. Mostly his sins."

"Oh," drawn out. "Sounds fascinating," like it wasn't.

Then Mom looks at Joe with the eyebrows-up eye. "Joe."

Joe's hands came up. "I swear, Dot, I won't pass many bad habits off on him."

The brunette said, "Night, fellows," like Monroe would have said it if she were a drag queen.

• • •

So zipped on 'ludes earlier, Jimmy'd not really checked out Joe's pad. Now he checked.

Hip place, Joe Joseph's was. A lot of stuff hanging on the walls that could have been expensive art. Too modern for Jimmy's eye. A Curtis Mathis TV the size of a small car. A Japanese stereo system to die for, speakers up to your chin.

It smelled of incense and cooking. Bead curtains in the doorways, candles around.

Not bad for an old guy. Jimmy thought it was a place like the Hef would have if he had a place in South Florida. Damn classy pad.

Joe told Jimmy to park it, disappeared into what had to be the kitchen—there was an oriental screen drawn across it, and Jimmy couldn't see but the layout seemed to be a mirror of Mom's place.

A shout: "Hey, kid, what you drinking?"

"You said ouzo."

Joe showed with a hookah about four feet tall. He sat it on the floor by the couch. Jimmy sat, checked it out. Joe went out, returned with a bottle and some glasses.

Joe did something to the stereo and Ravi Shankar fell out of tall speakers.

"Yeah. Good noise to smoke opium to, huh?" Joe grinned, held up a black ball the size of a marble. "You sure on this, kid?"

"Yeah. Let's do it."

They did it. Jimmy sailed, puked, nodded out in maybe forty-five minutes.

Man, did he dream—vivid, frightening shit.

[9]

Sometime before daylight, Jimmy pried himself loose from Joe's couch and stumbled home. His feet felt like two cinderblocks.

Slept hard, slept long. Rose about ten-thirty, still a little fuzzy inside and out but smooth.

A long hot shower called for Pop-Tarts and OJ.

Mom was congenial, fronted Jimmy a couple hundred till he got a job or got in school.

He said thanks, got some paper and an interesting mechanical pencil he found in a kitchen drawer.

Pop-Tarts made the juice taste like battery acid but killed the stomach rats.

Some stuff got jotted down on the college ruled paper—notes on Joe's story. Questions really.

Why, if Kathryn was so bitchin' hot, didn't he run off to South America with her, Mexico, wherever? He said he had the dough.

How'd he ended up in front of Many Ha-Ha's? Too easy, too coincidental. The car ready for them to ask for it.

What's an Auburn?

How'd his man, his cash man, know it was Joe who'd set Kelly and Kathryn up? Maybe Joe had told him how but they smoked so much reefer during story time he was hazy.

That thought led to a belch and another couple of Pop-Tarts, more OJ, and a short abbreviated version of the Machine Gun Kelly story on college ruled.

What if this guy was telling the truth?

Okay—doubtful. But what if? Either way, man told a damn good story.

"I gotta go see Joe, work out some problems I've got with a story."

Mom came from the laundry, flapped a pair of Jimmy's Landlubbers, bent them over an arm, bent them again.

"You're serious about this writing, aren't you?" A nice smile. Approving?

"Right now I am, Mom. Let's see how it goes. Give me a month or so."

"You've got it. *Bon mots.*" And a curious look.

Jimmy used the slider, rounded the hedge. No Joe. A look in the slider. More no Joe, but Iggy Stooge was ripping out *Nineteen-Sixty-Nine.* Okay.

Then a Joe. Coming from the hall, toothbrush in mouth.

He mumbled something, signaled Jimmy in for a landing.

Jimmy entered on Joe's retreating back.

The hookah was gone—the place was back to perfect. The long screen pushed against a wall with more folds than a concertina.

An orange breakfast bar was surrounded by tall stools with orange vinyl seats. Jimmy mounted one.

A couple of minutes, Joe returned.

"You just get up?"

Joe made a face without looking at Jimmy. "I been up since seven, kid. You just missed some eggs Benedict with nova and onion."

He went to the fridge, got a bottle, shook it good.

Celery. Knife. Gin. Black pepper. Lime. The bottle had a piece of masking tape on it. *Bloody Mary Mix* was written on the tape in Magic Marker.

"You want?" Joe pointed at the ingredients. "I make 'em with gin."

Seemed like Jimmy was going to say no, thinking how Joe drank a lot. Somehow it came out: *Sure.*

There was some washing, some chopping and slicing, then some tall cut glasses and some gin.

"Pepper?" Joe had the mill ready.

"Sure. Some."

Joe did both, one less—Jimmy's.

Two drops of Worcestershire allowed to fall dark and oily into the Mary mix.

Joe passed Jimmy's over, stirred his own with the celery, squeezed the lime wedge, tossed it in the mix.

Then Crystal hot sauce. Poke a finger in, stir well, taste the finger.

A big swig left pepper and pulp on Joe's lip. His tongue fetched the detritus; he said, "Jesus, that's good."

Jimmy mimicked Joe, never having had a Bloody Mary of any sort. It was good but needed salt. He mentioned it and Joe obliged.

"My doctor's got me on fake salt. I said to hell with it, quit using salt. Somewhat anyways." He reached over, grabbed the salt dredge, lightly sprinkled his drink. "So what's on your mind this morning?"

"Last night—nice trip." Jimmy salted liberally, stirred with celery.

"The coke and opium? Don't become friends with either of them, baby. They're fickle old crones, both."

"That being the case, thanks for the introduction. I got a question or two about the story you told me."

Jimmy got a fleeting flash of the eyes Joe Joseph had put on him before, the scary eyes. Like Jimmy was challenging him. Then they were gone. "Ask, kiddo. I'm all answers."

"What's an Auburn?"

"A turbo charged automobile, a race winner. Cousin to the

40

Cord and the Duesenberg—all fast sleds in the day. Handmade. What else you got." A grin with it like he knew Jimmy was pitching easy.

"How'd the money guy know it was you that set them up?"

"I told you—I called him, tried to buy Kathryn."

"But you told him to rot in hell."

"I had a reputation by then. I'd never been accused of being anybody's lapdog, but I did what I said I'd do. I said I'd put Kelly and Kathryn both on ice. Urschel wouldn't change the deal so that's what I did, kid. It's how you earn a reputation."

A pause to look at his sheets. "How'd you know Kelly was hanging out at Many Ha-Ha's?"

"The dinge, the one got me the car, Johnny Champlain. Guy played a mean slide guitar when he wasn't stealing cars."

"Come on. How'd you end up in Memphis?"

"I love the blues."

"Screw you. How?"

Joe enjoyed the funny more than Jimmy did.

"Knew a guy in Minneapolis-Saint Paul, a guy went by the handle Kid Kahn. Some of the loot had passed through the Kid's hands on its way upstream from a liquor deal. The cops had the Kid in the hoosegow. Had a couple or three other kikes locked up in there with him. Anyhow, kikes don't do so well in jail. Ain't in their disposition, you could say.

"I fly up there; the green stuff gets me a jail pass; I make promises to break later. The Kid tells me it's a guy named Barney Berman did the liquor deal. Barney's on ice too, him and the Kid both broke, no lawyer dough. I say, *Who was it Berman was trading with?* He's mum till we talk money; then he says, *Joe, I'm telling you, it was fucking Machine Gun Kelly.*"

Joe stopped but they weren't to Memphis yet. "How's your Bloody?"

"Fine. So. . . ?"

"So I needed to beat the Feds to Texas, knowing a kike's disposition to chirp like a canary when you put him on ice with

41

no dough. I left the Kid flush on dough but I couldn't get any in to this Berman guy—he'd chirp soon as the Feds leaned on him. I hit the airfield running, catch a flying tin can that coulda used a maintenance stop. The pilot bounced it down in Fort Worth—Mecham Airport. I glommed a rent car, kicked dust to Wise County. You're wondering why Texas, Kathryn's mother lived on a ranch outside a Paradise. See, if anybody anywhere knew how to find Kelly and Kathryn, it was the folks in Paradise, Texas, her people."

"How'd you know about Paradise?"

"I had a couple a brothers who didn't mind hanging out with tough guys and red-hots. This ranch was known for being a hole-in-the-wall for hot guys. I missed—the G's got there first and locked up Kat's folks and a few red-hots laying about the ranch. I gave it a week, let the dust settle, see if my client could get me a jail ticket. No dice. The Feds locked it down."

"What'd you do?"

"Found a guard with a taste for bourbon whiskey, a young wife, and flexible ethics. Got him to slip in an unloaded gat and a saw-blade to a guy was at Kathryn's ma's place when the Feds showed. The red-hot was a moke name a Harvey Bailey. I didn't know him personally but knew some about him. Enough I could play with him a bit. Word I sent was: I was a friend and would be in a black coupé across the street from the jail's back door. A few hours, here comes this Bailey fella who liked to rob banks and shoot people. Sees me, runs for the coupé. We lam out, headed north.

"By the Oklahoma state line, I knew I was supposed to take Bailey to Chi-town to meet the Kellys. That's if I was who I said I was. I wasn't so I dumped him, left him cuffed to an Oklahoma State Police bumper we came across in a diner parking lot.

"No dice in Chi, but I knew who knew Kelly there."

"Your brothers tell you?"

"No. A squid name a Eddie Doll. How I know him's a different story. Eddie put me on a guy who didn't really want to talk to me, but didn't want me dragging him in to see the cops more. His name was Joe Bergl. He didn't care to see the cops since they wanted to know about a certain car a his used in a robbery of a Federal Reserve messenger in which a Chi cop bought it."

"Bergl give you Memphis?"

"Yeah. But, like I say, he really didn't wanna. I had to convince him."

"How'd you *convince him?*"

The grin, then, "Kid, you really don't wanna know."

Jimmy thought about it. "Yeah. I do."

The grin.

"I put an old revolver next to his head—a thirty-four-forty—dropped a pill, blew out an eardrum."

"Jesus. I guess that'd do it."

"Works every time."

"What if that hadn't worked, Joe?"

"It did." No grin. A bold stare, like he was daring Jimmy to judge him.

"What if it didn't? How far would you have gone?"

"This business, kid? You don't ask yourself what-if questions."

More hard-eyed stare.

Jimmy didn't think Joe knew the answer, didn't know how far he'd have gone. He asked Joe if he knew.

Joseph shook his head, sipped his gin Mary. Told Jimmy such shit didn't matter. Said, "Go ahead, kid, ask me it."

"Okay. You found her so hot, how'd you do it? How'd you give her up? How could you?"

"That's the best question you've asked since I've known you. I'm not sure, baby. I think I knew she was as guilty as Kelly, maybe more. Maybe the author of the whole sad scene. Maybe I was scared of her, scared I'd end up like her third husband."

"How'd he end up?"

"Contact wound to his temple." Joe held up his Bloody in salute.

"Kathryn?"

A shrug. "The coroner said suicide." Good pause. "In spite of the fact Kathryn publicly threatened to do such the day before."

Jimmy let it soak in, said: "She was that good?"

"Yeah. Considering she was the product of bootleggers and whores, she might a been the best."

A piece of quiet, then Jimmy needed to know: "Why wouldn't she go with you? Why'd you say she couldn't do it?"

"First off, you gotta understand Kathryn'd been trying to cut her own amnesty deal with the Feds before the Urschel kidnap. Then much cheese fell on them, temptation, then trouble. I'm sure she was confused. The *why* you asked about? Seems to be a bonus amount of loyalty in white trash families. She coulda never gone without seeing kin. It's how she gauged herself. Measured how far she'd come from being a convicted prostitute."

Joe shook his head, grabbed the straw pork pie, slammed it on his head.

"Woulda never worked, kid. I never coulda laid in the sunshine, took up lawn tennis, croquet, polo, whatever else you gotta take up to be South American carriage trade. Didn't have it in me either, sweetheart."

Joe's face went off; Jimmy figured he was chasing a brief what-if.

"And, I tell you what, kid, she was one monkey-love lay too. You done with the inquest?" Joe rolled his head to face Jimmy.

"Yeah. I'll have half a Mary, no celery."

Joe poured Jimmy three quarters, topped his own off.

Before he turned back from putting the pitcher in the sink, his back to Jimmy, he said: "You still think I'm a lying old piece a crap?"

He turned and smiled like he was kidding, like they were best friends sharing a joke.

"I'm coming around. Where'd you go after Memphis?"

"Matamoros."

"That's Mexico?"

"Yeah that's Mexico. Lemme tell you about Mexico."

"Let's walk."

"On the beach, in the sunshine? Kid, please, it's hot out there."

"I gotta couple of grams of Lebanese hash and a seasoned chamber pipe."

"Then we should repair to some shady locale at the park and unleash this hashish and this tale of whores and gonorrhea, mobsters, kikes, guineas and gunsels and other excellent citizens. And how I pulled a damn dirty trick on the most deserving bum. That's gotta cancel out something I did somewhere, shouldn't it?"

"Man, I don't wanna discuss karma with *you,* of all people. I'm not even sure I wanna hear these stories."

Joe grinned, killed his drink, sustained a red trickle down his neck. A napkin dab on the fly. "Let's go, kid."

He said, over his shoulder, his head turned some, "You ever see a movie called *The Illustrated Man?*"

Jimmy hadn't seen the movie but Joe thought it was funny as fuck all the same.

[10]

The bottoms of my feet were about as tan as they'd ever dreamed they'd be. I had nearly sixty-thousand bucks in a couple of different banks. I was twenty-nine years old. High, wide and goddamned handsome. Didn't care a damn who knew it.

Mexico. Summer. 1934. I had gone damn near peasant in the last ten months. But not the Mexican booze—don't do tequila. Never agreed with my gentle constitution.

I didn't have pink elephants over it. Matamoros wasn't more than a bumpy hour's drive. You could fill your wish list in Matamoros you had the money. I had the money.

I went often. Bought single malt scotch for two bits. Clear Irish potato juice, aged Bushmills: two bottles, two bits. I bought a ten-dollar bottle of three hundred year old armagnac. I didn't even know what armagnac was. I bought two whores—sisters—for a month and a bit, then ran them off for slicing each other up with my kitchen knives.

Then a dollar's worth of miracle drugs at a Matamoros *pharmacia* ran the hybrid-clap off.

I was wearing only an undershirt, vaquero pants, barefoot. I had a straw sombrero, bent up in the front according to current fashion. I had my gun outside my pants for the world to see. It was Mexico, baby, '34.

I existed on a long, broken spit called Barra Jesus Maria. Only a few miles east of Carboneras but you couldn't drive there from Carboneras. The strip of sand, coquina, and lime rock created Laguna Madre, cutting the mainland off from the Gulf. Me? I had the Gulf on one side, maybe half a mile, the salty lagoon a few hundred yards the other way. Concentrated paradise. I could have lived there till I died. But there was the boredom. And there was that stubborn version of the clap perfecting itself along the border.

I kept reminding myself why I was here. Or how I'd ended up here—Brownsville was across the grand *rio* from Matamoros. Good for Brownsville.

Lots of shipping, lots of boats. Then one day lots of guineas and kikes. I was looking for a kike was rumored to be headed to Brownsville. The kike's name was Pearlie Friedman, and we'd had problems in LA back in '27. He was connected to forty of my sixty gees and some days I felt like earning a little more of it. I didn't have to, wasn't obligated to, just felt like it. Camped out across the lagoon from Matamoros; waited six-eight months.

Now I was bored. The nearly new Cord I'd glommed as a kicker in the Kelly deal was dirty and tired of being tethered in the dusty, bare front yard. So was I.

Drought, then non-stop rain. Trap doors in the clouds would open up and it'd rain drops the size of Buicks for an hour.

• • •

The clouds had compromised down to a drizzle earlier but kept a dismal horizon ready.

I'd brought my hand-made Mexican boots out to the porch of my little casa, had a pair of Argyle socks were knitted in Birmingham, England—two bits in Matamoros. Had a can of boot wax.

The porch: several cane-backed chairs and a porch swing I didn't trust. High plank floor. Everything covered by a tin roof—

rusted. I took a chair and speared the new socks with clean, tan feet that felt like riding up to Brownsville; eat some excellent southern cooking from a joint I knew was run by a Negress had a bum like two elephants were fighting in her pants. Brownsville had the food. Maybe had a Pearlie Friedman.

A local kid broke out of the sage and sorrel soaking wet. I threw down on him, nearly popped him.

He ran to the porch, leaned on it, wet and hassling. He was maybe fourteen and heavy with *Indio* blood—flat headed, almost puffy cheeks.

"*Señor.* . . ."

"Hey, hey. *Sal de la lluvia.*"

The kid smiled as if honored to get to come up on the *rico gringo's* porch. I tossed him a dishtowel from the table. He used it and talked.

"*Señor, un hombre lo busca.*" Catching his wind now.

Looking for me? The hell did I do?

"*¿Eres de Carboneras?*"

"*Sí.*"

"*¿Quién es el hombre?*"

"*El dueño de la tienda de víveres dice que se llama* Pale Anderson *de* Brownsville." The grocer was the center of the Carboneras universe: grocer, creditor, postman, constable, justice of the peace, and probably dogcatcher. Someone was looking for someone around here, they'd wind up in front of the grocer.

The kid folded the dishtowel carefully, placed it on the table in the same spot it was before I handed it to him.

I thought about what he said. I knew Pale, sorta. He'd spent some time in my old neighborhood when I was a kid. "*¿Cuándo se fue de Carboneras?*"

"*Hace una hora.*" Left an hour ago.

I nodded to the kid. "*¿Tomó un taxi acuático o el ferry?*" If Pale took a water taxi, he'd be here any minute. He took the ferry, then I had some time to think about all this.

"*El ferry.*"

I found a couple of silver dollars, flipped them at the kid. He caught them like he was made for catching silver dollars, one in each hand.

He peeked in his upturned fists, opening them like he didn't believe it. He believed. *"Gracias, Señor. Gracias."* And he jumped from the porch, ran off into the sage.

Shit, I was gonna offer him some of that three-hundred-year-old armagnac to knock the chill off.

[11]

It took Pale a couple of more hours to go south far enough to get a ferry east so he could drive north. I wasn't sure why he didn't take a water taxi across the lagoon, save himself some daylight. I didn't know what it meant—was it good or bad. He wasn't dumb.

He was tall, and pale as his name implied. He had a smile you could've put in the movies. The eyes screwed the package though—too close, too sure, too devoid of kindness. A wickedly smart cookie.

Pale uncurled from the back door of a Packard that went on for days. For all I knew its trunk was still on the U.S. side of the river. His black suit could've come from an undertaker's closet— black, Mennonite plain, off the rack.

I had put on a clean shirt with a starched collar, suspenders, dark brown suit pants, a tie with Felix the Cat winking. Brown and white wing tips, no suit coat. Pistola outside my pants—it was still Mexico.

Pale sneered at my wooden hacienda, sneered at the dusty Cord, put the mean eyes on me. "We know each other?"

"You knew the knock at a pig on Figueroa at West Fourth."

Pale nodded. "Yeah. You was a kid. What you been doin', kid?"

"Nerts."

"How you like not being a cop no more?"

I shrugged for Pale. Seemed he knew more about me than he confessed.

Pale smiled. "You didn't make no good cop no way."

"Yeah? Why's that?"

"Too much a the old neighborhood in you. You're from the wrong side a the tracks, Joe. Just like your brothers."

I thought about it. "Maybe so." I was serious.

Pale nodded. The sun illuminated his face on the upswing as it slipped under the brim of a decent Panama. "I hear you're lookin' for a kike."

"I hear you're running lackey for guineas and kikes."

Pale's cheek flinched, went to a grin, hands came out. "Hey, kiddo, it's the future." A tad of the Minnesota Nordic leaked out in the recovery.

"Not mine, Pale. You drive all this way to ask me am I looking for Pearlie Friedman?"

"No. Mr. Spaganetti requests your presence up in Brownsville."

I gave out some phony awe. "Eddie Spaghetti wants an audience with *me?*"

"I'd say it's stronger than *wants*, kiddo."

"No, baby. No can do."

Pale played shocked. *"No?* You sure about that no, kiddo?" He rapped a couple of knuckles on some glass.

"Yeah. Tell Eddie he needs me, send someone he can trust with the whole message."

A nervous punk had gotten out front passenger side and was walking around the front of the car. He had on a shiny light-blue suit with zoot-pegged cuffs, hair he'd stolen from a roadhouse crooner. Navy shirt. A tie in a nice shame-on-the-sun yellow. A hand slipped past a shiny lapel and into the too-long suit coat.

I went red-hot, pulled, crouched down a bit. The punk pulled the hand out, showed me his palm.

Pale's hands flapped dismissively. "Hey, hey, kiddo. Ice it a bit, huh? Chingy's got a letter, okay. Mr. Spaganetti thought you would react as you did. He forgives you. Chingy, the letter."

I stayed on the Ching's hand as it went in his coat again. It appeared with an envelope; I put some ice on it, let my piece drape.

Pale grinned, touched the brim of the nice Panama, said, "Good seeing you again, Joe."

"Yeah. You too." Nobody meant it. I took the letter from the punk.

Pale and Chingy loaded into the cattle car and dragged some soggy afternoon back toward Brownsville. I looked at the envelope, tossed it on the table. This called for some armagnac if anything ever did.

[12]

The letter lay there helplessly for two days while I watched. The Gulf breeze didn't want it. The fruit rats living in my attic didn't want it. Poor unwanted letter from the boss of Brownsville—Alberto, Eddie the Dry Cleaner, Spaganetti. Eddie Spaghetti.

Word was Eddie had a big press-iron in his office, which didn't seem irregular considering he fronted business outta dry cleaning joints. Supposedly you stole from Eddie, Eddie brought you in, put your head in the press, straightened your hair, kept you working for him. You seemed like you wanted to give him any more guff, he'd bring you in, let you see the press.

I'd never see the press. I'd never be in Eddie Spaghetti's office.

Third day, fate ran me down.

I was on the porch baking out a medium-sized hangover, minding my own business. I had one of the canebacks at a dangerous angle against the wall. I had nearly drifted off, maybe I had. The wind changed from hot cumbrous lagoon air to a clean cool Gulf breeze. Something fluttered beyond eyelids that were red to the sun. I cracked one of the lids, looked. The wind had tossed the neglected letter in my lap. It lay there. It dared me.

I cursed at it, popped the other eyelid, tore the envelope open like I hated it. I yanked the blithe stationery to attention. Either

Eddie had nice handwriting or had a secretary. The damned thing looked like the Declaration of Independence, that kind of fancy scribing.

Seemed to ramble on somewhat like the Declaration of Independence, too. I had to read it twice to be sure what it said.

Eddie had Italianized my name—Guiseppe Retti. Not even close. I was pure-bred American cur—issue of a Muskogee tumbleweed blown out of the dust bowl, blown to LA and married to a Spanish-Nez Perce half-breed from God knows where.

I appreciated the brotherly and inclusive gesture on Eddie the Dry Cleaner's part all the same.

The start was nance as hell: *My Dearest Joe.* I didn't know we were kissing close like that.

The letter blah-blahed some polite cordialities and morphed into a proposal for services—mine. Seemed Eddie needed me desperately to help an American of—Eddie's words—*high status* and an *excellent citizen* of whom I had certainly heard but Eddie didn't care to mention in this correspondence. Eddie also didn't mention his boss-hood or Italian heritage. The bastard just put twenty nice green hundred-dollar bills in the envelope.

So either I keep Eddie's money, say screw him, live in Mexico forever or go see him, get my hair straightened saying no thanks. There was a third choice—go find the guy kidnapped Charles Lindbergh's kid and buried him because that's what this was about anyhow.

I liked my hair like it was. I could live here forever—double screw Alberto Eddie Spaghetti Spaganetti. I could live where I damn well chose. Or I was dumb enough to think I could out-tough the mob.

The truth? I was bored. I was tired of the local whores. I got up, folded the twenty bills, packed the essential dry-goods and hardware in the Cord, said, *Don't go nowhere,* to Laguna Madre.

[13]

Big shot he played, Eddie'd been passed like a piece of chattel from the old Moustachoes to the new blood running things in the city now, the Moustachoes having all ended up dead and worse.

I skirted Eddie Spaganetti's Brownsville, aimed straight for another Brownsville. The Cord all but drove itself to New York. It was, after all, a Cord.

I knew a guy that knew a guy up there. The guy my guy knew could eat a couple a Eddie Spaghettis between his calamari and his clam linguine and probably not so much as belch.

The Cord and I managed to cross the nasty river and find a street called Livonia. Pulled on the curb a half block off Saratoga. Down that half block and across the street was a candy store stayed open all night long.

I watched a bit.

From the traffic going in and out Midnight Rose's candy joint looked like the local undesirables had uncontrollable sweet tooths.

I knew some by face and name but wasn't friendly enough to speak to any of them. Kid Twist Reles and Happy Maione came out laughing about something. Probably excited about some ice pick sale going on at Macy's.

A Buick with a bummed up fender, most of the oxblood paint

scraped off that whole side—the passenger's side—slid in. A slick galoot fell out.

"'Lo, Dukey." I'm talking to no one, only the windshield.

Dukey Maffetore. Not short nor tall, just slick-looking. Dressed in a black suit that could have been built on him. A lightweight. Somebody made by blood but not destined to ever be a major player. A messenger boy, a gopher.

But I knew him. He was a foul-mouthed bastard and could have been an idiot or not. He read comic books so I'd always assumed the first option. He wasn't who I was waiting on but he'd do.

The Kid dropped a shoulder, set up in a boxing stance as Dukey approached. Dukey went into his own stance. The Kid and Dukey danced, poked loose fists at each other while Happy Maione looked.

A few words, Dukey passed between the Kid and Happy. The Kid turned, kicked Dukey pretty good in the back of his lap. Dukey took it. He was a lightweight—Kid Twist wasn't.

Dukey used the door to Rose's; the Kid and Happy laughed their way into the back half of a black Caddy. The Caddy pulled away like it was the races, passed with a whisper; became nothing in my rearview.

There was a drugstore living between me and the candy store. I went in, enjoyed some mechanical air conditioning and that antiseptic smell drugstores manufacture.

I nabbed a couple of Superman comics and slid across some black and some white asbestos tiles to the pay counter.

A guy in a white coat with more than his share of nose and chin pushed some cash box keys, grinned a nasty one, showed me how his teeth could use more care. "I got some really good ones in the back—you know what I mean." He was nodding at my Felix tie. He'd seen Felix's naughty adventures. So had I, and a few million other people. Cause I admired Felix didn't make me a walking sandwich sign for pornography. Plus it pissed me off, his assuming I was that sort of boy.

I wasn't sure if he was the druggist or a soda jerk. Maybe both.

I said: "I know what you mean. How much for these?" I pointed to the comics on the counter.

The lech grin went where stuff like that goes when it's out of place. "Two bits."

"Two bits? It says a dime on the cover."

"Yeah. So what?"

I flipped him a quarter. He didn't try to catch it. It bounced on the counter and to the floor.

I shrugged up some apology.

The guy said he'd get it later; I said I'd see him later. I left him in the cool and the antiseptic smell, hit the sidewalk.

It was September and the autumn sun seemed too bright, hot on my hatless head. A knot of tattered boys were kicking a homemade ball in the vacant lot beside the candy store. A girl with olive skin and wavy dark hair watched with a toddler on her hip. She was just old enough to be a mother or a sister. Wasn't my neighborhood; wasn't my cross.

I used the door with a black-and-gold *Welcome* sign at gut level. More mechanical air conditioning inside.

A man with one lazy eyebrow and a simian amount of hair on his bare forearms leaned on a counter. "What'll it be, bub?"

"What's your best bond butterscotch going for?"

"Got some single going two for a sawbuck."

"Ouch. You people heard the Twenty-first got passed December last?"

"Hey, you asked. And it'll take State a New York till December after next to figure it out. Till then, it may as well be Prohibition still. Single malt two for a saw, bub. Take it; leave it."

"I'll take two. And tell Dukey Joe Ready's out front." I held up the comic books, smiled.

"You serious about the scotch?"

"Yeah, baby, and about Dukey too."

We had to look at each other a bit.

"I'll see anybody goes by the name a Dukey's here. Don't run off." The guy went through a door behind him.

Not long—maybe thirty seconds—the door swung out, the candy man pointed with his head. "Dukey says come on back."

I got some eyeball from fuzzy. Maybe he didn't like my Mexican suntan.

The counter swung around to an opening. I used the opening, used the door.

A hallway with sounds ahead. Man talk. Laughter. Cigar smoke.

Second door.

I used it, got a bunch of eyes, maybe a dozen sets. The room noise fell away.

Dukey stood, came at me open arms. "Hey, you bastards, look what the fuggin' cat's drug in. Goddam, Joe Ready, you son of a bitch."

I got hugged. I didn't know Dukey that well. He'd come out to LA a few times to bring info to my brothers—Matty and Jess—from the business run out of Midnight Rose's backroom. This room right here. They offed people.

"The Ready boys' little brother. Was a goddam cop once—watch his fuggin' ass."

The noise came back some.

I rubbed my chin. "Dukey, I need to see Pep." Pep being my key to the club: Ice Pick Phil, someone I'd known—through my brothers—since I was maybe fifteen. Pep didn't get the ice pick moniker busting ice for cocktails.

"Sure, Joe. Sure you do. Come on. Have a fuggin' drink with the bastards here. What for you need to see Phil?"

"I need him to put me in front of Anastasia."

"Sure, kid, sure. First a drink with the big boss."

Dukey flushed a pimply kid off a chair for me. I sat.

Six other guys at the table. I recognized two Bugsies—Goldstein and Siegel—Sal Spitole and an older gent. The older guy was Johnny Torrio, Johnny the Fox—once boss of Chicago. Torrio had the idea he could mellow a hot-head name of Capone so Capone could be the Chi boss and Torrio could go home to Brooklyn. Didn't work out that way for Johnny—he went to the hospital, then jail, then Italy. Looked like he'd finally made it home to Brooklyn. The low rung boys were Pretty Levine, a cold life-taker, and Moey Dimples, Saratoga numbers man. The rest of the beauties, standing and leaning, were muscle and gunsel.

Dukey uncorked a small-necked gallon jug, poured a round out to one and all, even the pimply kid. We drank to my health, or something, in Italian. We all said, *salude,* dropped the shine. Not bad stuff for homemade, you like liquor goes down like spring water.

Torrio watched me like I was a movie, like I couldn't see back. I showed him I could see back. I was free, white, and twenty-nine, and I didn't worship guineas. To hell with these guys with five nicknames.

Torrio must have read me.

He said:

"You a red-hot, Joe Ready? Different guys say you are."

"I got balls is all, Mr. Torrio."

It got snickers from the room like I was dropping one-liners. It got me a smile of sorts from Torrio. The foxy grin.

"Your brothers take contract on bums. Why do you not?"

"I'm not my brothers. I got something else I do."

More fox face, everybody watching the big boss play with me. "I could make you a wealthy man, Joe."

"I'm already wealthy."

I got pshawed or something. "What? You got a few grand in some banks somewhere. So what. You got a nice automobile. You lay around and get the clap from Mexican whores."

A spritz of laughter fell out the peanut gallery again.

Johnny Torrio said, "Shut up, you assholes. This kid's got more noodle than the all of you put together." A fatherly smile. "And you're wasting it, Joey. Wasting it on your something else—this

59

lookin' for people." His hand looked for something abstract in the air, didn't find it.

He reached across the table and gave me a little backhand slap. Not for real—playful. Almost affectionate.

"What say, Joey? You come play on my team?"

Honestly, looking back, I was on the fence. The charming old viper swayed me.

Luck prevailed, saved my weak soul once again—a punk came in, outta breath, tossed a set of keys on the table.

I recognized them.

The punk, maybe coked or junked, said "Me an' Piggy just glommed a cream-colored Cord, pulled it in the garage. You should see this thing."

I grabbed the keys, tossed them at the punk.

Everyone watched the keys hit the punk in the chest, fall to the floor. Not Torrio—he watched me.

When the rest of us looked back up, I had a Savage .38 revolver the size of Florida on the punk.

"I'm gonna chat a few more minutes with Mr. Torrio here. I get done, my Cord's not sitting on the curb out front, I'll take it real personal. You hip?"

"Hey." Twin hands up, palms out. "Sorry, Mister. The keys was in it."

I asked again was he hip; he said he was hip.

"Then you go put my car back where you found it and put the keys back in it. *Capisci?*"

The punk nodded, got my keys off the floor. "Sure, mister. Right now like soon enough?"

"If that's sarcasm, pal, I'll pop you one in the arm right now. Wanna be popped in the arm?"

"No, sir. The car'll be out front."

Dukey told the punk, "And don't let no fuggin' body else take it neither. You listenin', asshole?"

"Yeah, Dukey. I gotcha."

I looked back and put the big Savage away.

Johnny Torrio said, "Such a damn waste, Joey. You're breakin' my heart."

Torrio made a motion with a finger. "Pour us another, one for the road."

Goldstein said, "You leavin' us, Johnny?"

"Yeah, Bugs. Me and sweetheart here gotta go see Meyer."

Siegel said, *Lansky?* like he didn't believe it.

Torrio nodded, said, "Yes *Lansky.* We've become politicos now, so we do favors for big shot heroes. Don't we, Joey? *Salud.*"

We all drank to big shot heroes. *Salud.*

[14]

Lansky didn't love me like Johnny Torrio did; I could tell he didn't.

He acted like he didn't trust me, but he was Meyer Lansky and there would be money involved if we went to the dance together. And not no dusty two gees outta Brownsville, Texas. We'd talk tall cheese and we both knew it.

Lansky's first: "I hear you're a smart boy."

I thumbed at Torrio. "He heard I was red-hot. Seems contradictory, huh?"

Lansky eased back in a giant of a chair. I wondered if his feet touched the floor.

"You're a long way from home, Joe Ready, to be going cute on me. You think I like cute?"

Jesus. Screw the guineas, screw the kikes.

"I think you'd like to look like a regular gee to Thom Dewey. Good luck. Even if we deal, good luck."

Lansky did some eyebrows. "Oh? We deal, you deliver, huh?"

"Mr. Lansky, this ain't brain surgery. It's pretty common knowledge the guy's passing gold tickets in Jersey. The cops weren't stepping on each other's manhood and your guys weren't a bunch a meatball gunsels and worse, the fix woulda been in on this guy last year. Yeah. I deliver." I gave Lansky a couple of beats, showed him my stuff. "I want twenty on top a Spaganetti's two and I want Pearlie Friedman."

Lansky and Torrio talked with their eyeballs some. I couldn't hear a word of it.

Could have been a secret buzz button, could have been clairvoyance—a goon came in. Lansky talked in his ear. The goon glanced at me briefly. I still had my gun so I grinned at him.

The goon drifted; Lansky said: "I can't give you Pearlie. He's way back, old neighborhood."

I worked my pauses again. "Then I don't make you look good, get that fat-faced cross-dresser off your ass." I meant Hoover.

Lansky worked his own beats. Said: "I could make you."

No beat, I said: "No you couldn't. You couldn't even fool me with Spaganetti. Me ending up in your—" I looked around, "—office should tell you something."

He laughed. Maybe with me.

Lansky put the happy face on Torrio. "He's a pistol, Johnny."

"I say, huh?"

"Yeah. You say. How about eighteen gees and Pearlie's current whereabouts?" The last to me.

"You say Brownsville, deal's off, I keep Eddie's two large for coming up here."

Lansky did a study on me. He could've written a term paper he took so long. "You want Pearlie Friedman bad enough to walk by eighteen grand, I gotta know why."

Not that it was any of his business. "When I was young and foolish enough to take being an LA cop seriously, Pearlie crossed me up. He's a kidnapper. It's become a nasty term you hadn't heard."

Lansky watched me. I wondered what he saw.

"So this is Pearlie Friedman's fault? This whatever it is I don't wanna know about some kidnap?"

"I don't really give a damn if it's Pearlie's fault or not. I'm gonna nail him for it. I make eighteen grand off it, fine. I make two grand, fine. Either way, I'm nailing Pearlie Friedman."

I looked from Lansky to Torrio. Torrio was foxy-faced, probably enjoying the perversion.

Looked as though Lansky had forgotten me and Torrio were in the room—a good two minutes went by.

Then: "Whatchu think, Johnny?"

Torrio said, no sag, no hesitation, "Give 'im the guy, Meyer. Pearlie's no good no how. The kid here's got 'im runnin' scared. He's no use to us." A pause, a shrug. "And this kidnap thing he's doing. . ." he made a circular motion in the air with a couple a fingers, ". . .ain't the way we're goin'. *Capisci?*"

Lansky nodded, turned to me. "Sixteen grand and Pearlie Friedman."

"You said eighteen."

"Now I'm saying sixteen."

So what if I got beat outta two grand? I was beat by the king of the kikes.

I put out a deal sealing hand.

Lansky looked at it, grinned at Johnny. "Kiddo, you don't deliver you'll be sorry you shook my hand."

"I get done with this Lucky Lindy thing, I'll call for Pearlie's new address. The goods aren't straight dope, you'll see me later anyway."

Lansky closed his eyes after starring into mine. "Johnny, he's a pistol."

"I say he is, huh?"

Lansky opened his eyes, leaned forward, grabbed my hand when it wasn't expecting it. The grin surprised me. "Like these guys say. . . ," a head was nodding at Torrio, ". . .*omertà.*"

I squeezed the little Jew's hand. I said, *omertà* back at him like I was born with a garlic press in my mouth.

[15]

Torrio stayed. I was sent back to Midnight Rose's—Spitole and Irving Bitz, the two guys Meyer gave me who'd been in the newspaper would be there to tell me what they knew.

I could see nerts blooming from that meet.

A couple of two-bit bootleggers. Lindbergh's frantic search for help put him on Bitz and Spitole—God only knows how that little parley got set up originally. They bilked Charlie, or more likely one of Charlie's benevolent friends, out of a few measly grand. The Lindbergh camp got nada but promises to pony up a kid. Didn't happen.

The kike and guinea club was looking bad over it and Lansky said these boys, Bitz and Spitole, would be ever so helpful. If not, I should let him know such.

After the rap about Bitz and Spitole, Lansky had chopped the big pow-wow. I'd gone arms up, palms out for more.

I got a wink that Torrio wasn't in on, and, "Talk to these bootleggers first. Things will be swell. Go."

I went, rode in the front of Johnny Torrio's car. I forgot was riding in the front my idea or the guy driving.

After a few turns, the driver said: "I got some dope for you."

I said: "What's it taste like?"

The magilla liked it. I got an awkward right paw in my direction. "Sammy."

65

I gave him my hand and my name though I'm sure he had the name.

He said, *"Joe what?"*

I said, *"Sammy what?"*

We swapped a couple of pretty healthy grins.

"Give."

He gave. "You are to know some stuff. Somebody maybe don't want somebody else to know what the first somebody tole another somebody—" sing-song, melodic. "Ya know?"

I didn't have a clue but I played the optimist. "Depends on who the somebodies are."

"You could be right. I'm only a messenger, Joe. See me drivin' someone else's car? I ain't the brains in the arrangement."

I could tell. Mentioning it seemed a bit wet so I let it go by. "Tell me things, Sammy."

A finger, the index. "One: ain't no one to know none o' this, where you heard it. *Niente. Capisci?*"

I rolled a coaxing hand.

Another big finger. "Number two: you report straight to Mr. Lansky. No one else. *Capisci?*"

I put out the yellow flag. "Hold on. You work for Lansky? We're in Torrio's car. . . ." I'm slow. "Ah. You're not Torrio's driver."

"Nah. His guy hadda go do a bad number two. Some soured wine or sumpin'."

"I bet. Give up three."

A longer third finger. "Three: The cops can't know nothin' neither."

I'd kinda included that in the index finger rule. *Ain't no one to know* seemed inclusive as hell to me.

"Tell me something I don't know, Sammy. You're breaking my frigging heart here."

The pinkie. It had to be the one. I could hope. "There's a guy in Hopewell used to work for us, guy name a Abe Wagner. Find him."

66

"What's his sin?"

"Besides cheap white linen suits, bootlegging."

Seemed to be a lot of bootleggers around these days. The confused end of Prohibition left a lot of sharp fellows without work. But like the candyman at Midnight Rose's said: nothing had really changed much. If you could find good untaxed bond whiskey cheap and move plenty of it, you could live in a brownstone, act like regular folks.

And if a moke could pick up a jacked load from time to time, had discreet associates to distribute it, he could knock down some mortgage payments, get the wife's hair processed every Friday and send Junior to military school, get his chubby, spoiled ass out of the house. Bootlegger had grown to cover a lot of ground.

"Why am I gonna find him?"

Sammy grinned good, probably like he would when he was sticking an ice pick in your ear. "Now this, *I* think, is the very best and most informative part. Listen up, Joe."

"Baby, I'm sucking the words right out a your mouth."

"This guy Abe the bootlegger passed some a Lindbergh's gold notes off on a guy we know, a guy down at the docks sells different stuff. Name's Po Po. Po Po calls somebody who calls somebody and so on. I go pick up these notes. Guess what?"

"None of them were Lindbergh notes."

"No, stupid. All of 'em was, all Lindbergh notes."

I clammed. Nothing to say. Still wasn't my serve. I'd yet to see the first nickel of the sixteen-large.

Sammy wasn't solving any great human issues any time soon, but he saw it. Saw my qt, knew I wasn't barking for free anymore.

An envelope that felt like it had sixteen gees in it hit the leather seat by my thigh.

"This Abe guy, he's embarrassed the family, Joe. He took bad money and lammed. Now everyone thinks he stooled cause the cops nabbed him, then cut him loose. The cops had nerts but some stoolie blabbing how Po Po's got some Lindbergh bills. Po Po, the only witness, suddenly went to Detroit for a vacation, couldn't be found, even by the Detroit cops."

"Maybe out fishing."

"Duck hunting sounds smarter this time a year."

This big kid with the serious pomade habit wasn't sounding so dumb anymore.

"But if Swartzkopf was to pinch old Abe. . . ," Norman Swartzkopf was superintendent of the New Jersey State Police.

"You're followin' good, Joe."

We rode some. I felt it coming from across the trestle.

"The job could be let out to the boys who work outta Rosie's for a few hundred bucks, but a certain party is willing to offer the sum of an additional five thousand dollars you wanna take the contract on this bum. The party considers you'd be speaking to Abe anyhows, feels it is an adequate offer."

"And if not, I bet you're free to accompany me to the prom, pop Abe in the head."

"Yes. I've been authorized to do something like that." A business like pause. "Course you don't get the extra five gee."

"Sam, I appreciate the candor, but another five gees at this point would seem like gluttony. Tell Mr. Lansky to be patient. I visit Wagner, he'll flush and fly. You guys get the lead out, you might catch him on the wing this time."

"Mr. Lansky feels very strong about my involvement. Very strong."

I looked at the envelope on the seat next to me, patted it good-bye. "That case, tell Mr. Lansky I said, thanks anyway. *Capisci?*" I slid the envelope at Sammy.

He slid it back. "In that case you have his blessing to go it solo. I'll drop you at your car." Another block or so Sammy said, "No need wastin' time on Bitz and Spitole. Two bit cons. They'll be lucky they get around Mr. Lansky on this in a vertical condition, you get what I'm pitchin'?"

I tried to leave Meyer Lansky's money on the seat.

Sammy wouldn't have it—"Hey, Joe, don't forget the cheese." Envelope out at me.

My hand didn't seem to want to touch it.

I could always take it over to Jersey, get a room, lay it out on the bed, see if your mob money looked any different from your garden variety currency, see if it looked any dirtier.

• • •

The Cord took me on down to Trenton and I did find a hotel. One that looked like it had a safe and a house dick.

Could be I was being edgy for no good reason except some serious people knew I had sixteen grand. I lost the sixteen, I *still* owed Lansky. Put him advantaged—either I deliver or pony up sixteen large.

Was a highbrow flop. You couldn't stay here you didn't have a nickel or two. Twenty feet up to a dome ceiling. Wasn't the Sistine, but it wasn't bad—a naked angry angel was in hot pursuit of a smiley demon with a couple of naked angel frails under an arm. The bad guy didn't look too worried, even with an arrow through his tail. Columns boiling over at the capitals like marble waves. The counter was frigate-sized, maybe cherry wood.

The nance on the counter was the same soft fluffy nance I'd seen on hotel counters in lots of towns.

He quoted rates and I asked didn't the management know the country had just gone through a depression.

He said most of their guests didn't seem to be too depressed despite the economy.

We both grinned. Just because a guy's a fairy doesn't mean he can't be funny.

I filled out a registration card, dealt out some dough, and got a key with a celluloid tag attached.

A Mex dressed like an organ grinder's monkey grabbed my old leather case. I told him to hold on a minute, used Spanish. The little guy actually looked at me, at my face.

"Sí, Señor."

I asked the nance did the joint have a decent safe. He said so far, so safe.

I passed an envelope over, signed for it under the clerk's signature. He gave me a copy and a smile.

"Anything else, Mr. Joseph?"

"No, pal. Me and *mi amigo* here got it."

I showed the Mex a palm, urging him along, gave him a *por favor.*

The trek to the elevator wasn't many miles, but the knee-deep wine carpet made it seem like work.

I should have looked at the key tag. One-oh-six was on it. I showed my bearer and we changed trails.

The room was three off the lobby. The fairy knew his marginal guests, knew who needed an eye kept on. I'd try to hold it down, not wear out my welcome.

I tricked the lock and the Mex was past me and was opening my case before I could stop him.

He must have liked guns. I had a few and they seemed to make him smile.

I pulled a double sawbuck, said, *"Para mi hermano."*

It brought me the international gesture for clamming: a finger to lips.

The Mex pulled the door nearly shut behind him, stopped, and spoke in as fine an English as you'll hear in New Jersey. "Sir, if you'd care for anything that's not on the room service menu, ask for Fredrick."

I laughed; the Mex laughed.

"Bring me a bottle of something made in Scotland, something the Scots would be proud of, Freddy. You need another sawbuck?"

Freddy wagged his head under the monkey hat. "I'll bill you when I get back. No lady this evening, sir?"

"Maybe later, Freddy. I'll let you know."

"Please do, sir. I'll be back shortly with your bottle and some ice."

"And you'll have a tall cool one with me."

"Yes, sir. Anyone can *habla* East Texas Spanish like you do, I'll surely have a drink with."

The door clicked shut.

I went over, flipped the thumb-latch, locked the door.

Under some roscoe and some shirts was the sixteen gees. I pulled it out, counted it.

A rough carpet covered most of the floor of my room. I moved a small writing desk and some chairs and flipped the rug back. Spread a hundred-sixty engravings of Franklin evenly on the floor. Eased the rug back, put the writing table back, put the chairs back and looked nonchalant as possible until Freddy knocked. The wait wasn't long, maybe a butt and a half.

I did the honors against Freddie's better judgment. We drank to long life and prosperity. Drank to the future. Drank to Nueva Laredo and Los Angeles. Drank to having five drinks by five o'clock in the afternoon.

Freddy got sincere, told me his name really wasn't Frederick but some name based on an arcane *indio* dialect that his grandmother's people used. Said he could hardly pronounce it sober himself.

I owned up, told him my name wasn't really Joe Joseph.

He said he didn't think it probably was. "I thought you were a Fed until I opened the bag. Jesus, a German sub-machine pistol? A sawed pump gun. Got buck shot in that one?"

I nodded. "Single aught."

Freddy nodded. "Fans out better'n double aught, huh?"

"Yeah. And falls down quicker you got collateral standing behind somebody."

I poured; Freddy tonged ice.

He held his glass out. "To kind-hearted hitters."

"Whoa, Freddy baby. Not me. I get in tight situations, but I always got ties to the. . . ," I thought, ". . .legal side. Maybe I use the fence freely."

"A paladin?"

"A private license, but mostly I'm a guy with a good hard head and a rubber jaw. And some interesting guns in my travel case."

"I can see you as that. Like in the pulps?"

"No. Like pissing in empty liquor bottles and skulking in dark side streets. Sleeping in your car, crapping in the bushes. Real romantic. I gotta hemorrhoid; I got intermittent double vision in my left eye. My nose has been broken four times, set three times." I grinned, held up my iced shot. "But I got enough money for the rest of my life in a couple a banks, and I'm still vertical."

Freddy clinked glasses. "Here, here. Well said."

Freddy intrigued me mucho. The guy had a head on his square shoulders.

"Where'd you go to school, Freddy?"

"The Normal School For Indigenous Children on the U.S. side of the river. A wonderful school with a damning moniker, don't you think?"

"I think. Then what?"

Freddy grinned. "It show?"

"Yeah, it shows."

"University of Mexico—Doctor of Internal Medicine."

"Trouble there?"

"Political."

"And no papers here?"

"And no papers here."

I pointed at the hootch; Freddy bought us one apiece.

The single malt was amber nectar. I swished it around the ice cube, watched the striations align.

"Freddy, baby, I got a guy you need to know. He's in LA but that might be better than coming into existence in Trenton."

"Hey, Joe, I know some guys too, but I got a wife, two kids and a mother in a rent house in one of Trenton's half-decent neighborhoods. I'm not saving a whole lot."

72

I'd have bet he wasn't. "You trust the guys you know? When you get the dough, you trust them?"

A shrug which meant, *not really*, which meant, *no*.

"What's the toll?"

Freddy gave me a fatalistic snort, sarcastic laughter. "Two, three grand to paper the whole family. More to get my license transferred."

I nodded. Hell, I knew Meyer Lansky. John Torrio, too. Close friends of mine. I was a guy could make promises he'd have to keep when he sobered up.

"Freddy, I get you papers, do I get free doctoring the rest of my life?"

"Joe, I'd give anybody that deal. Don't kid. It's not real funny right now."

I held my glass up. "I'm serious as Walter Damn Winchell, *mi hermano*. Drink to it, goddammit."

We drank.

Seven o'clock, Freddy went home to his *esposa linda*, the *mijos* and his *madre*, still not convinced of my sincerity.

I rang up room service and ordered clams on the shell, red wine and an antipasto tray. Tossed an order of calamari on top. Made sure everyone would be on the same diet this evening should a party spring to life.

• • •

The food was between decent and not bad, and the excitement came earlier in the evening than I'd expected. I'd sucked my last clam down, pushed the tray into the hall, shut the door. Sharp voices came from the direction of the hallway, but sounding farther away, like in the lobby.

I wrapped a bandana around my face, pulled on my hat, brim down. All I needed was a gat. I grabbed the burper.

No one in the lobby—I'd peeked.

A yelp.

73

Somebody had slugged the nance in the back room.

I yelled, "Trenton Police. Come out hands up, eatin' carpet, mokes."

Nada.

Then a guy comes out like he was catapulted. He hit the counter, stood there.

I didn't drill him. It was my favorite nance.

"Shake it, sweet pea."

The nance shook it out the front door.

I tried again, same authoritative voice. "Sergeant, they don't come out in thirty seconds, open fire."

Maybe count of ten, two mokes come out shooting figments, never did see me in the shadows of the hallway.

I knocked them both down with one rip. Finished the chore with another quick burp.

An axe-faced guy was on the carpet leaking life. I didn't know him. I stepped over his quiet body.

The other I knew. I pushed the gray felt off his brow with a toe.

"Sammy, Sammy, Sammy. The family'll be so disappointed."

Sammy moved his mouth like a fish on the sidewalk.

"Bye, Sammy."

Sammy died; I went to my room, crawled in bed, and waited on the cops.

One pounded a half-hour or so later. I got up, ruffled my hair, pulled on my pants and told him I was a sound sleeper—all I heard was a few pops.

• • •

Next morning, all the cops and cameras gone, I'm checking out and the nance thanked me.

I said, *For what?*

He said thanks all the same—room's gratis.

"Nice town. Maybe I'll come back sometime."

74

"I wouldn't. The police made me open the safe to see what I had."

"They don't like baseball headlines?"

"Maybe they're not fans. *Arrividerci*, Mr. Joseph, and thank you once again."

No Freddy. I humped my own bag, bag in one hand, in the other Meyer Lansky's envelope full of newspaper cut up the size of bills. One hundred dollar bills.

I turned a corner and bumped into a short, thick man who smelled of nickel cigar smoke. He'd be the house dick.

"Grenz, house security man."

"Yeah?"

"Yeah." A thumb like a banana jerked over a shoulder. "Like twinkle toes told you, don't bother with our asphalt no more."

"Sure, baby. You like sports?"

Grenz wrinkled his face.

"You like baseball?"

More wrinkling, then, "Yeah, I guess."

I handed him the envelope. "Happy reading, baby."

Grenz took a look. "I knew you were tied into the noise last night."

"Yeah? And I wondered was your absence a coincidence or did someone cross your palm with something? Maybe that's how come we both left it where it was. Don't you think that's best?"

He looked at me, sucked his teeth some. Slapped the envelope on a palm. "Don't come back, buddy." He walked away, pitched the envelope in a can.

I gave his back a spare center finger.

Freddy had my car on the curb, door open.

He took my beat case, stowed it backseat.

Freddy had no telephone but lived next to the neighborhood *carniceria*. I got a number and some instructions on how to get him on the store's pay line should I need.

Freddy got two of Lansky's bills; he palmed and pocketed them sight unseen.

[16]

Every town the size of Trenton has something to bait hopheads and every town the size of Hopewell has a hophead who can't get to Trenton. I went to dinge town and got some bait—a couple of half-load bindles—pure Chinese white. A quick taste proved it potent.

The taste and a shot of scotch took me to Hopewell in good spirits.

My positive attitude paid off, got me a punk with quick eyes making quick promises.

Someone had busted his upper lip. It looked ugly and made him talk funny. We agreed on a bar in a naughty part of town. Did I know it? No, but I'd find it.

I wore two guns. Didn't need either.

The hypo vibrated in, spotted me. A lot of head wagging went ignored; he came over.

"Hey, fella, you see me give you the sign?"

"Un-huh." I blew some beer head onto the bar, took a swig.

"Well, drink up and let's go."

"Un-un."

"Un-un? What for's un-un?"

"There's not a quieter or sleazier place in Hopewell, baby. Here or nowhere. The skag's yours but I gotta few sawbucks for some skinny dope on this fat kike. You got somebody knows something, then tell him to come on in, have a warm beer."

The barkeep and I smiled at each other over the board on two barrels. I guessed the real bar was out being painted. The barleyman's shirt could have used painting, too.

"Well, I don't know what he'll say."

"Ask him when's the last time he saw five fins in one place?"

The punk was gone.

A bit, the door let some sunshine in. I didn't look.

A quiet voice said, "Mista. Mista." Dinge voice.

I still didn't look but the sweaty barkeep did.

"What?" More like a bark.

"Sir, could I speak to the gentleman at the bar?"

"Nah. You ain't comin' in here. No niggers allowed."

I said, "Even with a ticket?"

The barkeep ran thumbs up and down some nervous suspenders. "Ticket? The hell you talkin' about?"

"This." I put a fin on the bar, smoothed it out.

Sweaty nabbed the five, said, "Make it snappy." To the dinge: "Come on in but don't touch nothin'."

The voice said, "Yessir, yessir. Sho won't touch nothin'. Sho won't now, boss."

Someone shuffled up behind.

I said, "Sit down."

The voice said, "Nah, sir. I'm fine right here, sir."

I said, "You got a ticket. Sit."

The bartender looked at me, jerked his head.

A man sat on the stool next to me.

I turned, read his mail.

He was that beat Negro who could have been forty or sixty. Jersey or Mobile he'd be the same guy. Eyes so liquid they could run off his face any second, the whites yellow as a nicotine finger. Stoop labor back, hard labor hands. A rummy in a decent suit coat, ragged bib overalls and no shoes.

"You wanna drink?"

The barkeep jumped in, protecting the fragile exclusiveness of the dive. "No, un-un. Ain't no niggers drinkin' in here."

I grinned, said, "Yeah?"

The barkeep came down, said, "Not without no ticket, they ain't." He had brains; so *what* they were in his wallet?

I gave him a ticket for my Negro friend and my friend selected a shot of bourbon. It must have been the way the dinge honored it. Whatever—it made me say, "Tell me a story and I'll go a double."

"Plus the twenty-five, sir?"

"Plus the twenty-five. Spill."

"Thank you, sir. You a gentleman. Okay, here go, sir. This Hebrew gentleman you lookin' for, he baldheaded, wear a white linen suit all a time, white shoes?"

"Yeah. You got him for me?"

"How much it worth I got his neighborhood but not his particular cut, sir?"

"You could find his house, I'd be more generous."

"How 'bout a kicker? Man met me at the park by the lake ever day four-five days. Give me a twenty to go get him a pint a shine. Sho did now. Give me two dollars jes for makin' the trip. Shine wasn't but a dollar."

"Yeah?" I was ears up.

"Yessir. Then a couple a shine boys tell me 'bout how the state police lookin' after them twenties I was usin'."

"Your buddies tell on you?"

"Not yet, sir. But they always the future. Sho is, now."

"You tell the man in the white suit?"

"Yessir. He give me a five that day, sent me to get his pint. I ain't never seen him again."

"You know why I'm looking for this man?"

"Yessir. I got me a good suspicion. It's about them twenties, I do. That liquor sho was out the right bottle. Sho was."

I got out another ticket. To the keep: "Give the man a double." To the dinge: "What's this park by the lake called?"

• • •

Dope looked straight on the locale. Jewish deli, temple down a block, some Yids on the street. Too many to make a cakewalk out of spotting my one certain kike.

If this guy Wagner was doggo in any classical sense I'd never glimpse him. Aunt Moira or somebody would be doing his running for him, him peeking out the eyelet lace curtains.

Then maybe not. This neighborhood, the domestics would have been fetching Abe's gefilte fish.

Okay, totally new approach—try being smart. I called Freddy, waited long-distance for thirty-five cents worth, asked could he get to Hopewell? He could.

We shook hands at the bus station two hours later.

In the Cord, on the way to the park, I skinnied Freddy. He liked. Liked the whole set-up from Matamoros on.

We leaned on the car, studied the crowd.

Freddy said he'd be back in a bit, went over and stood in front of the deli. The little Mex worked a couple of Negresses in maid outfits, then nabbed an older Mex fellow in a chauffeur's outfit.

The chauffeur had nervous eyes. He took Freddy and a bag of produce to a Rolls. They loaded, disappeared like a sigh.

I found two fingers in a scotch bottle, leaned on the car, and played with it till a cop cruised by, eyeballed me. I showed him a face of upright citizenry and held the hootch down inside the car window.

The cop must have bought the face—he drifted. The Rolls sighed into view.

Freddy got out, smiles up.

He never faltered, got in the Cord. I read, broke my lean, and met him inside.

"Go north."

I went north.

Freddy said, "I think it'd look better I was wheelman."

79

I dug; pulled curbside.

Fire drill and Freddy was wheelman.

A left or two, a right or two, Freddy put the Cord to bed under an elm that must have dodged the Dutch disease.

"Down two, across the street. Big lavender thing with the fancy porch."

Freddy meant the cornice work—very ornate. Roccoco Jersey.

"Lots of you guys doing domestic in Hopewell?"

Not even a glance, Freddy said. "What? Us doctors? I'd bet not."

Nailed me so through and through I took it like a man.

A little bit of stony silence, Freddy said, "The people he's with got a Mexican maid. The guy in the uniform? He's her father."

"Freddy, you're made outta gold, baby. Let's go get a bottle, piss away the afternoon, see where fat kikes go for kicks in a berg like Hopewell."

Downtown liquor store; industrial row for an icehouse; glasses in a dry goods store.

The Glenfidich wasn't good enough for Freddy. We found a Mex joint hidden pretty well in dingeville. Freddy brought out greasy fried plantain, limes, tequila, some dried meat. I didn't ask for specifications.

Sidebar: last time I ever drank tequila or ate non-speciated meat products.

Freddy drove us back to the stakeout, put us on the same piece of curb.

We sat—we drank.

We each had a stash joint. We herbed.

Then we ate. And drank.

Then I puked on the curb and was okay again. For a while I was okay. As long as I laid off the tequila, I was okay.

Abe showed about quarter of eight in a green DeSoto—he and a woman. They went into the lavender house without knocking.

Too easy on how it was falling, so to spice things up Abe exits like ten minutes later with the dame and now two more dames— oldies. One of them maybe Methuselah's first wife.

It must have taken them an hour and a half to get to the DeSoto. Then granny balked, Abe trotted back to the front door, leaned in far enough to make noise, trotted back.

Not long after, what could have been the first Packard limo built came from ivied gates. The foursome loaded on, sailed away. We tagged along a safe few lengths behind, Freddie minding our manners for us.

One thing for sure—Abe Wagner wasn't doing much doggoing. That'd be one to cipher over a long green Cuban. No it wouldn't—Lansky used me to flush the guy so his boys could do Abe outta town, outta state, do him where no one's looking.

The Packard had an open chauffeur's cab with a closed coach behind. The driver was as dark black as the Packard. Could've been from sitting in the open cab.

His eyes shown white like a caricature of a Negro. I didn't mention it to Freddy. He'd have thought me prejudiced.

We went to a place named Lenny's. Freddy and I had lamb shanks. I'm not sure about Abe and his party—they got a private salon.

The shanks were decent and we took care of our debts, and took toothpicks from an aluminum dispenser out to lean on the Cord.

Abe came out alone.

He walked east on the sidewalk, toward us but across the street.

I told Freddie to get the car primed and I followed Abe on foot.

A rough fellow in a Mackinaw jacket came from a cellar stair, spoke to Abe.

I pulled up short, went back, leaned on the car some more.

Abe and the Mackinaw chatted quick, exchanged envelopes, and retreated in different directions.

Abe went back to the restaurant.

The lamb and starch had sobered me up enough I needed a drink. Freddy did them up neat, dry, straight and high. Two of them were like midnight dew.

A skinny hour, Abe and party came out; the Packard appeared like it had a summons bell in it.

Abe, the babe, and the two old Jewesses piled into the Packard. The dark Negro took them away.

Back at lavenderland, the blue hairs got out. Abe and babe no got out.

Abe and babe try a bed and breakfast joint beyond the city limit sign maybe three miles. The big Packard bent in the middle and headed homeward.

A second story light comes on in a bit. Silhouette looks like Abe. Then the babe. Then the both, cuddled up like kittens.

Freddy said, "What's your version?"

"Same as yours. They know someone at the desk—no luggage, straight to a room."

"Should I see who they know?"

I looked from the window to Freddie. "Say how."

"I could be looking for a job. I got good experience and references."

"At ten-thirty?"

"I just got into town. I'm a real go-gitter." Freddy had gone border Mex. "What can it hurt, *Señor?*"

"Get out and ply your wares. Freddy, you know there's a big nut for you when we get done."

"Original deal—the good papers—I'm tranquil."

I nodded; he walked over to the entrance.

Two shots and three ready rolls that tasted like smoking nothing through a new sock, Freddie was back. He'd gotten the job, started Monday morning at five so he could take out the trash before the gentry awakened.

"You got a stair on the inside. It's off an open courtyard, three sides. A stair on the outside leads to the wrap-around porches we see."

Twelve foot of overhang jutted out from the main structure. One ceiling was another floor and so on for three floors.

"The exterior stair has a padlock on it after dark. A large Schlage."

"Can we cut it?"

"Cut it?" Freddy looked shocked. He wriggled his digits. "These fingers are magic, my friend. We need cut nothing." A smile. "I noticed you got a pick set in your bag."

I dug the bag from the boot, found the picks. Freddy rolled a couple in his fingers and then into a fist to hide them.

We walked boldly and directly to the gate. I played innocent and Freddy played the picks in the lock.

Freddy's work with the feelers made me wonder about him some more. A lock clicked and Freddy swung the door back, did a go-ahead gesture with a horizontal hand. I went ahead, quit wondering. Freddie may have had a normal education for an indigenous kid, but he'd damn sure been around some since.

"Bring the lock. I don't wanna get locked in."

Freddy put the Schlage in a front pocket.

Four turns corkscrewed us to the second floor porch. Down a few windows to Abe's room.

The woman must've had a mouth like a tunnel—when she laughed, it sounded like a train was coming out of it.

Abe would laugh back at her occasionally only Abe didn't sound so sincere.

The Mex and I leaned on the rail of the porch, smoked ready rolls, toyed with a flask I had in a pocket. We were waiting on who knows.

To make conversation, I said, "The woman seems like a screamer, you think?"

"Yeah. We go in, man, she's gonna yell her head off. You got a plan?"

I thought about it, laid one out. "I'll knock her out. She'll get a good one off, but I'll sap her mid-hoot."

"*Amigo.* You're not serious, are you?"

"No, but I can't think of anything else that sounds like it'd work."

The quest went unresolved—Abe came out the French door of his room. He lit a cigar, said something inaudible over a shoulder.

Shirt sleeved and tie-less, the big kike strolled across the balcony, leaned on the rail. Like we weren't there.

Then we were there.

He said: "You got business with me?"

I said yeah and the scene went off script.

Short on a long one: Abe went over the balcony. Caught a foot on the rail. Hit the ground flat on his back. Hit it pretty hard. Startled hell outta me and Freddy.

The startle broke, we bolted for the stair.

Four quick downward turns, a jog around a corner.

Abe's still on his back. The moaning was awful.

"The hell's wrong with you, pal?" I was serious.

Some moan.

I asked Freddy did he catch it. He said no, he didn't.

"Abe." I said it loud, in his face. "You think we're here contracting?"

Two floors up, a voice said, "What's going on?"

I turned, looked up at Abe's babe. Forty going on fifty, red hair she wasn't born with. She was broad, more so in the shoulders. Wore a hungry divorcee dress—one of those gay print things hung over meaty shoulders by two-inch straps.

"I believe this fella leaned out too far and fell."

"Oh-my-God. Is he okay?"

"He's just had the wind knocked out of him. We'll get him up. My friend's a doctor of internal medicine."

She thanked God for that but it sounded more like something she just said.

Freddy had Abe's belt when I turned, pulling up, saying relaxing things to Abe.

Abe caught breath way down in his diaphragm, hauled air in like an airplane propeller. At that point in the evening it was just another awful sound.

Freddy stopped bouncing Abe, Abe caught a second breath— and started giving Freddy hell about being too rough. Called Freddy a *dirty little spic.*

I squatted, leaned in close to prone Abe.

"Abe, you say something else stupid, I'll put my shoe in your mouth. Shut up and listen."

Abe couldn't shut up and listen.

I looked at the Jewess. "Could you toss us down some ice in a towel? Your husband's neck needs it."

She said, *sure,* twice like a New Yorker would, and drifted.

I put a number ten Johnston and Murphy in Abe's mouth. He shut up.

Enough is enough. "Listen, you bootlegging scum bag, you don't wise up, you're gonna be so dead you won't need giggles in a backwater inn. I got your nuts, Abe. Got 'em in my pocket."

Abe's face didn't get it.

"Five grand's what you're worth to me. Five big fat grand, sweetie."

Abe's face still didn't get it.

"Abe, they know where you are. Sit up like a man when I'm talking to you."

He sat.

"Less'n a grand, Abe. That's all you're worth in Midnight Rose's back room. Think about why Lansky'd give me five to treat you like a bum."

Abe knew. Same reason Abe was laying low in a side spur stop like Hopewell—the Lindbergh certificates.

He had to be sure. "You guys from Texas?"

Freddy wanted to play, said, "LA."

Abe said, "Figures. And I *bet* your name don't end in no vowel." The last came at me.

"Sometimes. No, Abe, I'm no part guinea. I'm unconnected to the big happy family in the city. And I passed on the fat sandwich cause I'm chasing somebody's upstream a you. You ain't shit to me one way or another."

Abe put out both hands, one at Freddy, one at me. A bit of tugging, we got his rotundness fully vertical.

"So whadda you want? And one a youse needs to find my cigar."

85

I hit Abe in the side of the neck with a right hook. The hook took him down to a sitting position.

Abe made some funny noises down there, cleared his throat, shook his head, said, "Or not, if neither of you don't feel like lookin' for it."

"Abe, get the hell up and tell me where you got those gold tickets. And please lie to me so I can punch you again in the same spot on your neck."

Freddie and I got Abe vertical again.

The woman was back squawking about, *Here's the ice.*

Me and Abe eyeballed.

"You sure you passed on the contract?"

"Abe, baby, if we were motivated, one of us woulda put an ice-pick in your ear while you were on the grass."

Abe nodded a big head, told the woman to toss him the ice, drink some wine, let him discuss a proposition with these investors.

We got the New York double-sure, some ice and her broad backside.

Abe said he could use a drink.

I had one in my pocket; I said I had one in the car. We took a walk, three pals out for a stroll.

To the Cord. Me and Abe in the back seat like royalty but him with ice on his neck.

We did some Scotch; I felt like a good smoke, mentioned it to Freddie. He grabbed cigars from the dash pocket, green Cuban numbers, passed two back, kept one.

Second shot Abe wants to know what's in it for him.

"Abe, baby, I've put a shoe in your mouth, punched you pretty hard in the neck. The hell you think's in it for you?"

Abe put some thought on it, puffed his cigar like an Indian.

When he spoke, it wasn't nonsense. "That sorta ante, somebody else as unattached as youse'll take the contract."

I shrugged.

"I'm worth five grand? Why come? I mean, even considering the source a them twenties."

"Clean, good talent ain't cheap, baby. You get a year's worth a Rose's for two grand. But quiet guys don't wake up for pocket jingle like that."

"You seem to know a lot on the subject."

"Blood related to it. I'm a Ready brother."

Abe nodded. He'd heard the name.

He should have. Quiet, cool killers. You didn't want northeastern fealties to come into play, get the Ready boys. Good boys, no noise, good to Mama—put her in a big house in Pasadena. Got her off the reservation and she drank there till she died. Her boys out there plying their wares, do a bum—go home to LA, act like regular folks.

"But I don't take contract, Abe."

Abe looked at me to see if I was joking—or faking. "And all you want's the guy with the certificates? Why?"

"Same as what makes a stooge like you worth gees, sweetheart. Lindbergh. He's a *hero*, you hadn't heard."

Abe went cagey. "You two ain't cops? Tell me you ain't cops."

I said, "Yeah, I'm Swartzcopf. That's Melvin Purvis driving the car."

Freddy waved the cigar like he enjoyed being Melvin.

"Come on, Abe. You got no value at this point beyond your immediate whereabouts. One phone call to Lansky your ass is worth tall bucks, alive."

"They'll kill me. Why's it better to let them do it by selling me to 'em?"

"Cause you're worth those tall bucks, and my conscience is full-up right now with more pressing dilemmas. Talk to me, Abe, for God sake. I'm getting tired of you."

"The guy lives in the Bronx. I hooked him up with a Harlem crew—niggers own a floating club. Sure, I've turned a few bills on my own, you know? I gotta make the dough."

"Yeah we watched you turn some tonight. What'd you manage to pinch off the tiger's tail?"

"Come on, man, I'm doggo over this crazy family stuff. I gotta make the dough where I can make the dough, right?"

87

"Right. You got a name and address? I know you do."

"Richard Houke, a Dutch guy."

Freddy looked back. "Boss, this canary keeps singing long-song, we're gonna need gas."

"Get gas, baby. Abe's getting ready to lie to us. I'm gonna punch him; then we're gonna take him up to the Bronx where he's gonna show us something to make us not invest so much as a nickel phone call in his impending demise."

"I ain't going to the Bronx, fella. Do what you want, I ain't going to the Bronx."

I hit Abe in the jaw, put him to bed.

I had a little noodling phase while Abe was chilled. Laughed to myself about the big cluck going off the balcony. Poor Abe—I really messed up his evening.

Bet the henna-haired Jewess wondered what the hell happened to big-shot Abe after he took the dive. She'd drink too much wine, conk out, wake up in her wig and the temptress dress. She'd be pissed at Abe, swear to never speak to him again on the cab ride home.

The smell of the river woke Abe. He snorted, looked at the open window by his head.

Abe picked up his chops pretty well. "We in the Bronx yet?"

Freddy said, *All but.*

Abe said catch an ave, run to Two-Hundred Street.

Freddy drove the Cord along the narrow streets like it had a hinge in the middle—was a beautiful thing.

Freddy, after a bit: "Give me an avenue, pal."

"Twelfth, then Two-Hundred Twenty-Second Street."

A few turns, Freddy needed more.

"Number seventy-nine. Garage off to the side."

"New looking garage?" Freddy looking at Abe in the rearview.

"Yeah, I guess, now you say it."

I turned to put my body fully aimed at Abe across the back seat.

"Abe, you jerk me, I'll get Freddy here to gut you, put you on a

88

fence in the desert to cure when he goes home to see his mama this fall. I'm going up there, see this guy. You're straight, you win."

"Listen, buddy, I'm straight. Guy's a tight-lipped dude, but always got the tickets. Three'll get you four all day long."

"Whatcha say, Kid?"

Freddy—the Kid—said, "I say I go to the door, see who lives there."

"Nice. Okay with you, Abe?"

"Sure. His old lady's name is Anna." Lots of *ah* to it.

Freddy drifted. We watched him drift. A tumbleweed was never as subtle as Freddy crossing dusty Two-Hundred Twenty-Second Street to the modest white house. The house didn't look loved, like it was probably a rental. I could be wrong. The tenants could be busy with other stuff than shrubbery.

A dark haired woman entertained Freddy's foolishness, asked him inside.

A few minutes, he plowed back to us and the Cord and the scotch.

"Anna Hauptmann, two *n's* on the end. Saw a stack of mail. But the guy's first name really is Richard."

"Where's Richie?" Curious me.

"At work, or not. It wasn't so clear. I told her a friend told me I could get three for two on pesos for U.S. twenties here."

"Yeah? And she said. . . ?"

"She said maybe. Richard'd be home soon, I should come back."

I said, "We'll wait." Cuffed Abe on the jaw. "Right Abe?"

Abe put out rug merchant hands. "Come on, guys. I delivered, didn't I?"

Freddy looked over the back of the front seat. He shrugged.

I said, "Kid says, *So you say.*"

Abe rolled his eyes.

"I could knock your Jewish ass out again you want. You do seem to spend raw time better kayoed."

89

Abe thought he'd be okay if I could pony another shot or so of that honest scotch I was pouring.

I ponied two times three before Richie showed.

The guy was drunker than we were. It took the sidewalk and more to contain his stagger-step.

Second step up to his clapboard, he went to one knee. Stewed like Italian tomatoes. Good for the home team.

"Tell him you got a gee's worth of Franklin's portraits for whatever gold certificates."

"I told the wife pesos."

"So what. You were testing. Here."

I counted a grand off Lansky's dough.

Abe was eyeballs on the roll.

I counted twenty, passed them to Abe.

"Abe, sweetie, when I say you can scat, you need to go invisible. Now. Don't go back, roll the redhead, say bye to Auntie Whosit. You need to go. Now. From here to out of sight."

Abe took the two gees; looked at me hard. I said, "Sympathy dough, Abe. I think the guys at Rose's are gonna run you down. I give you running money maybe it eases my conscience."

"So, I can go?"

"No. When my man gets back, we'll see."

Abe nodded. "Why'd you give me the cut now?"

"I just wanted you to know what you'd be missing you screwed me."

Abe held the two grand in his fist until Freddy got back.

"Two for one, *hermano*. What you say?"

"Anybody care in Mexico if U.S. twenties are tickets or not?"

"No comprende, Señor."

"Freddy makes another grand, Abe gets to go hide out some more. I love happy endings. You need a ride, Abe?"

"Nah. I'll take the bus outta here. Ain't no one suspecting me in the Bronx?" Abe checked me good. "Right? Ain't nobody looking in the Bronx?"

"No, baby. You're free to go. Tell him, *Vaya con Dios*, Freddy."

Freddy told him, did it good and Spanish.

[17]

Things broke easy. Next day we followed Richard around some. Post office, hair trim, early lunch at a pretty greasy diner.

After lunch we rode some more. Stopped at a gas station.

"Pull in Freddy—gas up."

"Yessir, boss." Putting some Amos on me.

"Cut the funny. Give me one of those twenties."

I got a handful, kept one, wrote Hauptmann's tag number on the bill.

There was a goober in a peaked cap wanting to help me.

"Fill it, baby."

Hauptmann paid and was on his way out.

"Hey, buddy, you got change for a fifty?"

The Hun's eyes looked like he was gonna cry.

"No. Not today. Sorry, Jack." He sounded sorry.

"How about a sawbuck? Got change on that?"

Hauptmann gave me five ones and a five. I passed him a weary sawbuck, put the five and the ones in my breast pocket.

The guy inside saw the whole exchange from over Richie's shoulder. I was liking it.

The restroom was around back. I used it for a temporary office. Took out the twenty-dollar gold certificate, added another twenty and a ten, put it all in my breast pocket behind my display kerchief. Hauptmann's cash went in my pants.

I came out, went around some storefront glass to a glass door.
"How much?" across the gravel lot, at the pump jockey.

The goober said a dollar and a dime.

The glass door leaned away. The guy inside wasn't happy. He was eating fried chicken and something else from a lunch pail. The pail wasn't new. His scowl wasn't new. And nothing got newer or happier because of my interruption.

"Says a dollar ten. All I got's two twenties and a sawbuck. Fella outside just now broke my emergency fifty or I wouldn't have that."

"I can do the sawbuck."

I put it all on the counter. The dirty guy took the ten but I caught him admiring the twenties.

Eight-ninety—in ones and dimes—came back at me.

I was poking at one of the twenties. "You know, something about that fella, how he was skittish, and then he gives me those two gold certificates. I wrote his tag number down on one a them. See it?" I tossed it on the counter.

Greasy wiped his hands on his overalls, felt my twenty. He leaned over, held it up to a brown, soiled paper taped to the wall.

"Well, lookit here." Greasy smiled. "That there's some a the Lindbergh kidnap money."

"Yeah? Shouldn't you call the cops?"

"I guess I should. You know, he had a foreign accent too, didn't he?"

"Yeah, I noticed. Know what? I bet there's a handsome reward tied to this deal."

Greasy studied. "You saying even split?"

"No, baby, I'm too rich already. I just ride around with my faithful Tonto solving crimes. Hiyo, Silver."

"Hang on, buddy."

I stopped. I let him say it so I could counter.

"How do I know you're not the kidnapper?"

"I got an LA drawl. My man Freddy? Straight up border town

Mex. This boy had a Swedish sounding accent or something, like *you* said—the newspapers say the cops are looking for a guy with an accent." I grinned good. "But if it was my twenty, why would I point it out to you? And you're keeping the money. Damn, man, can't you see I'm just being a good citizen because I can afford it? See that Cord automobile out there?"

"Yessir."

"I got that as a bonus on a job. A *bonus*. You know what one of those costs?"

"No, sir."

Neither did I.

I did innocent hands. "Call the johns, get your reward, forget about me and Tonto. Let us ride quietly into the sunset." I left him with a smile and a tip of my hat.

A car pulled across the gravel, put some dust in a small dervish coming across the hot street.

When it pulled past, I walked to the Cord, got in.

"Where to?"

"West."

"What's west?"

"The sunset, my faithful companion, the sunset."

"You know I got a family in Trenton, right boss?" Trenton was northeast of us.

"Let's pretend Trenton's west, Freddy, and get the hell outta town at the same stroke."

"Into the sunset, boss."

After dark and dinner at a damn good backwater inn, I called the number Lansky'd given me.

A few purrs, a moke says, *Yeah.* Not even a question. These guys needed some Emily Post piped in.

"Yeah," like he had said it. "Lansky close by?"

"Who's this?"

"Tell him it's Ready."

"Which one?"

"Would it really matter, precious?"

93

I got Lansky.

"You iced Sammy and the two of you so close after your chat."

"Caught him stealing, baby. Shot another fella too you hadn't heard."

A little amused noise, then: "Yes. A man called Cat."

"Your job's done." Like that. Flat. Nothing in it.

"Yeah? Tell me about it."

"Read it in the newspaper in the morning."

Some q.t.

"A twenty grand sign up, Joe."

"You been talking to Torrio?"

"Yes. He wants you in Chi."

"What'll Lucky say?"

"He's too busy out trying to get arrested by the police and get deported. I'm thinking he wants to live in the old country very badly."

"What about Capone?"

"Kiddo, a caveman like you'll eat 'im."

"How you know that?"

"What don't eat Joe Ready, Joe Ready eats. I know you, Joey. Better'n you do."

I filed the confidence, said, "I pass, Meyer. Thanks all the same."

"I tried. All I can do is try. Good luck with Friedman. I never cared much for him anyway. Too impudent." A pause. "By the way, this week's sheet has him in Canada."

"Which side?"

"Yours."

"Bye, Meyer Lansky."

"God bless, Joe Ready. Offer stands. Any time you should care to defect."

I told him I'd think about it, but I never did.

[18]

Only two questions on the Lindbergh story."

Late A.M. on Joe's patio, reefer going. Joe Joseph, or maybe Ready, worked up a lungful, passed to Jimmy. He was grinning. Knowing what's coming.

"The hell's Ready?" Jimmy toked, watched Joe.

More grin. "Me, kid. Joseph's my traveling name."

Like that explained it. *Oh yeah, a traveling name.*

"You traveling right now?"

Joe shrugged his head to one side. "What's your second question?"

"You believe Hauptmann kidnapped the kid?"

"You been reading up on Lindbergh?"

"Yeah, went to the library first thing this morning." Pass the doob back to Joe.

"I wondered where you were. Yeah, I believe it was Hauptmann. But it doesn't matter, see. He had the loot, all but the few gees he'd been able to roll. If he didn't do it, he knew who did. Same thing, to me. Had he ponied up a pigeon, he coulda dodged the hot chair." A shrug. "He never nickled anyone up but a dead guy. He did it." Joe puffed, ducked the roach in the ashtray.

Jimmy accepted that.

"This Pearlie Friedman. What'd he do?"

Joe exhaled, puffed his cigar. "Keep listening, baby. We'll get to Pearlie."

"You ever catch him?"

"We'll get to him. Trust me, kid. Matter a fact, I'll tell you a short one in the morning while we're fishing. Clue you in on some a Pearlie's work, one a my biggest fuck-ups—just so you'll see I'm not quite perfect."

"Fishing?" Jimmy didn't do fishing, told Joe so.

"We'll take my poles, buy some bait and beer, drown some shrimp. It'll be fun."

"How early we talking?"

"Why does it matter? You're not getting any tonight."

"Yeah, I hear you."

"Let's try coffee at eight, see how it goes."

Sounded good to Jimmy. He thought morning fishing meant a pre-dawn attack. No way. Not in Joe Ready's world.

• • •

In Joe's world, nine A.M., after coffee and doughnuts at eight, means Miller time. He walked to the bait shop at the center of the pier, disappeared through a spring-loaded screen door.

Jimmy finished his second cup of coffee. He'd brought it from Joe's at Joe's insistence. Seemed in a hurry. To get Jimmy out, maybe? Ah shit. No way. Jimmy buried the thought of Joe having a woman in the bedroom. He'd shown it to Jimmy—round bed, satin sheets, strobes and blacklights. The Hef's bedroom, but in West Palm. Very hip.

Whatever, man. The ocean was fine this morning, the sun sprinkling diamonds on the low, undulating turquoise surface.

Joe appeared with a six-pack and a bucket. He sat the bucket between them, passed beer around.

"You gonna bait your hook?" came with the beer.

"Are you?"

Joe shrugged, "Maybe," sat in his lawn lounger, found dark shades, lay back. A few seconds passed; he sipped, sat the beer on his abdomen.

96

Jimmy put his hand in the bucket, got spiked by a shrimp. It made him curse at the little bastard. Who'd have thought a freakin' shrimp could stab you?

Joe peeped an eye, rolled his head to see what Jimmy was doing. "Don't let those mean old shrimp whip you, sweetheart."

"Screw you. Where do you hook these dudes?"

Joe's other eye opened. "You're shitting me, right?"

Jimmy said, *Yeah, just shitting,* hooked the shrimp through its tail diagonally.

Joe muttered, *Jesus,* found the thin floppy straw hat Jimmy'd seen before, put it over his face.

Jimmy pushed the button on the reel, let the shrimp plop on the planks. The shrimp thumped around pretty good for being tail hooked.

He reeled the shrimp in to about face level, studied it, swung it over and let it hang by the hat.

Joe said, down under there, "Smell reminds me a my second wife."

Jimmy laughed, stood and dropped the shrimp over the rail. It hit the water and was gone.

The wind was outbound from Jimmy's side of the pier, and he was trying to watch his line, see where it was drifting.

"Jimmy," loud, close.

Jimmy looked over a shoulder. The Saul guy from the party— his mom called it the mixer.

Jimmy spoke on the way to upright from his lean on the rail, said, "How are you? Saul, isn't it?"

"Yeah. You got a good memory. You guys doing any good?"

The guy was smiling big. Jimmy hoped Saul's Polident held.

"Drowning shrimp. You?" Jimmy looked back, reeled up.

"Just got here. Fridays I fish."

Joe said, *Yeah,* as a question, pushed the hat back.

Saul grinned, said "Yeah, every Friday. How's it going, Joseph?" while Joe pulled the hat back down without a response.

The guy smiled out and drifted to the end of the pier, maybe a hundred feet, a little more. Jimmy watched him unfold and uncoil and unpack.

"Set the drag light and make sure it's unlocked." Meaning the reel.

"Why?"

"Cause you're gonna set it down eventually, and I don't care to lose a fifty-eight dollar Penn reel."

Jimmy obliged but it took him some time finding the right knobs.

He quit acting. It showed—he'd never been fishing in his life.

The rod propped on the rail just right so Jimmy nabbed a beer, sat on his lawn chair.

"What's that Saul guy doing?" from under the hat.

"He's still unpacking but he's got two rigs baited and in the water already. He's looking. Hey, Saul what's-your-name."

"I think he said it was Goldstein. Nervous guy Saul is."

Jimmy hadn't noticed. He was dorky by Jimmy's ruler.

"Whatever happened to the guy who fell off the balcony?"

"Abe Wagner? Got a lead breakfast in Minneapolis, St. Paul one."

"The mob?"

"Sure the mob. The guy copped a disguise but he couldn't shut the hell up. Couple a gunnies caught him at a breakfast joint, killed him over two scrambled, toast and bacon way I heard it. Maybe it was God getting his Jew ass for eating pork."

Jimmy'd have to remember that one. Put it in his notebook.

"You get this Pearlie guy?"

"No. And Lansky'll die in debt to me. He swears otherwise, but he knows he owes me."

"What's the deal on this Pearlie guy, Joe? What'd he do?"

"Kid snatcher. Good at it if collecting a ransom once in a while is good. I ran across him in LA in '27. I was young as you almost and a cop, you can imagine that. Pearlie set up a kidnap, then lammed when Big Joe Parente, boss a Frisco and everything south, got the ass. It didn't go well, but I'll tell you that one later.

I'm gonna tell you about one in Tacoma, Washington, kid name a Charlie Mattson. Had Pearlie written all over it. I coulda had him—did have him—but I got too smart."

[19]

Thanksgiving '36 came and went like a whisper in church. Ma had died spring before last and I didn't care to break bread with either of my reprobate brothers and their respective current molls.

Back among the naked simians, back in LA. Living in a carriage house behind a rich man's house. The rich man knew a rich man I knew and neither spent a whole lotta time any-one-where. It was offered—I took.

I had a wheelbarrow full of money, a new car, and thought I was pretty damn pretty. Lay by the pool, got a tan. Wore white breeches and buck shoes. Wore my shirt open at the collar. About as waggish a period as I ever had. I was pretty damn pretty all right. Even prettier when I'd load up on coke four-five times a week.

Some shorts dropped by from time to time. Hollywood made hummingbirds of the lovelies. Hollywood, the pretty, red hibiscus full of the nectars called fame and fortune. I bedded my share—I was young, I could, I did.

A girl named Delores—I'm not sure on the last but it was surely something sappy and contrived—was on a wood chaise by the pool. She had worn a white two-piece, but now the top was lying on the table. I'd retreated to the double shade of an umbrella-covered table in the shade of a respectable eucalyptus.

My Filipino houseboy came out, shouted: *Hey, boss.* He knew to announce himself, knew what an unsuspecting soul might find around here when the gentry was amiss.

"Yeah, Peach?"

"You got phone call. Big shot from New York, boss. You come."

"Who is it, baby?"

"He say tell you is someone who know his loxes and bagels."

My-my. The chief kike his-own-self.

"I'll be back, toots. Gotta call I gotta catch. Watch those things don't swell up in this heat and explode."

Delores took it like King Tut's mummy.

Peaches had the phone, saying, "Yes, sir. Hold please. Mister is here now. Please."

Coming from the afternoon heat, the mechanical air conditioning was frigid. I had on trunks and had a towel on my shoulders and it was still cold.

I took the phone, said, "Lansky?"

A guy who spoke through a slit in his face said, *Hold on.*

I held. Thirty seconds, I dumped the call.

Peaches looked puzzled. I stood by the phone.

It rang.

I said, "Yeah?"

"The hell you hang up for?"

"The hell you keep me waiting for?"

A tsk or two. "Joey, Joey, Joey. So-tough Joey. LA Joe. The Cali Kid. You got more?"

"Yeah. The You-put-some-tattered-info-on-me-about-our-mutual-acquaintance Kid."

"Sorry. I gave in good faith. The guy gave it? He won't do such again."

"Wow, I'm feeling better already, your good faith buoying me up."

"You're a smart kitty, Joe. But you can get too smart. Even a kitty like you can get too damn smart. Even way out on the West Coast."

I heard. I'd been reprimanded properly. It probably didn't show since I didn't care much.

"You know it's still daylight out here and I'm working on my tan."

"Okay, Smartie. Your man's around Seattle. Done that Weyerhaeuser thing. That went swell for him so now he's supposed to be setting another one up before he moves on." Went swell for Pearlie maybe but a couple of other mokes were in jail for it.

I thought on it. The Weyerhaeuser kidnap had been Pearlie's type of deal—pick a kid up at school with a good story. Seemed like a chauffeur's uniform and a half-assed story could get you a hall pass most anywhere chauffeurs hung out and picked up kids.

"Seattle's a big city. *Around* Seattle's even bigger."

Lansky laughed. "Not so big you can't find a guy name a Abbey Franks owns a restaurant in the waterfront area. It's called . . . hang on."

Someone got shouted at. The someone mumbled off phone.

"It's called Frankie's Fish House."

"Why am I looking for Abbey?"

"He's got an address for you."

"You can't tell me?"

"Abbey'll have to talk to you some. It's his town."

"Beautiful. This good dope this time?"

"Yeah. He's in Seattle. Straight dope."

I made a motion to Peaches to let him know I was thirsty. "You're finally tired a the guy, aren't you, Meyer?"

"Think about it, kiddo. We don't need this kinda advertisement. The guy was once connected to our club as we've discussed before. To the cops, once a wise-guy always a wise-guy."

"Isn't that kinda how it is, dad?"

"Sure, after a point. This bum never got close to that point."

"I appreciate the leg up."

"Just go take care of our business. And, Joe, listen up. Should our mutual friend Pearlie fall into the hands of the authorities and start singing, I'm holding you personally responsible."

"Yeah? Why's that?"

"I gave him to you. Now he's your responsibility. You should maybe get on up to Seattle quick as you can, Smartie. Whadda you think?"

Lansky didn't wait for a snappy comeback. I was glad; I didn't have one.

I parked the phone, ate the drink Peaches was holding out.

"One more, boss?"

"Bring the bottle, Peaches."

• • •

I was driving a Duesenberg SJ that year. I sent the frail home and Peaches and I loaded it with a couple of travel bags. Went north for a thousand miles or so.

The Duesie wasn't brand new, but nothing on the open road could touch it. The sled would do over a buck in second gear. Peaches would blast by bush-league cops in chalky little one-store towns like they were backing up.

Some meandering, some sight seeing, we pulled by the Seattle city limit sign three days later.

It was raining. As far as I can attest, it always rains in Seattle— a pale mist that mutes everything else.

There was a decent hotel on the water, not that the climate cared. From the window off the suite's common area the view could have been water, jungle, or a glacier. I could see rain.

Peaches got us unpacked, came up with an excuse to go out and ramble. I wished him well, told him don't get shanghaied, gave him ten bucks mad money.

He was leaving in a two-toned shirt with a western yoke in cream and tan, zoot pants in dark chocolate, oxblood and white wing tips. The grease dripped off his hair. He was everything the Filipino houseboy should be on a Friday night. I told him so.

Before he pulled the door, I said, "Hey, baby, jokes aside, this ain't LA. Keep an eye on the back of your lap."

"Sure, boss. I be careful. Maybe Seattle should be careful too, huh?" Peaches did his magic act with the thin pig sticker he carried—the sticker wasn't there, then it was there, then it was open, then it was twirling on two fingers, then it was gone again.

"Go, my son. Embrace the night."

"Yeah, see you, boss. You need something?"

I thought about it. "Nah, I'm fine. I got hootch and a couple a reefers."

"Okay, boss. Later."

"Later, Peach,"

Seattle better watch out. Five-three Peaches and his bone-handled butterfly knife were on the street.

[20]

Saturday about two I left Peaches and the big Duesie on the curb and dashed through a drizzle to a place called Frankie's Fish House. It was nicer than the name insinuated.

I shook off in a foyer, checked out the room. Oh yeah, this was the right joint.

Lots of guys who don't pull off their hats just because they're inside. Wearing suit coats buttoned up against the December chill or to maybe hide hardware.

Straight to the bar, no sit down, say, "I need to see Abbey."

A bartender in a white shirt and bowtie said, "Abbey who?"

"Abbey A-friend-of-a-guy-in-New-York could lose you and Abbey both in the lint in the back corner of his sock drawer."

I noticed the bartender had a wandering eye. Maybe it was glass. "Who should I say's askin' should this Abbey guy be here?"

Separate them by three thousand miles, you get the same script. Strictly B-movie stuff.

"Joe outta LA."

"Okay, Joe outta LA. I'll go see."

The barkeep raised a tall bridge at the end of the bar and used a door. It led upstairs—I cold hear his heels bumping the treads.

I waited too long, smiled at a one-way mirror high up on a wall over the bar.

The bowtie clomped back down the stair. The door opened. He liked me now.

By the time he got to me, I could see his molars

"Mr. Franks says please have a cocktail while he closes the meeting he's in."

"What's your best here, precious?"

"Canadian. Care to try it?"

I tried it, liked it, tried a double. Liked it twice as much.

You had the hat club in the back, but all other was only two older Jewish couples at separate tables. The old Jews were sitting up front. They seemed to be enjoying themselves and the food.

Half a finger in my glass—second double—the door swung open and three hats came out. Two went out the front door; one joined his look-alikes in the back.

Another moke stepped out, threw a *psst* at the barkeep. The barkeep looked over. The guy nodded at the door. The barkeep said, "Mr. Franks says please come up."

I drained my whiskey, put down a fin.

The keep said, "No charge."

"Then call it a tip, sweetheart."

A door was at the top step, no landing, but a sign said, *Welcome.* Another said, *Keep Out.*

Me and the magilla escorting me didn't even knock. We just stepped up into the room.

The restaurant was quaint, fish camp suave. This room was from a magazine.

Polished redwood paneling up sixteen feet interrupted by fir timbers of a lighter color. Same with the ceiling but more ornate, boxed off in geometric patterns. Maroon leather and dark carved wood lived between the walls. Three straight back chairs and a rocker faced a fireplace. A fire was going but no one cared. Larger versions of the straight backs with some height on them huddled around the centerpiece, maybe eight of them. Like tugs attending the Queen Mary. The flagship was a desk. Maybe twelve foot of desk. Solid teak, dark as sin, carvings from a prior Chinese dynasty. Goddam art if I ever saw art.

There were three other doors, one for each wall, but not a window in sight.

Gentle gaslight fell from the ornate boxing overhead. The desk had a lamp on each end. The lamps were jade—more dead dynasty junk brought up to modern standards, drilled and fitted for Edison's light bulb. One was a demure maiden. The other was an angry bent Kabuki flautist. Beautiful, incongruent to the Western mind.

No one home but the guy behind the desk. The door clicked and the moke who'd brought me was history.

The desk could have been bigger and not made its owner look small.

I've seen tall people and I've seen fat people and I've seen tall, fat people. I never saw anyone the size of Abbey Franks.

Maybe—maybe—no more than seven feet tall. Weight wise I'd bet four centuries you put him on a scale could sing that high.

At that altitude, he seemed comfortably hefty.

He stood, put out a hand the size of Monaco, showed me some decent dental work.

"Mr. Ready. Glad you could come. A friend says you've contracted on a bum. . . ."

"Whoa. No contracted. No."

His large frame went back a few inches. "I know your brothers. I admire their work on this coast. You guys and your Jesuit education. Brainy guys. And please sit."

"Yeah, well, Mr. Franks. . . ."

"Abbey. Please, I'm Abbey."

"Then make *Joe* outta mine. What I'm saying, I'm not my brothers. I don't do contract. I do kidnaps."

He looked puzzled and he wasn't a simple man, wasn't a benign, goofy giant.

I blew out some air, dropped into a chair. "Could we get a drink? And could someone go out, tell my driver to come in out a the rain."

Ask and you shall receive. The gray felt that had brought me up came from a different door than where he'd exited. It made my nape bristle. I felt myself up for a gun. Found one under my left arm.

Abbey, as I now referred to him, ordered a Canadian and whatever I wanted.

I wanted a double Canadian and a double Canadian chaser.

Abbey told the moke to bring a bottle, a couple of big glasses.

Abbey leaned in, knucks bristling with short dark hairs. "I'm some confused. New York says you're here to shut a certain party down. Am I wrong?"

"Yeah. I'm here to ruin his day." I winked.

He weighed the wink. It was lead but I was hoping it passed for gold.

"Yeah. I see what you're saying, pal. No need anybody discussing things don't need to be discussed."

I grinned like I was the Cali Kid. "Yeah. I love it when I can tell the truth to a grand jury, say all I heard was some nothing. Don't you?"

Our libations came; the goomer drifted.

We toasted friends in New York.

Abbey poured another.

I reached for it, feeling no pain.

A hand like an anaconda came up, grabbed my hand at the wrist bones.

"Meyer said make sure you understand the arrangement. You understand, right?" A stiff squeeze came with it.

"Abbey, sweetie, I could play this cute, prod you in the nuts, tell you I got a seven-sixty-five Mauser pointed at your gut. Not much of a load unless you're up close and got a Filipino houseboy knows how to drill out the slug, fill it with mercury, and plug it back with lead."

I smiled. The big guy smiled—he was thinking about it. I grinned a sharp one to help him off the fence. "Baby, it's gonna look like a street car went out your ass you don't let go a my arm."

Abbey held pat. "I watched you, bub. You ain't made a move since I nabbed you."

"The gat's been out since your palooka came out the wrong door."

Franks let me go, said, "He's gotta quit that. Listen, pal, you're gonna turn this bum out to the cops, don't do it in my town. How 'bout it?"

"You got my promise."

He cocked his huge head. "You make Meyer Lansky angry, friend, you're screwin' up."

"I'm a Jesuit school kid, remember? What's one Jew more or less to a choir boy like me?"

A nod. "Meyer said you were a smartie."

"That's what he calls me."

"Smartie?"

"Yeah."

A grin. "He likes you. Told me to work on you."

"You sound like you know him."

"He's my . . . like you could call a goombah. Yes, I know him well. He likes you. He would give you a city."

"Wow. Then I could be like you—King of Seattle."

He grinned, poured us a drink.

He held high, said, "To one crazy goy son-of-a-bitch—here's to you, Smartie."

We drank to Smartie.

[21]

I scoped the house Abbey clued me to. Working class section but decent. Nice clean lawns, two- and three-bedroom wood houses. The world up here was built of wood it seemed.

Peaches got out of the car. Dragged a half-wit excuse to the front door while I lay doggo half a block east.

Beef steaks half off—even more if you'll just talk to Peaches. His idea. Clever little bastard Peaches was turning out to be.

He came back proud, maybe five-five today. "Got it, boss. Lady say no need much meat. Husband, her and friend all leave day after Christmas. Only need little meat."

"Get in."

"We go get meat?"

"Yeah. I'll take a loss on it if it'll get you friendly, baby."

It went qt for a while. I said, "Merry Christmas, Peach. I forgot all about it."

"Yeah, boss. I also forget."

"Think Santa'll find us way up here?"

"I think Santa stop lookin' for me and the boss many Christmas back."

I found a butcher away from the lunch-pail neighborhood, gave Peaches a few bucks.

He came out with half a bag and change. Poked the change at me.

"Keep it. I'll owe you big we wind this up, baby."

110

"We okey, boss. You pay good. I drive a Duesenberg, sometime. I got snappy clothes, two-tone shoes. We okey dokey."

I put the Peach back at the scene of the crime, watched him to the front door, watched him talk himself inside. I slid across the seat and turned myself back into a passenger.

A few minutes, smiling Peaches came at me, doing a near gavotte. He told me how he sold the lady the sack of meat for exactly half what we'd paid.

"Hey, boss, good news. I tell lady I need cheap job, paint house, cut bush. Workie workie all day long, one dollar." Peaches leaning on the Chinese part of his heritage, going Charlie Chan with it.

"What lady say, Number One Son?" Putting the Chan back on him.

"She say can only pay one half one dollar. I say okey, is good. Do bow, say I go home now, come back paint house, cut bush tomorrow for one half one dollar."

"Ah so, Number One. What say now?"

"Lady maybe wonder why handyman drive Duesenberg, honorable Father."

"Maybe you ride bus tomorrow, Number One."

"Maybe tomorrow you drop me out of car next block over one."

Peaches sparked the Duece, pulled off the curb.

He'd done well. Clever bastard.

• • •

Standing back up in a copse of evergreen somethings. Car over a couple a blocks at a garage getting shined up. The trees kept the mist off some, but I had an intermittent drip off my hat brim.

Pearlie showed himself in undershirt and suit pants, suspenders dangling, about ten A.M. Came out on the porch, watched the lady shove Peaches around the yard in the gauzy mist.

The lady saw Pearlie, came across the yard to the porch.

111

Pearlie pulled her up on the side, a two-foot leap. When she was on board, they embraced, kissed deeply. Then some chat, close-faced. The woman brushed the droplets from her hair, doing it like a girl. She wasn't a girl.

Then another cat came out the screen door. The clench broke in Olympic time. Some innocent milling around by Pearlie and the woman.

The other guy was in suit pants, no shirt, shoulder rig. Not a bad fashion statement but a little Spartan for the climate. Lotta hair on his frame.

Hairy yelled something at Peaches. Peaches bobbed his head, went to clipping double time at a low evergreen hedge.

An hour or so I got bored, snuck off. Picked up the Duesie, sought out cold beer and less dampness. Found both about two blocks south.

Halfway through my second jar, Hairy showed up. Got on a shirt, a tie, an open jacket, wet hat. No over garment.

He parked next to me, flapped his hat. "It's fuggin' rainin' again. God, I hate this place. I swear I'm gonna mold, all the rain."

I reached down, found a regular fellow smile, a goombah smile. "It's dry in here, buddy. Have a beer. On me."

"Yeah, I will. Hey!" Too loud at the kid pulling tap.

The kid looked.

"Quick one here, kid. Hop-hop."

The guy looked me over. Must have liked the cut of my clothes. He said, "Where you from, pal? Frisco?"

"Please. With this tan? LA, baby, all day long."

"Yeah? Me and my partner spend time in LA. Whadda you do to pay the rent, Jack?"

I looked at my beer; I grinned at my beer. I looked at the moke; I grinned at him.

I shrugged my shoulders said, "Whatever it takes."

The hairy one grinned like he knew the secret handshake. "I git it, buddy. Same with me and my partner. You got work here or just lookin'?"

Another shrug. "I'm always ears out for work. Whatchu got?"

The guy checked me out good this time. "Big dough, sweetheart. Big dough. Lemme talk to my partner, see could we use somebody else."

For a patsy maybe. I looked at myself in the mirror behind the bar. Could be I looked like a patsy. I'd been made one before. Once a patsy always a patsy, right?

The keep showed with a beer, didn't smile till I told him put it on my nickel. He went away.

I put on a good face to apply for the offered job.

"Baby, I'd appreciate it. The boys I came up here to see went red-hot, got run outta town. I need a grubstake to get back to LA." I showed him some dental work. "And I ain't real particular what it is long as the heaviest lifting is pocketing the pay."

"I hear you, fella. That's how I see it too. Say, you ever borrow a car?"

"Only from people I don't know. You need wheels?"

"Yeah. Somethin' fast."

I drained my beer, signed to the bartender for another.

"I was to *borrow a car*, where should I bring it for you to look over?"

It earned me another good hard look. "Two days, right here. Five o'clock. Got it?"

"Got it."

"Okey, pal, I gotta shove. It's Christmas Eve and I ain't bought the old lady nothin' yet. You know women."

I knew his. I'd seen her making smoochie with Pearlie Friedman a bit ago. I didn't mention it. "Yeah, baby, I know women. That's why I'm single."

We drank to knowing women.

He drifted.

I did a quick shot on top of the beer, paid up.

I drifted. I'd have business outside to attend.

Yep. My car door was open and a pair of legs dangled below it. The legs pushed up, turned over sideways. Someone was hot-wiring the Duesenberg.

I woke up the Mauser roosting under my left arm, held it inside my overcoat.

A soft step put me on him. Up close I could hear breathing and grunting under there. Sounded like it was giving him a go.

In one move I put my weight on one of the ankles, rammed the door into both legs.

The other end of the legs cursed then got quiet.

Guess it was my turn. "Broad daylight out you're gonna steal my car. The hell's wrong with you, mac?"

I pulled the door back, looked at the back of Hairy's head.

Stepping off his ankle let him turn to see me.

His face took a bit of embarrassment, added some relief, put it in the shaker.

"Hey, buddy, this yours?"

We'd been the only two guys in the beer joint.

"A car like mine out front and you don't mention it? I *think* you're gonna try and steal it. Why the chatter about boosting sleds?"

"Come on, buddy. You don't look like a moke would own a Duesenberg."

"It's used."

He grinned. "Can I get up?" He was still on the floorboards.

I let him see the Mauser putting it back in its nest. "Get up. Jesus."

Hairy got himself upright, put out a hand. I wouldn't take it.

"Okey, pally, I get it. Hey, you move okey. Real okey. I gotta fill my compadre in on ya. We still on for five o'clock in a couple a days?"

Hairy was all smiles. I wasn't.

I played it on the muscle. "I'll think about it."

"Ah, come on, pally, don't be sore. Okey, show you some faith: Four-twelve Patterson. Two streets over. Come see me day after Christmas. My wife's ma'll be there all day tomorrow."

I knew the address. Peaches was doing slave labor there as we spoke.

"I'll think about it."

I got in the car. Through the window I could hear him saying I moved good.

The guy didn't have a clue how good I moved.

[22]

Peaches and I spent Christmas day in the hotel drinking TNT and smoking dynamite, watching it rain on Seattle.

After a decent room-service dinner we exchanged gifts. Peaches gave me a bone-handled pig sticker like the one he carried; I gave Peaches a grand.

The thought counted and we both acted more pleased than we really were. It was Christmas and we were pretty much all the family either one of us had—Peaches' family was across a broad unfriendly ocean full of dead men; mine was in the graveyard or on the road to perdition.

Then it was holidays be damned—I had work to do. I had to figure what Pearlie and his hairy partner had going on and figure how to set them up for the trip to the cophouse. To hell with Abbey Franks and his town.

Peaches was inside; I almost was. Near enough. If I couldn't work it from that set-up, I should go get a real job.

"Peaches, you hear these guys saying anything?"

"Nah, boss. Lady talk yak-yak." Doing his chinaman.

"Yeah? *What's* she say?"

"Don't drop paint, don't cut bush too much, don't step mud into house." Then a smile intended to represent sly. Peaches had enough Chinaman in him he always looked a little sly to me.

"Give, baby. Don't make me work for it."

Peaches poured us another nibble of some pretty old brandy.

116

"Lady say she waste one half dollar on work. She say soon everybody gone. She say she go buy big house in California. She say soon. Only cut bush, paint house for mother."

"Yeah, I figured. They want a car tomorrow, next day. A fast car."

"Bank heist, boss?" Back to LA Peaches.

"Could be. The tall kike's a kid snatcher. It's all he does far as I know."

"He good at it?"

"Maybe fifty-fifty. But I think it's only due to good luck. He ain't that smart."

"No. Nobody there too smart, boss."

Then it should be light work for a professional like myself.

I went out on the balcony, stood in the mist, smoked a joint of jazz musician Mary Jane. It was cool but strangely not cold, not as cold as Northern Cal would be right now.

No way you could bring a kicking kid to that neighborhood. You might-could wear your gat on your hairy chest and no one's gonna mind. But a kid scream or two, somebody's calling the coppers.

A cabin. A farmhouse. Somewhere wide open to make sure no G-men are associated with the cash. A flag on a fence post, a note. A few more flags and notes. A fast exit path that police radios can't outrun.

Oh hell, the Weyerhaeuser kid was from Tacoma. What if it's up there? That was a wild card. Maybe. I stepped back inside.

"Peaches, sweetheart, you meet anybody in this burg knows who's got the dough?"

Peaches thought. "Maybe, boss. I met a Chinese girl who work for city councilman."

"If you had a phone number, you could maybe call her, ask her where the money in Washington State lives."

"Sure, boss. No need. Girl tell me she maybe go to Tacoma. Big money. Councilman in Seattle is maybe not even doorman in Tacoma. You know it?"

"Know it. Not far down the road. You ever steal a car?"

Peaches showed off his purplish gums. "Sometimes, yeah, boss. How about you? Maybe when you are young?"

"Yeah, baby, I know how it's done. I think we need to pinch a car."

I could buy one, *call* it hot, but if it *was* hot, I could weave it into the set-up, add a year or so on at sentencing.

"Tomorrow, Peach, we'll kill two birds with one stone. Go up, check out Tacoma, lift a bucket off some *in absentia* rich guy. Whadda you say?"

"I don't know nothing you say, boss, but *Tacoma, lift* and *rich guy*. I say sure."

Christmas '36 fell into the out bin. But not without a soft bang. I let Peaches talk me into a couple of Chinese whores to make the season a little more merry. Can't speak for Peaches, but me and my butterfly? Merry as hell.

• • •

Next morning, on the way outta town, Peaches stopped at a Chinese apothecary, got us some preventative medicine for the encounter Christmas night. It could've been eye of newt for all I knew—I took it all the same.

Peaches driving, Tacoma didn't even get the Duesenberg warmed up. Some ogling, some asking, we found the carriage people.

Peaches' Chinese girl was dead on. Money. Big money.

We glided, ooh-ed and ah-ed. The big Duece fit right in.

A Packard with a city block or two between the driver and the passengers went around us, loud as a silk scarf rubbing a bowling ball. A couple—young—walked long-legged horses on a broad grassy shoulder, hand in hand, infatuated faces. Love or a reasonable substitute.

I couldn't remember what it must've felt like. I once could remember, but it seemed a long way off. Now I was infatuated with whores and bums, expensive drink, exclusive establishments, exotic dope. I'd seen too much of the wealthy to lower myself to rub shoulders as equals with the lot. I could be sad; I could be a sick SOB when I could justify it. But I couldn't sustain life living in the nether between sad and sick, that nether where the wealthy dwell.

I shouldn't judge. I've kept all my poor kid habits and developed my own shrill version of the wealthy's bad side. I was a damn mess. Nineteen thirty-seven coming at me like a Buck Rogers space ship, I was flirting with a cocaine addiction, had never dropped enough rope to allow my anchor to catch hold anywhere, had walked off from every meaningful relationship I'd ever enjoyed—personal, professional, metaphysical. You name it I'd walked off on it.

But, on the positive side: I was gainfully employed, did well, worked very little for my gain. I was more lucky than smart, only lonely when I wanted to be.

I'd become some dumb B-grade noir movie—wealthy, suave, carefree playboy solves crime for peace of mind and betterment of the world between jumping frails and boozing it up. So where was my peace of mind? Where was the better world?

Maybe I was feeling a little sorry for Joe. Maybe I was feeling the weight of the coke leaving my brain. Maybe the goddam rain was driving me nuts. The weather here was wrist-slashing stuff. I ever got to that point, I'd definitely come here to do it.

Peaches pulled me off the happy thoughts with: "Hey, boss, look. Somebody packing for trip."

He slowed the car, pointed out a circular drive that eased around to sideswipe a three-storey wooden calamity. No style, nearly no windows. A tall box with no unpredictable lines. The limestone porte-cochère looked like it had been bought somewhere else, trucked in and attached as an afterthought a few drinks later.

The grounds rescued the scene. Tall healthy shrubs, ancient trees, perfect lawn grass that had retained some chlorophyll here and there. The flora wandered off over a hill behind the ho-hum

119

house, fused with the forests beyond to become dark silhouettes in the misty rain.

An attendant in boots, riding breeches and a leather jerkin over a collarless shirt wrestled a trunk into a Caddy's boot. Several lesser cases sat on the flagstone drive.

The driver straightened, lifted a peaked cap, and wiped his forehead on a sleeve.

We drifted past like we were part of the rain.

"Looks good. Wonder what's in the garage?"

"Boss, I see six door. That many door they maybe got what we want."

"I hear you talking, baby. What say we grab a corned beef on rye and a beer somewhere till Ma and Pa get the Caddy on the road."

"Maybe somebody stay. Gotta plan on that, boss?"

"We gotta plan on that, Peach."

If we had a plan on what Pearlie Freidman was piecing together, we'd be aces.

[23]

Peaches landed at a diner straight from the primer on the subject of diners. Chromium counters, low round vinyl stools on swiveling pedestals, booths with more vinyl on the seats, something like Bakelite on top of the chromium-edged tables.

I did a corned beef; Peaches did the blue-plate.

The corned beef must have been bought by an older Jewess—there wasn't a hint of fat in it. Didn't need it; the rye was greasy as a backroom full of politicians.

Peaches raved about the meatloaf and roasted spuds.

The joint served a brown Canadian beer that had plenty of character. Could've been colder though.

We stuck around to see what a couple more beers were doing. Last gulp, I dropped a buck, swiveled and stood.

There was one of those glass counters where the cash box was. I left another buck or two, told the guy the food was good.

He looked like he didn't care a damn if I liked it or not.

I refused the change. Told him to put it in a jar and get his smile muscles fixed.

He was a big, shovel-faced moke with dumb eyes. He didn't like me when he finally figured what I'd said.

• • •

Peaches stalled two hundred yards down from our pigeons, put the Duesie on the broad shoulder.

I got out the hootch, played with it straight from the neck some; schooled Peaches, scribbled some nonsense on the back of a slip of hotel stationery.

Peaches rolled the car across the flagstones, stopped like it wasn't his car. Screeched forward to the garage. Did another abrupt stop.

He jumped out, went around and began lifting garage doors. About number four I was out with my slip of paper with the doodlings on it.

Five went up. Six up.

Three bays were full of antiques. Two were empty; one held a low Studebaker roadster, a President.

I thought about the trouble a two-seater would cause for the three at the house in Seattle. Somebody would have to sit in the rumble with the luggage, in the rain. It sounded like fun. I wrote *Studebaker* and *President* on the paper.

Peaches found a registration over the Studebaker's visor. Tossed it at me. I grabbed the name: Gerald Millerford Grodin.

The piece of paper had all the necessary data needed by the time I got to the front door. I grabbed a brass ring in a brass horse's mouth and banged it pretty hard.

Hard enough—a young woman in a domestic's outfit answered. "Yes, sir?"

"City Garage. I'm here to pick up Mr. Grodin's Studebaker for service while he's out a town."

She said, "Mr. Grodin's not out of town. Mrs. Grodin is. It's her car."

I felt blood rush to my upper regions. God, don't let the man be home.

"But wait please. I'll get Mr. Grodin."

I was in this deep, no use running off now.

I grabbed a couple of good breaths, signed for Peaches to get the Duesenberg ready to flail.

The maid returned with a key, holding it like a tea bag by a little ring.

My knees stiffened up. My heart eased down.

"Mr. Grodin said to take it and no hurry. Missus is visiting her mother for two weeks."

She dropped the key into my open fist.

Goddamn I felt good. So good I didn't feel bad at all about being morally corrupt.

I took the roadster, drove hell out of it back to the hotel in Seattle.

We let a couple of valets park the sleds, remembered the way to the hotel's watering hole.

Peaches and I leaned on the bar, parked rears on high stools with arms and backs.

The bartender acted glad to see us. Asked me was I drinking the Canadian reserve this afternoon.

"Bring me something single-mead, old. Surprise me."

The barkeep pointed at Peaches. "Brandy, Peaches?"

Peaches nodded. First-name-basis-Peaches.

"What now, boss?"

"I'm gonna take the car over later on. Maybe you should go on pretty quick, tell them your wife's sick and needs medicine or something. See if they'll let you in. Take that little Italian .25 in my bag."

"Nah. I'm fine, boss. Just fine." Peaches patted his front right pocket. "No good with guns. Maybe shoot the boss."

"We wouldn't want that."

"You think it might go tough, boss?"

"No, Peach. You just never know. Plan is follow them, let them do their dirty deed, put some cops on them when they light down."

Our drinks came; the keep bought one for himself. The three of us saluted. The bartender drifted, as a good bartender will.

"Boss, what happens they get away? You use your gun then?"

I sipped. I would have answered but I didn't know. The

character from the beer parlor, the one wanted to steal my ride, I had no particular quarrel with. I hoped he didn't get between me and Pearlie Friedman. I had a score with Pearlie. However we settled it would be fine with me.

Peaches hit me on the shoulder as he turned and slid off the stool. "I go, boss. See you later, huh?"

"Yeah, baby. I'll be along directly. Keep your ears on."

I had a few more with a guy in the mirror behind the bar. He really didn't look like the kind of fellow would steal your automobile.

[24]

Nine o'clock: showtime.

I put the Italian .25 on my ankle, traded out the Mauser for a .45, put my new shank in a coat pocket.

I consulted the mirror, found a darker tie, so navy it was nearly black. A powder blue dress shirt, a navy gabardine suit, a pair of black Johnston and Murphy slip-on dress shoes. A navy felt hat, black satin band, capped me. I looked the well-dressed gangster anywhere.

I took my nattiness down the elevator, put it in the Studebaker, drove it across town.

No car in the drive but lights on.

I could see Peaches and the woman moving about inside. Boxes were on tables. The woman was going to be excited about the roadster.

She came out on the porch and looked at it sitting in the drive, me sitting inside.

I waved. She didn't

I stepped out and realized it had almost stopped raining. The weather here was like a leaky faucet—no matter how hard you turn the handle, it continues to drip.

"Evening, ma'am. I was meeting a fella here about a car."

We'd see how that fit.

It got tight quick. She pointed, said, "That?"

"Yes, ma'am. This fella requested fast." I nodded at the Studie. "It's fast."

"It's a toy. That won't do. Won't do a'tall."

I put out hands. "Lady, this fella home?"

"No. He'll be here shortly."

"He at the beer parlor a couple a streets over?"

"I suspect."

I nodded, said, "Evening, ma'am."

The Studebaker backed me out to the street. I held up for a car coming pretty fast.

The car braked, swung through a shallow ditch, and died in the yard.

It was an Olds coupé, the one with lots of nice gadgets including a hot plate and coffee percolator, but no guts, no power.

Hairy and Pearlie fell out of the Olds show pony, looked hard in my direction.

I pulled back in.

Hairy went happy; the woman was yapping at the back of his head. He turned, said something to Pearlie.

I popped my door, put my feet out.

"Hey, buddy. I wasn't sure you'd show."

"You said you need a car. I said I need some dough to blow this burg. We dealing or not?"

A beckoning hand. "Come on, pal. Meet my partner. Pete, this is . . . I never did catch your name."

I didn't catch his either. Didn't have to. The woman bawled at him from the porch, bitching about the car I'd brought. Called him Harold but it sounded more like *hurled*. Told him the car was a toy. She had some pretty sharp language for a woman, moll or no.

"Joe." I put out a hand to Pearlie. I'd never seen him up close. At a distance once, the back of his head once. He'd laid his baby blues on me once, briefly—so far as I knew. "Nice to meet you, Pete." But all I could think is how I wanted to pull the .45, bust a cap in Friedman's brain. I played with him like he was a Pete, not a Pearlie.

126

Pearlie might not have gotten a good dose, but the cockroach instincts tickled his survival nerve just a touch. I could see it in his eye, feel it in his handshake.

I had a cure for that, he wanted to play. We'd play tell-the-truth, see how that worked.

"Do I know you from somewhere, fella?" Pearlie was looking inside me.

"Could be. I was a cop for a few years. That it?"

Pearlie smiled. "Maybe, pal, maybe. Where'd you cop at?"

"Dallas." Well, not the whole truth.

Peaches stuck his head out the door opening, called the woman.

"I doubt it. I don't think I ever been caught so much as speeding in Dallas. Nice town you like Mexicans. Why'd you quit copping?"

"Didn't quit. Got fired." I pointed at the car. "Old habits got in the way. You got a badge, you can pretty much drive off in anything you want." I shrugged. "Mexico was a short jump. Why would I wanna copper anyhow when I could do ten times that boosting sleds and sleep late?"

He seemed okay with it. His itch was soothed.

"You fellas drink whiskey?"

"Hell, yeah." Harold did.

"Sure, pal. Let's sit on the porch, chat some."

I grabbed a fifth of scotch from the Studebaker, followed along to the low porch.

The three of us perched around a table. I asked for glasses.

The woman cursed some but came up with three, none like the other.

I put two good shots in each, raised my jelly glass in honor of good luck, clear roads, unmarked bills. Pearlie and Harold amened and we drank.

It made Harold whoop and put his pickle jar down too hard on the table.

"That's good stuff, buddy. Fill 'er up." Harold pushed his jar at me.

127

Mid-pour Pearlie said, "Go easy, partner. We gotta have clear heads tomorrow morning."

"Aw quit bein' wet, Pete." Harold knocked the whiskey back, pushed the jar at me again.

I poured him a pickle jar full, looked at Pearlie, got down to business.

"Pete, the lady says the Studebaker won't do. How about it?"

"Maybe. Can Hazel drive the Olds good enough so's she could make it to the cabin?"

Harold took a gulp. It made his eyes water up. He made an *ah* noise, drug it out, belched, said, "Not a chance, pal. She's never had her wheels on a highway. Here to the grocery is it. Hey, Joe, how about the Duesie you were in the other day?"

"Not for sale, sweetheart. I got the papers washed across the river, got the block and heads restamped. Not for sale."

We sat on our problem a bit.

Pearlie pointed out how he didn't really want Hazel along tomorrow anyway.

I offered. "You guys need me in on this deal, I'm ready."

Pearlie said, "What deal, fella?"

I shrugged. "Somebody's looking for disposable, fast automobiles, I start fantasizing."

"Hey, Pete, maybe the chink could drive the Olds."

Pearlie was watching me drink. I put the obvious out there. "I could drive the lady where you need for a C-note."

"I could get a taxi for ten bucks." Pearlie. But he was thinking.

"Yeah, but could you get any discretion with it, Pete?"

Pearlie looked at Harold.

"Why you lookin' at me, Pete? I'm good on the guy. He catches me. . ." a quick peek to see if Hazel was listening ". . .tryin' to pinch his ride and cuts me slack. Then he shows in a damn fast and for sure hot car. The cops ain't got bait like that." Harold jerked a thumb at the Studie.

I tossed the registration on the table. "Owner's outta town— that baby's cool as an early fall for two weeks, sweetheart."

128

Pearlie checked it out.

"What were you doing in Tacoma?"

"Stealing a car."

"Why there?" Pearlie threw the registration back down.

"It's where the money is, Pete. Ain't you heard?" I grinned like Johnny Torrio.

"Yeah, I heard. Okay. You run the lady and her stuff down the road some, wait for us. I'll give you the Franklin when we get there."

We looked hard at the other for some seconds. Pearlie broke first, said, "You don't know who I am. I'll tell you I'm somebody's got friends with long arms. *Capisci?*"

Oh, Pearlie baby, if you only knew how long your friends' arms are. *"Capisco."*

Then to make up, he says. "We come in hot, need a gun, you for sale?"

"Baby, I got my own hardware back at the hotel. I'll get red-hot anytime you get the dough. Coppers don't phase me—I was one; I know what they're thinking in the clench."

Harold finished his jar. "Yeah? What're they thinkin. How they'd love to pop a cap in you?"

"Nah. They're thinking the same thing you are but got less motivation not having jail over their heads. They just wanna go home end a shift."

Harold poured his own from my bottle. Pearlie watched me. I shrugged.

Harold said, "See, Pete, I told you he was a smart kid."

I stood, stretched. "You gonna ditch the Olds?"

Pearlie looked at me.

"Come on, baby, ain't nobody getting anywhere fast in that slug. Strictly a parade float. You got something fast and clean at some rendezvous point. I ain't a psychic. Maybe I just done some a what you're doing. I know how it's done." I put a couple of completely innocent hands up. "I just need a ride back to town is all."

Pearlie nodded. "Sure, pal. You get here early tomorrow?"

"What's early, baby?"

"Eight-nine."

"I'm here. The chink need a ride back to Chinatown?"

Harold: "Yeah. I'm tired a his whiney attitude. Buddy, you mind I pour me another healthy one 'fore you split?"

"I'm leavin' the bottle, baby, cause someone's gonna find me two C-notes for that Studebaker so it can spend the night."

Pearlie punched Harold. "Give the man the two bills before he ups the price. Thanks, pal. That's white as hell of you."

I was alla sudden Pearlie's friend.

Harold shouted at the chink, called him that.

Peaches ran out, humbled, a model four bit a day servant. "Yes, big Mister?"

"You need to get outta here with this man. He's goin' downtown. You're goin' with him. Go on, git."

"Oh, please, big Mister, please. Must have half one dollar for workie so hard so long." Peaches had his hands together, cupped, out and ready to receive his alms.

"See the lady. I got real business here."

Harold pulled a decent roll, unwrapped the piece of wire that held it. Peeled off a hundred and five twenties. I thanked him, gave him the key and registration.

Peaches had the woman at the door, hands out, at her. "Okay, lady, please I go now. Must have money. Wife so so sick. Need pill to breathe. Please, lady."

Hazel huffed, turned and grabbed her purse. She came out with a long wallet, unzipped a pocket. After a rummage, she came over, dropped two bits in Peach's palm, huffed, dropped another nickel.

"Oh, thank you, lady. Thank you, big Mister. Thank you, other Mister." Then my turn. "Oh, new Mister, so please you give ride." A few bows. I wasn't sure the little ham wasn't going to kiss my hand.

Harold finished one drink, made one, like it was all one

practiced exercise. "Listen, shut the hell up and go get in that damn Oldsmobile fore I throw you in it, chink. Now git."

"Yes, big Mister. I come tomorrow, workie-workie."

"Yeah, do that. Make it noon. Take a taxi and tell him big Mister'll pay him when you get here."

"Okey, big Mister. Okey. I get cab on telephone now."

"No, tomorrow at noon. Right now get your chink ass in that Olds." Harold sat up, pounded a fist on the table, said, "Now."

Peaches ran off, speaking in tongues.

"See you fellas in the morning."

Pearlie said, *Sure;* Harold thanked me for the whiskey. The woman came through the open door, wallet in hand.

Behind me she wanted to know who'd pinched the three hundred dollars hidden in her secret pocket.

Sounded like fun but I kept moving.

[25]

So far, my big mistake was what got me in the game—the roadster. I couldn't get in on act one since we couldn't all get in the car and someone had to get the woman and her notions down the road. I was chauffeur; I was out of play.

Peaches and I had talked options over breakfast. Peaches could follow Pearlie and Harold in the Olds. But the President would walk off and leave it. Which led to I take the Olds, Peaches takes the Duesenberg. The Duesie was too recognizable; worse than the Olds. Buy a new sled, something fast. I do that, now I got Peaches alone, one on two—I'm still committed to taxi driver. To hell with it. We'd ride it like it sat, wait on them at the rendezvous. Even if it was a kidnap, I'd get the mark when they got there. We'd get candy when we stopped for gas in case it was a kid.

• • •

"You told me to write it. You gonna tell me *how* to write it too?"

Harold didn't look good this morning. The scotch bottle sat—barren, used up. Not unlike Harold a little.

"Harry, my handwriting. . . ." Pearlie watched me approach. He didn't speak.

I'd backed the Duesenberg down the drive, then backed

132

on up close to the porch. I got out of the car and ignored the conversation, turned to give the boot handle a twist.

Behind me was the whispering, then shushing. Then a few seconds of ear-piercing silence. Ignored but not forgotten, we all let it go, got sunny-side up.

"'Lo, Joe." To my back.

I raised the trunk-lid and turned. "'Lo, Harold. 'Lo, Pete."

Pearlie nodded. I nodded.

Somehow, somewhere, buried under a million years of evolution was that bell. It tolled from his collective fathers—a long, long chain of graceless survivors. He knew and later he'd tell himself he knew if he lived. He'd curse himself when he found out it was me turned him out. Good. I'd cursed him for some nightmares.

Right now I smiled. "Wish the Chinese boy was here."

Harold flapped a hand. "Aw, we ain't takin' all she's packed. Hell, half of it ain't even hers. Belongs to the house. We rent it furnished."

"Shall we?"

Harold and I did. Pearlie sat, his eyes followed us, followed our movement, but he wasn't seeing us. He was someplace else.

I'd been thinking kidnap or robbery. Now the tidbit I'd got about the note. That was telling me probably the latter. Nappers, as a rule, scram, make contact later. Works better. Gives the family time to panic, then feel grateful. You leave a note, it's all about money to a rich guy from that moment. He's even gonna wanna barter some, talk you down soon as you call.

Too much talk equals curtains in a chair or a chamber depending on jurisdiction. A rope or a firing squad in a couple of remote states.

Good nappers were noisy as a bucket of steamed clams.

Then the fast ride I'd furnished for the deed. Two seater. You could get someone else in it, but you couldn't hide them well. They'd like the Studebaker roadster if it was a boost job.

Maybe I was trying to ease a future guilty conscience. My stomach got funny and I asked myself if I was so sure it was a heist, why was I buying candy?

133

I loaded the Duesie while Harold and the woman fought over which boxes he was going to hand me. With several skirmishes and a few pitched battles, I had Hazel and her boxes in the car.

She was mad as any gun moll ever was. We could hear her muffled curses from inside the car. Harold told her to shut up a couple of times while he and I had a bottle of beer for breakfast. I got some decent directions written on an envelope.

I dusted out while Harold was getting his second helping on breakfast.

Pearlie said nada. He came out of his reverie, grinned at me. He made a pistol with a hand, shot me with it.

I grinned, shot him back, put him in my dual rearviews.

The lady was okay until I went the wrong way at the first stop sign. "Hey." Nasally.

I found her in the mirror. "What?"

"Where you goin?" She whined it out.

"I gotta pick someone up."

"I don't know. We can't take nobody to the cabin."

"Wait'll you see who it is. You know him."

"Who?" About five miles long, like a wail.

I used some shoulder; Peaches came from a grassy knoll brushing off the seat of his pants.

I slid right; the Peach got under the wheel.

The Okie said, "Oh," doing some octave work on it.

We rode, me reading the directions to Peaches.

Hazel said, "Hey, Chinese boy, whatever your name is, I ain't payin' you today. This fella brought you, he pays you."

Peaches turned a bit, winked his left eye. In the most unaffected California version of English he said: "Lady, that particular arrangement is over. It was fun. The pay was pretty pitiful but I understand you're a bigoted cheapskate as are your two associates."

I was impressed. I'd never heard Peaches do much beyond his Philippine-American patois or his Chinese act.

I wasn't alone—the woman said, "Oh, my Lord. This ain't good, is it?"

Nobody said was it good or not.

• • •

We slid out of Seattle, caught a familiar highway south. The directions dodged us east before Tacoma.

A few miles uphill, houses got rare. Some rough road for a good long time and signs began pointing to a place called Bonnie Lake.

Our directions followed the arrows. We rode on a ridge over the lake that let us see for miles. We'd left the rain in Seattle. Here it was cloudy but dry. We made the last turn, used a key on a padlock and chain across a wet, suspect rock bridge.

I left the chain down as previously instructed, got back in. A quarter mile, mostly down, we found what I'd call a shack. I was still looking around for this mentioned *cabin* when Hazel said, "Well, here we are. Home-sweet-home."

Guess one man's shack's another's cabin.

I let Hazel go first, check for haints or cops with heavy fingers and such. No goblins, no coppers.

Hazel ordered Peaches around some, not smart enough to change gears.

He was the gentleman, tolerated her rudeness and her open bigotry.

You're a better man than I am Gunga Din.

• • •

The shack was a decent place to wait you happened to have a wait to sit out. Nice view, nice air. Quiet once Peaches lost his grip on chivalry and showed the woman his knife trick. Told her she didn't mum up he'd cut her tongue off.

"You leave her alone?" I was sitting on a dead fir tree that had grown old and tired and just fell over.

"Yeah. Where's she going, boss? The woman couldn't escape if we were downtown LA. She couldn't run across the street."

"Why'd you hink me on the accent?"

Peaches pulled up some trunk. "Boss, you wanted a Filipino house-boy. Chop-chop. Make lady laugh. Boss, I'm an actor and I can't make the kinda dough you pay me on a stage, in front of a camera. Not even in a backroom live blue show."

Some quiet, then more:

"Boss, it started off I needed a job. I played my cousins from the motherland, affected their speech. It worked; I got the job. Then, I got to like you even if you are a lazy hedonistic drug addict. I couldn't tell you. It'd be like I was juking you all along."

"Weren't you?"

A beat. "Yeah, I guess. I still gotta gig?"

"Long as you want it, baby. Just don't try it again."

• • •

The wait went to twenty-two hours and some.

I'd put the mojo on the Studebaker at six that eve with a phone call at a grocery down the hill a piece and a half. I knew the cops were on the car statewide within an hour or two, had to be.

Quarter of ten the next morning, no one but Harold showed and he looked like he'd been pistol whipped pretty badly. The Studebaker was muddy and tired.

The pulped-up face didn't keep him from looking surprised when he came in the shack. I had the big .45 government-model Colt out.

"Where's Pearlie?" I tried to make my face look like it wasn't his friend.

Harold wasn't the smartest boy in town but he caught it. "Who?" Playing dumb for me.

"Come on, baby, you can give it up. I gotcha."

"Oh, hell." He spun around, hand to mouth.

The woman came from the outhouse, saw Harold's face, and put out an unenthusiastic little scream.

"Oh Lord. Oh Lord." She looked around. "Where's Pete?"

I grinned at Harold, said, "Who?"

Peaches laughed while no one else did.

Harold said, "She don't know nothin'. What kinda cop are you?"

"No kind, sweetheart. I'll ask once more where Pearlie is and you're gonna tell me. You don't? I'll put my associate on you and your old lady. Peach, show the man some of your stylings."

Peaches put the bone handle knife through the paces, put some pepper in the act.

Harold looked back at me, stood mute.

The wife says, "Harold," pulling it out.

"Harold, baby, looks like the man pistol whipped you. You showing in the Studebaker tells me Pearlie's stooling me and you both out and we'll see cops here two-three hours. Beyond that— if that's not enough motivation for you—this guy Pearlie is no one you wanna be involved with. The kike and guinea club in New York painted a target on him. Let it go, Harold. I won't kill you, but I tell these clubbers you balked on me. . . ." I shrugged at the inference.

Another long, whiney: "Harold."

"Holy Mother of God." Harold fell into a chair. He looked fagged out. He let his head roll back up, found me with his eyes. "Buddy, you got any drink?"

"I'm not your buddy, Harold. Yeah, I got a drink a whiskey. You tell me where Pearlie is, we'll have us a shot or two."

"Buddy, I'll tell you it all, but I could sure use a stiff one right this minute."

I wagged my head at Peaches. He got up, went out.

"Spill it, Harold."

"Okay, we go to get the kid, leave the note. I go in, bandana on my mug. There's three bigger kids there. I nab the squirt, put the note down on a counter. I point my gat at these other three, tell 'em to hit the floor. I drag the kid out.

"The little bastard started kicking and yelling. I put my gat away, slapped him a time or two, settled him down. Got him out to the car. I put him on the floorboards under my feet and we vanished.

"I'm thinkin' we're comin' here like the plan was laid. Nah, Pearlie takes a side road up into some woods. We take the road around, come out by a big field. Sittin' in the edge of the field is this blue Caddy Pearlie told me he'd sold. I'm thinkin' Pearlie's makin' lotsa plans don't include me; I get the jits knowin' somethin's goin' on. We stop, get out, get the loudmouth kid out." Harold looked up. "Thank God."

Peaches had come in with a bottle of whiskey and a couple of those chromium collapsible cups. He popped the cups up, poured, passed both to me.

I gave Harold one of them. He knocked it back.

I sipped at mine, pointed at Harold's cup. "Peaches? Would you be so kind?"

Peaches was kind, all the way to the rim. Harold ate it in one big bite again.

The wife whined at him, just his name. He told her to shut the hell up. She did.

"You were telling me about the loudmouth kid."

"Yeah. Little brat. Tellin' us we're stupid, we're gonna get caught and go to a Federal prison. Get this: he says, *Just like the stupids who kidnapped my friend.* I says *Who's your friend?* He says, *George Weyerhaeuser.* Pearlie tells the kid all of 'em didn't go to Federal prison.

"Then the brat asks Pearlie why'd we only ask for twenty-eight grand? His buddy George got two-hunnert grand. Pearlie tells him we asked two hunnert eighty gees. The kid says, *You think so?* He said he read the note while I was threatening the older kids with my gun. Says the note said twenty-eight *thousand.*

"I'm startin' to feel funny. See I wrote the note and I ain't so

138

good on numbers, particularly the big ones. I ain't bad with words, but not numbers.

"Pearlie says to the smart kid, write on a paper what he saw. The kid writes what he saw word for word, hands it to Pearlie. Pearlie gave me a paper, says write two hunnert eighty grand on it.

"I did. I *thought* I did. Like I say, I ain't so good on numbers."

"But you ain't bad on words. I heard. Peaches, pour Harold one. Where's Pearlie? Where's the kid?"

He looked punk, swallowed only some of the drink this time.

"Pearlie said I wrote twenty-eight grand. I tell him he shoulda wrote it. We do some shovin' and the kid starts laughin'. I tell 'im he'd best clam. He says we're so stupid we can't even write a decent kidnap note. Why don't we just let him go, give his dad some money so he won't prosecute us.

"I slap hell outta his chops and he runs. Little bastard could run. Pearlie says he gets away, we're both goin' to the chair."

Harold stopped, looked at his feet, both hands around the cup.

I could feel this load coming like a full-out freight train, straight at *me*.

He drank, drained his cup.

"So I shot him."

I drained my cup, pushed it back flat. I reached over, pushed Harold's flat. Put the caps on them. Both went in a coat pocket.

"Peach, grab the bottle."

And I shot Harold in the forehead with the .45. He went over backward in his chair, bled on the floor.

The woman keened a shrill and urgent aria for the exit scene.

[26]

The hell do you say?

Jimmy didn't know so he stood there, leaned against the rail of the pier looking at Joe.

"That bother you, kid? Me telling you about popping the guy?"

Some waiting, some wondering. Then: "Is that a true story? I mean for real, Joe?"

Joe made a serpentine motion with his hand. "The truth rambles back and forth with time and memory, but, yeah. The big pieces? Sure it's for real."

Some more quiet—ocean quiet if that's quiet.

"Why'd Pearlie leave a note? You said notes aren't the best way."

Joe smiled at something Jimmy wasn't in on. "Maybe change up on his MO. Pearlie'd been a busy boy. The Feds were getting wise. Hell, I don't know, kid. If I could think like a highwayman, I'd *be* one."

Jimmy nodded like it mattered. "You call the cops, an ambulance, anything?"

"What? After I capped Harold? Why? He was dead; the woman wasn't staying anyway." A shrug. "I gave her five grand for her loss."

What?

Jimmy must have been looking pretty hard at Joe.

Joe said: "You're thinking maybe it was for my conscience. Maybe you're right or maybe I don't have a conscience. Maybe I was tired a guys killing kids in front of me."

They stared a bit longer.

Then Joe said, "You're gonna judge me, fuck you, kid. You don't know shit yet. You get to be my fucking peer, then judge the hell away."

Joe got up folded his chair, said, "Take care a my fishing shit. Put it on the patio when you get done." And walked down the pier toward land, chair under an arm, hand on hat crown against the wind.

Jimmy shook his head, turned and looked at the ocean, snorted out a little laugh. He looked the other way down the pier, out toward the ocean. Saul looked over, wiggled fingers in a wave. Goofy bastard.

Jimmy didn't wave. Fuck the old dudes. So uncool. So old. So out of tune.

Fuck 'em all.

And all liars. Jesus, what a story. Like you'd tell someone you hardly knew you committed cold-blooded murder. Tell them you shot someone in the brain.

But Jimmy could dig it, felt good when the story went to that part. Like in a movie when the bad guy gets it.

That's all it was though—a story. Who'd this guy think he was kidding?

"Hey, Jimmy, want a soda?"

Jimmy turned knowing who it was.

"Nah, Saul, I'm good. Gotta couple of beers left."

"Yeah? You doing any good?"

Jimmy wrinkled some brow.

Saul clarified. "Fishing. You catching anything?"

"Nah. I don't think I'm trying, to be honest."

"You want, I'll teach you. I been here ten years. Caught everything there is to catch here. Your pompano's prime you wanna eat it. But now your permit, that's the ultimate. I could show you how to rig a line to catch a pompano or a permit, you want."

"Nah. I like my style. But I do appreciate it, sir."

A hand flap. "Aw, no sirs. How bout Saul?"

The guy was annoying. "I think I'm gonna pack up. Me and Joe were just getting some sun anyway."

"Yeah, I saw your friend leave. He lives next to your mom, right?"

"Yeah."

"Strange guy. Strange guy. Say, I hear your writing is going good. Whatcha working on?"

"Just jotting down some stories."

"Yeah? What're they about?"

Jimmy grinned, got a beer and didn't offer good ole Saul the last one.

"You wouldn't believe it, Saul."

"Try me."

"Buy the book. See you, sir." Dismissing a sixty-seventy-year-old guy just like that.

Saul nodded for a few cumbersome moments, then decided his rigs needed checking and split.

Jimmy pulled in a lungful of the ocean air. The smell of the sea was strong today, thick and enticing like the smell of sex. Maybe he should cruise the park, grab a hippie chick with hair under her arms.

He decided to let someone else kill the bait shrimp and the last beer. Gave them to a guy looked like he worked for a living, had a kid with him. The guy was grateful, the kid overwhelmed. Made Jimmy feel good even if Joe had bought everything.

Joe wasn't on the patio so Jimmy leaned the poles against some wall, went in his mom's slider—he'd had enough Joe today.

"You and Joe fish?" Rhetorical.

"Yeah." Rhetorical. Then: "What's for dinner that's not fresh fish?"

"Pot roast. Do you want a sandwich, now?"

"Sure. Turkey?"

Jimmy went in his room, got his notebook.

"Can I get it to go, Mom?"

He came out, plopped at the bar.

"You and Joe are getting chummy, huh?" Mom.

Shrug. "Wild. . ." almost said *ass*, ". . .stories, Mom."

"I'm glad you've found a friend." A mom smile.

Jimmy wasn't sure. Something . . . something. Like Jimmy was getting to look through only the red lens at a 3-D flick. If he had the green lens, too, maybe he could see the whole show, see what it was coming at him.

[27]

A dragon in a nurse's costume stuck her head in about eight. "Visiting hours are almost over, Mr. Ready."

Joe rolled his head in her direction, but didn't bother looking at her.

"This is my kid, I'm dying—he's staying, lady. You make him leave, I'll die right now just to spite you."

The dragon cackled hard enough to break her make-up. "Your son can stay as long as he wants. We've got Jell-O."

"Great. Go to the morgue with green Jell-O in my gizzard. How 'bout a shot a scotch, sister?"

"Mr. Ready, you know better. Press the button if you need us."

"Sure, sweetheart."

The nurse released the door and it hissed shut.

"You ever figure out why Joe shot that guy?" Joe talking about himself like he wasn't here.

Jimmy nodded. "You told me why. It just took a while to make sense."

"Good. Tell the story and I don't wanna hear about you jumping hippie girls or anything. Forward to after I got over being mad at your punk ass, me and you back at the fishing hole like Andy and Opie."

Joe tried a laugh. It fell to a whispery noise. He got his breath back, said, "And that fucking pompano."

"Permit."

"Sorry, kid—it was a pompano."

"Then you tell the story."

"Okay, so it was a permit. Lemme have a sip a that water there."

Jimmy rolled the bed table under Joe's face, pointed a bendy straw at his mouth.

While he was in close to Joe, Joe said, "I love you, kid. I know you never did want a daddy and I don't know what we had, but you're like family, maybe closer."

Jimmy lay a hand on Joe's arm. All bone. "I love you too, Joe. Like it or no, I'm gonna tell the part about catching the fish."

"You got to, go ahead. But keep in mind I'm ninety-eight here. I could go any second."

Jimmy agreed and grinned. Went in a pocket, pulled out a flask, splashed it at Joe's water. Joe said Jimmy was from God. Then Jimmy told about the fishing trip. And the fucking permit.

• • •

Joe had acquisitioned a grocery cart with its identifying nomenclature gone. A hot grocery cart full of lots of fishing gear. Joe saying he was gonna show Jimmy how to fish for real, eat the slimy bastards for dinner.

According to Joe, high tide was ten-thirty. High tide seemed important, especially incoming—they hit the pier at quarter after nine.

The bait shop supplied shrimp, sand fleas, frozen squid, and two six packs. This was stacking up to be some serious angling.

There was a big ass Haitian guy where Joe wanted to angle, so he gave the dude a ten, sent him down the pier wealthy, sporting a smile.

Jimmy grabbed a shrimp.

Joe said, "You're not even close to bait yet, grasshopper," doing it like the Kung Fu guy on TV.

Jimmy put the shrimp back in the bucket.

"And you don't hook a goddam shrimp through the tail. Now listen."

There was some hook talk, some stuff about weight and sinkers. This test, that test. Something called *snelling.*

Joe showed how to hook a shrimp, parallel with the tail, going in the insect underside of the thorax, coming out at the tail's tip.

"Something wants to eat that shrimp? He's either gonna be hungry, suck it all down, or be finicky, nibble the best part like you or I would."

Made sense to Jimmy. He acted like he knew what he was looking for in the tackle box, gave it up. "Help me here, Joe."

Joe tossed a hook, a couple of sinkers at Jimmy.

"Use the little Penn. The black rod. Yeah."

Jimmy rigged. Didn't quite get the snelling thing right, but after two or three tries the line stayed in the hook.

"You didn't put your sinkers on first." Joe held out the line clippers.

Jimmy looked at Joe but didn't say it. He clipped the hook off, slid the sinkers on the line. Got the hook tied first go.

Got the shrimp on second go. First go the shrimp got on the pier and pounded like a flamenco dancer. Second round Jimmy impaled him, tossed him in the salty sea.

Pretty good—landed a sea bass post haste. Too small so he took a dive.

Then some sand fleas. Joe said he didn't think it mattered how you hooked them long as you were humane. This from a guy who told you he shot someone in the head.

Joe caught a nice bonita. Big son of a gun. Colors the rainbow hadn't heard about. Back in the drink—Joe said the big ones had cie-something, would make you sick if you ate them.

The sand flea did it. Jimmy got a couple of decent sheepsheads in the bucket.

Then the permit. The son of a bitch the size of the A-page on your daily paper.

Joe saying how it was a big sheepshead, all that would eat a sand flea.

The fish'd get flat way to you, make the line sing like Eartha Kitt. Made Joe drive backseat.

Don't break the line. Don't let him strip the reel. Don't point the damn rod at the fish.

Trophy fish. Some watchers. Some oohs and ahs when the fish flashed at the surface.

A guy from the bait shop heard about the struggle, brought a seine net on a long rope down.

Third run the guy snagged the fish with the net. Jimmy's line popped, hit the bait shop guy in the face. He said, "Jesus," but held on to the rope.

A little insincere chivalry on Jimmy's part—how the line popped and the guy with the net actually caught the fish—Jimmy took his fish at the bait guy's insistence.

Only its fore portion would go in the bucket, maybe twenty inches of him. The rest, a good foot and a half, wagged like a white flag after a siege.

"Nice pompano, kid."

A guy older than Joe said, *No, it was a permit.*

Joe begged hell out of his pardon. The guy made a case about dorsal fins or some nonsense. Joe said a permit was just a big pompano and this one wasn't permit size.

A guy about half a dozen teeth shy of a set said, "It's a permit, buddy. Ain't got nothin' to do with size. It ain't like a flounder and a fluke."

Jimmy didn't know a flounder from a fluke, didn't care—he'd caught a damned permit.

The crowd thinned as it will do after the headline act. Joe grinned.

"Nice fish, kid. Best I ever seen come off a this pier."

Jimmy touched the drying tail. It stuck to his fingertip.

The backside of the bucket went away. Liquid hit Jimmy in the face, filled his eyes, momentarily cost him his sight.

Then the crack arrived, milliseconds later.

Joe took Jimmy over his chair and to the boards of the pier.

Jimmy could feel the water from the bucket on his leg and knew they'd turned it over.

Another crack but no percussion.

Then what was left of the bucket spun like a top; the crack followed.

Joe's arm was over Jimmy's head, both kissing the pier.

Then the ocean hitting the sand at the pier's beginning. No sea birds yet, then a shrill *cheerie*, then more, like it had never happened. Jimmy raised his head a little.

A pelican landed on the rail, looked at the wrecked bucket. He looked at Jimmy.

Then a siren. Way off but destined for here.

A shout: *Hey, are you guys all right?*

Jimmy realized it was aimed at him and Joe.

Joe said, *Yeah.*

The siren was prominent.

Joe rose to his knees for a quick moment, went down on Jimmy again. Nada.

He rose, said, "Get up. It's over."

Jimmy sat, looked at the ruined bucket, said, "They shot my damned fish."

Joe said, "Twice, baby. Somebody don't like pompano."

Jimmy didn't mention the permit thing. Too freaked.

And here come the fuzz. West Palm fatties. Sharp as a perfect circle.

Wanted to know first why somebody'd shot the fish.

It was worth a laugh. Jimmy started, Joe caught it, six or eight guys around went feverish. They all laughed off some stale, nervous adrenaline while the top cop didn't get it.

The uniforms gave way to dress pants, shirtsleeves—short ones—and blithe ties. There were some cameras and some Baggies full of pieces of plastic, pieces of fish. Somebody dug a slug out of Jimmy's permit, bagged it.

A detective talked it over with Joe and Jimmy while uniformed cops scoured the shoreline.

Nobody knew nada. Joe asked the cop would it be all right if neither he nor Jimmy left town till this was over. The cop didn't think it was too funny.

Some *nos* and shrugs, the detective started picking on the people that had been behind Jimmy and Joe, across the pier.

Joe jerked his head at land.

Jimmy made a face, not sure they'd been officially dismissed.

Joe hissed, started loading his fishing equipment in the grocery cart.

Jimmy shrugged it off, lent a hand.

The two of them bumped off maybe ten-twelve feet, the cop said; "Mr. Joseph, Mr. Cotton, I'll see you both later today. At these addresses you gave me."

Joe flapped a hand at the guy, bumped on down the pier.

Jimmy tarried, played good citizen, said, "Sure. Thanks, officer."

He caught up to Joe. Over the noise of the cart banging on the pier, Joe said, "Why didn't you give him a blow job, kid?"

"He's a cop, Joe. I got. . ." Jimmy looked back ". . .a couple a reefers in my pocket. Jesus."

"You thanked him for being a rude, yokel cop. And he ain't no officer—he's a detective."

"Yeah. Lieutenant something."

"Hernandez. Lieutenant Detective."

Lot of authority resentment for an old dude to be copping Jimmy was thinking.

Maybe it was fishing. Or the ocean. Last time on the pier Joe was edgy—he and Jimmy'd had words and nobody'd shot at them either.

Jimmy let it go. Let the cadence of the rubber wheels bumping take them to terra firma. Took the helm of the cart across a band of sand, pushed it to the complex—no words involved.

The gear got stashed in a closet and Jimmy sat on a barstool.

Joe looked over, took a pull out of a cut glass decanter. The liquid was sunlight caught in garnet. "Whadda you still doing here?"

"I was hoping to get the chance to turn down a slug of whiskey."

Joe sat the decanter on the counter. He rolled the top after it. The top clinked.

Jimmy grabbed the decanter, took a good slug. It was velvet until it hit your stomach. The stuff landed like molten lava.

Joe did another, put the decanter back on the counter, stuck the top in it.

"Kid, don't ever let anybody push you around. Don't matter who it is. They might get the idea you like it. *Anybody* would include the cops."

Another slug for Joe. One for Jimmy.

"Who shot at us, Joe?"

"Look at my kitty cat getting curious, asking good questions."

There it was again—that something that was going on beyond this story-telling business. Beyond Jimmy's vision, but he knew it was out there.

Why mention it? Jimmy figured he could step out anytime, right? See what this ended up being about for real.

Joe fired up a joint, knowing the cop said he'd come by.

"Wanna go out on the patio?"

"Nah."

Joe got out scotch, ice and a glass, got good and stewed, watched Jimmy a good bit.

The joint put a glow on the late morning, sending it to the surreal world of memories.

Some quiet, then Joe said, "You want out, kid?"

Like he'd read Jimmy's mind.

Jimmy wagged his head. "Nope."

Joe said, "Good. You might wanna get your fancy spiral notebook and your mechanical pencil—I got a long one."

"This one about Pearlie Friedman?"

"Sorta. This point, I'd about given up on him. I looked hard enough I'da bet he'd left the continent. Pearlie went so doggo even Lansky couldn't ferret him out for a few years." A snort of a laugh. "Then I found him, in Lansky's back pocket."

"You nail him?"

A headshake. "Nah. I was the one got nailed. Damn near beat to death. My whole face was redone by some incredible Cuban surgeons. Nah, I was chasing a couple of other bums, Alvin Karpis and Harry Campbell. Friend's a Pearlie's. Backed right into him. Nearly died for it."

"Worst mistake you ever made?"

"Nah, kid. Worst ever was letting Pearlie and Harold go through with that kidnap, kill that child. Anyway, lemme tell you about Cuba when she was young and ripe."

[28]

Rags and riches this shamus game. One day you're down to some nice expense money and a rent car. Next day you're counting twenty grand. Day after that you find out a little lark of a caper you never expected to see a nickel from pays off forty-some-odd legal gees. The lark: I'd papered a Mex doctor who then opened a clinic in San Diego and subsequently got rich. Doctor Freddie sent me half of his first three years' take as a symbol of his gratitude. Forty grand—I sent back thirty, kept ten for my troubles getting him, his family, and his degree from *UNAM* okay with the state of California. Not to diminish Freddie's capabilities or integrity, but even ten gees falling on you outta the blue is a nice hunk of luck.

You ride the wave, another hunk of luck falls on you—you call Meyer Lansky and find out Meyer was in Cuba. Talking to Batista. About God knows what. I didn't care much. A guy I was interested in seeing was meeting a couple of fellow kidnappers there. I was on these other two birds and we were going to Habana.

The Miami flight was fleet and uneventful. No one cut up.

Not even the guys I was shadowing, Alvin Karpis and Harry Campbell. Their wives were with them and it got a little loud in the hangar before the flight. We'd settled in nicely once in the air, everyone brown bagging hootch, nipping liberally.

I left them at the airfield. Habana wasn't that big I couldn't find four people, one of them pregnant—seemingly severely pregnant. Watched them to a cab, wrote the cab's numbers on my hand with a pen. I was off duty; I was fagged.

The Nacionale had a room for me. A cab put me on the curb under a nice wide porte-cochère. The clerk was slick as oil, didn't look like he'd trust me or anyone.

I asked was Mr. Lansky here yet. The clerk said, *Who?*

A good bit of eyebrow and a conspirator's grin came with it.

"Anyone fitting the description shows, tell him Ready's in. . . ," I looked at my key, ". . .six-twelve."

"I shall, sir. Should someone fitting that description check in." His English was smooth and correct.

I winked for both of us. "Tell him I don't answer in my room, try the bar."

He assured me he'd pass the word on, asked about a hop—I patted my small shoulder bag, gave him a shrug gratis.

I turned, took in the Nacionale. Church. Maybe cathedral. No, no—monastery. Moorish influence. Deco influence. A damned busy place for an establishment bigger than some countries. I rambled a bit.

Gardens off arcades. A big ass cannon in one of the gardens. A restaurant, named after Corregidar *Somebody* that was a little smaller than a hay field.

My affection grew. A bar made for Habana sat behind a bold arch, neon a suggestive shade of pink quivering around it.

Cigar smoke, card games, whores. Heels and aristocrats. Cheaters and chumps. Rumba music and loud, bold talk.

A girl in pasties and a singular triangle of cloth danced on a tall round barrel. She could have been twelve or twenty; couldn't tell. She knew what hips were for. Her hair was the exact color of new copper—an unlikely shade on her nut-brown skin. She eye contacted me and I felt it all the way to the bottom of my fly.

Nothing sanctimonious going on in there.

Nor on beyond where the roulette wheels clattered and collective *oohs* and *ahs* would drift back through the bar.

My travel bag wasn't fit for a place like this. It was all full of gats and pills and picks and knucks of brass.

I took my junk up to six on an elevator that moved like a rocket and stopped like a hearse.

The lobby was acres of marble and granite. The stones were left below—I stepped onto a cloud of buff. Soft putty-colored walls under subtle sconce lighting.

The carpet was rough going, but I only had a short wade to my room so I didn't break out the snow skis.

A nice heavy lock clicked like it meant business and let go an eight-foot door of solid mahogany. A bird of paradise and some other jungle items were tastefully carved in it. Was a nice door.

Familiar carpeting beckoned me inside.

I've stayed in a lot of joints billing themselves as class joints. They bow before the Nacionale.

The room went on a couple of city blocks to a set of French doors; the view went right out the door and landed on Habana Harbor. The pale water twinkled and winked like it knew something I didn't.

Lots of deep, brocade-clad furniture. A bed with maybe a couple of Caddies hidden under it. Forest green walls over a high mahogany wainscot, more mahogany trim below that.

Behind a Chinese-red door was tile. Black and white checkerboard walls with ebony trim stood on patterned pink marble and neutral limestone. The floor flowed to a turquoise square at its center. The turquoise bled out to the deepest cobalt blue I'd ever seen. Claw tub and washbasin the same shocking cobalt.

Man. I could live here till I died.

I crawled to the center of the big bed. The trip plus life the last few weeks had exhausted me, so I punched up a couple of pillows and waited on the sandman.

He found me down in the cushy lux and dropped a hook that sent me flying into a deep cobalt sky.

[29]

A telephone in every room—quite a convenience. So nice, so very nice. Unless you hadn't slept in a couple of days and were finally manufacturing z's, out like a Van Winkle.

Ring ring ring, fast and urgent. The house phone.

I'm thinking I'm getting Lansky.

I get a redhead named Selma. She was a nurse-stewardess for Pan American Airways, and PanAm was the owner of the can we hopped from Miami to Habana aboard.

We chatted in Miami some and she'd dared me to meet her in the bar at the Nacionale. Wanted to teach me the rumba. I said I was open-minded, wouldn't miss the chance.

"Well?"

Nope. Not Lansky. Too aggressive for the little Jew.

"'Lo, Red. You in the bar?"

"I thought we were going to call me Selma. Yes, I'm in the bar."

"Ready to rumba?"

"I'd say you should be the one to answer that. I think I've made my intentions as clear as possible without looking sluttish. See you in a few, Joe."

Click.

Brush for the teeth, brush for the hair, brush for the shoes, wings on my feet, through some suggestive pink neon.

Red wasn't hard to spot. She was the striking redhead with the school of sharks circling her.

I shooed them away, took her arm and waltzed us to a table on the patio. We had some dinner and some sheer innuendo. Afterward, she kicked her shoes off, smoked a cigar, and drank brandy like a man.

The night was stellar and the mosquitoes busy elsewhere. Second, maybe third brandy, Selma asked: "What's your line, Joe Ready?"

"Pardon?"

"Your profession?"

I grinned. "I'm a private detective."

"Sure you are, honey. And I'm a famous Latin flamenco dancer."

"Whadda you *think* I do?"

She weighed me, squeezed out the brandy by squinting. "The way you held on to your bag, I thought cash. No—you don't look like a travel bag full of money."

"Thanks."

"So that leaves lots. Drugs. . . ."

"They move the other way."

"Guns. . . ."

"Not bad."

"You could be on the run."

"I'd prefer *on the lam* if I were. For what am I lamming?"

"No crimes of passion. You're too cool-handed for that. I got it. Drunk driving—you killed some people. Someone famous. No, no. A mom and her baby. They're going to hang you for it."

I looked disappointed. "Drunk driving? All the sinister I look is drunk driving?"

Selma smiled, leaned forward, her feet below the glass tabletop searching for shoes. "No. And I don't go out with gangsters, so I'm keeping my imagination animated. Don't disappoint me, Joe."

I took her hand. "I'm no gangster. And, trust, I've had plenty of opportunity."

Hand squeeze, nice look. "I just bet you have, Joe Ready. You care to go upstairs, do the rumba?"

Went up to my room, did the rumba.

Selma the Red seemed pleased to find I already knew how to rumba.

Second dance, the telephone went urgent. It went ignored. It would be Lansky. I couldn't tell him to wait, but I could skip answering.

Not long after the races, the ringer rang again.

Selma nabbed it, said, "Mr. Ready's room."

Her gaze came around to me. I was trying to stare her strawberry nipples down. I glanced away, saw her furry red eyebrows.

"Sure, fella. Smartie's right here." She held the phone out. "It's for you, Smartie."

"Yeah? Who is it?" I knew.

"Meyer Lansky."

"Yeah? He tell you that?"

"No. I recognized his voice. He flies us quite often." A smile said she knew who Lansky was.

She stood, gathered her accoutrements, and let me enjoy seeing her walk to the loo.

Oh yeah—Lansky.

"Hello, Meyer."

"Smartie." Warm, friendly. "The hell are you, kid?"

"Good. You?"

"Yah. Fifty-fifty on good days. Who's your secretary? I recognize the voice. The memory associated is pleasant but outta reach."

"Remember a sky waitress with PanAm? Tall redhead?"

"Chest out to here? Yeah. I compliment, Smartie. I didn't know you did so well."

Like he called to see who I was playing bouncy bed with. Small talk, lively attitude, the your-pal-Meyer touch? He wanted something. For his sake I hoped it wasn't a big deal.

I'd never learned to move in Cuba too well. The goddam place was stable as a neurotic spinster. Changed dictators every twenty-

157

thirty minutes. This time of year was as peaceful as it got. It was *zafia*, everyone was working, everyone had money, everyone was happy. Maybe not the students. They seemed perennially sullen.

"You in the Presidential Suite?"

"Where else? Come on up, Smartie. The chef's doing something special for dinner. Join me."

"What if I said I was busy?"

The redhead came out of the bath, ensemble intact. "Bye, Joe."

"Hey, wait—Meyer, hold on—Selma. Where you going?"

"Bye, Joe. I told you: I don't date gangsters."

"Wait. I'm no gangster. Hold on. Talk to Meyer." Back in the phone, desperate. "Meyer tell her."

The door closed and Lansky said, "Tell her what?"

"Never mind. What time's dinner?"

• • •

Dinner was at nine. I knocked at nine-oh-five and ignored the two military guards by Lansky's door. A magilla in a tux answered my knock, head-wagged me in.

Lansky's suite made me feel like I'd been slumming all afternoon. If I'd brought my good field glasses, I could've seen the three-piece combo—piano, bass and clarinet—at the far end of the room.

You could entertain the Swiss Army in here if the Swiss had an army worth entertaining.

Wasted expanse. There were two men in the place. Lansky and a guy dark enough to be local. They sat in an area arranged for conversation around a fireplace. The fireplace was cold. The other man's eyes were colder.

The eyes were jet buttons, eyes that knew something about death. I didn't like him and I hadn't been introduced yet.

Lansky beckoned over, called me Joe, not Smartie. Called the other guy Colonel Batista. I'd heard the name. He was the grand puppeteer of all of Cuba—for right now he was.

The little guy started life two years ago as a sergeant—an army stenographer. Now he'd become *Colonel* Batista. This time next year he'd probably promote himself to general. He didn't look like any stenographer I'd ever seen. Thirty-five or so and a slick package in his doorman's duds.

The news rags called him mulatto. No mulatto. Yes Creole. *Mucho indio.* Thick black hair made fast to a head that sloped from forehead back. And the eyes.

They skinned me. They flayed me. They filleted me.

I said, "Don't get up. Please," just for fun. Shook Lansky's hand. "How are you, rabbi?"

"Watch it, Smartie. Say hello to the colonel."

I did.

It didn't move him to words.

I didn't embarrass myself with putting out a hand to be ignored by the arrogant bastard.

If we'd been in the States, I'd've maybe sat on his peaked hat.

An empty chair seemed a good choice to keep me from a firing squad, so I used it. I still got broadsided.

Batista said, "The red haired woman is very beautiful."

"Yes. I agree. You know her, Colonel?"

"I met her this afternoon. I had her brought to my office after she left your quarters." He watched me to see how I liked it, how I took it.

I didn't like it but I took it.

My peripheral: Lansky over there enjoying the show.

"I'm flattered you find me so important." A nice smooth smile I'd brought with me from the mother country. "You being such a busy man. The strike, the students."

"The communists, the guerillas, the mothers for better candle wax." He brushed all the distractions away with a wisk of a hand. "And you. All these gangsters you chased here. Do you have a plan for dealing with them?"

Lansky laughed like he wasn't a gangster. "Of course he doesn't, Colonel. He's a brash character. An opportunistic hunter of other men."

"Is he any good?" Like I hadn't shown up yet and it was still him and Lansky and the three-piece combo.

"I wouldn't want him after me." I got a wink. "And I'd make him rich he'd let me. But he won't."

"Too pure?"

"Too dumb. Hey, Smartie, you wanna jump in defend yourself go ahead."

I smiled some, poured a shot or three into a tall tumbler from a crystal decanter. Tonged some ice, sipped.

I smiled, held the whisky up in admiration, sampled, liked.

Said: "Whadda you want, Meyer?" Said it and watched Batista.

[30]

Not much to ask. I get my guys, Karpis and Campbell, trussed like turkeys. All I had to do—to get these birds special delivered to Miami—was find a man named Antonio Guiteras, hand him a letter. An invitation, really, according to the colonel.

Okay, I'm not Disraeli, but I'm not a too dull boy. "Why me?" The obvious was out there like big white panties.

"Yeah, Colonel, why him?" Lansky helping out. I looked at him, looked pained. He shrugged, sat on a smile.

"Do I find him, let you kill him, or do I just go ahead, pop him one in the head myself?" I'm still looking at Lansky, talking to Batista.

We stewed on that, Meyer warning me with his quick Yid eyes, scolding me. I looked back to Batista.

"Neither. I only want this letter delivered to him. He wants to leave Cuba. I want to help him." Hands dismissed. Innocent hands, a stenographer's quick, lithe hands. "It's easier than killing him."

I doubted that.

"You and your resources can't find him, how do I? I know maybe three people here."

Batista relaxed, seeing me drawn in to his opera.

"You will pose as an American magazine writer. A reporter."

I shrugged. "How?"

"Coincidentally, there is just such a young man under house arrest at the Columbia barracks. He flew here from New York City, New York, to talk with Guiteras, to interview him."

Coincidentally. "This guy say how he was to make contact?"

A cold stare, a near smirk or smile or a nervous grimace. "Yes. He was quite co-operative."

I bet he was.

"Look, Colonel, I'm not an actor. That's what you need. This isn't my sort of spice. Sorry."

Batista didn't hear *no* much, I guess. It made him flush.

"Did I mention we're holding the woman until you've completed your assignment?"

I got the juice under control, said: "Come on. I hardly know her. Why don't you pick up the registration clerk? I talked to him for almost five minutes?"

"If you wish, we will."

The bastard.

"Meyer." I spoke to the little man but kept my eyes on Batista. "Say something, Meyer."

Lansky cleared his throat. "Colonel. Please. This woman's totally unrelated to anything. How about it?"

Batista used up some time like he had to consider. Then: "No, Meyer. I must insist and overrule. No, the woman stays under arrest until we complete this matter."

"Colonel, I insist." Lansky playing along, not sounding very convincing.

I'd been hemmed in. A couple of cold, heartless, murderous bastards knowing a chump like me'd act goofy over some short he hardly knew.

Hemmed in didn't mean I had to act like a rat in a bucket. It meant I negotiate.

"First off: win, lose, or draw, the redhead flies outta here. Two: I see anybody even looks like Spanish blood behind me, deal's off. Three: I want Pearlie Friedman, when he gets here, as part of the

162

deal. You fellas talk it over, let me know. I'm in six-twelve—oh that's right, you two know where I'm at."

I killed the liquor, stood. "And, Meyer?"

"Yeah?"

"I don't know Colonel Batista, but I do know you. I hear okay on all three I'm looking at you to see it happens with the frail."

Two powerhouses, each to his own, and both of them looking like they'd like to put me on a spit, roast my insolent ass.

"Tell him, Meyer. We deal he can turn the girl loose." To the colonel: "I keep my word."

"As you said: I don't know you."

"You know Lansky. Work it out. Just let her go; show me some good faith."

I turned, walked for the double doors that opened to the hall. Twelve-fifteen feet Lansky began chuckling. It got louder, became a near cackle.

Then: "Habana, Smartie. You want it? The Nacionale, Club Montmartie? I'm gonna put up a place'll make the French Riviera look like Trench Town. All yours, kiddo, you want it." More laugh.

I wagged my head, used the door.

• • •

It was Lieutenant Andreu. I knew it would be Sergeant or Lieutenant or Ensign *Somebody* waiting in the hall. I didn't slow down for the introduction—made him talk to my back, run to catch the elevator.

The doors closed and he said—tried to say—"Mr. Ready, I am Lieu. . . ."

"I heard. Give me a phone number."

He had it ready, efficient bastard he was.

"When shall I expect your call?"

The no accent at all got me looking.

"Yale?"

"Harvard."

"Political Science?"

"Economics."

He was tall as me at a touch over six foot. Thinner—me at a buck eighty, him at twenty-thirty less. Glasses. Unblemished uniform. Polished boots. Looking everything like the future of fascism should look. I didn't like him much—maybe he grew on you.

The elevator squatted gently; doors opened onto the sixth floor hallway.

"When shall I hear from you?"

I stepped out, turned. I had a smile. "What's your name, Lieu? The first."

"Eduardo."

"They call you Eddie?"

"Some do. They call you Joe?"

"Yeah." Lansky calls me Smartie and I don't know why. I didn't feel so smart. "Lansky'll call me, tell me do we got a deal. I'll call you."

"I'll know before you, I suspect."

"Then come on up."

The doors began closing. Eduardo pushed a button and they withdrew.

"It's easier to leave the island when you go with the tide."

I nodded, looked at his shiny boots. "I've heard versions of that before. You ever heard the one: *don't shit a shitter?*"

He said, "I don't think that applies in Cuba, Joe. Be seeing you."

And the doors closed.

I leaned over after five beats, pushed the summons button. Not long another set of doors opened, an arrow over the door down pointed. I went downward times six.

The street was crowded and loud. Every day was Carnival here. Drunken American women gaggling and honking like geese. Drunken American men in adopted leisure outfits, acting like schoolboys at the state fair. A little Spanish blood, more in control, more aware of the hungry ones moving through the crowd, looking for a weak soul to cut out of the herd.

I shoved through, not caring who I pissed. A big blonde guy who could be on a billboard told me to watch where I was going. I urged him to have sexual relations with himself. He wanted to brawl, so I popped him one on the jaw, sat him on his pretty, tanned ass.

No one took up for the beefsteak, so I walked on, tried not to shove. A side street came up, and I popped from the gelatinous masses. It was cool. More people than I needed but not like the boulevard. I could breathe.

American blues came from opened wood doors. Only red lighting inside but for the stage. The stage was washed with pale blue spots mounted directly over it. A man in a pork pie—a black straw job—sat on a backless stool. Half-sat, one cheek on the stool, one leg on the floor.

He had chin whiskers and a black enameled guitar. A green medicine bottle was on his number three finger. When he danced it on the strings, it sounded like the lamentations of angels.

I was drawn in, bellied up, ordered a Bloody Mary for the nutrition. Sipped it, watched the stupid in the mirror, listened to the hat singing how he was going. He didn't know where he was going, but he was going. *Baby, do you wanna go?*

Story of my life. I never knew where I was going. Come on— Lansky'd said it. Others had said it. No style was my style. I had the blues, but I could still dance.

Maybe Batista was a bull-shitter. Maybe Selma was in her room. Maybe she'd flown out. Maybe I should call, find out.

I gave the keep a twenty, told him to do me double but clean scotch this go while I found a phone booth.

He said a gentleman of wealth and taste like myself could use the wall telephone in the kitchen for a dollar. He was American and blacker than sorrow, bald as a prepubescent eggplant. Rosebuds for ears. Hazel eyes. Big enough he could go anywhere, sleep there should he want to.

Red Selma answered in her room. The inner vibration receded.

"How's things, Red?"

"Well, well. Nice kettle of fish, Joe Ready. I can't come; I can't go. I can be in my room. There's a guy with a nasty looking gun and a brown front tooth on my balcony. His name is Angel and he comes inside to piss." A beat. "How are you?"

Hmm. "Look, Selma, I'm working on it. Okay?"

"Okay? I may lose my job. I screwed you with no raincoat between us—I could be pregnant seeing how I'm ovulating."

God. Don't say ovulating.

"I've got two more guys with big guns in the hall. So what is it you're working on?"

"You're not at Columbia Barracks, okay? Selma, I'm not a gangster, okay?"

"Sure, okay. I don't know what the hell you are, Joe. I know you're trouble. I know that's your business. I knew it first time we spoke." Some heavy silent stuff, then, "Take care of me, Joe. I'm depending on you."

"I gotcha, precious. Hang tough. I'll see you tomorrow, next day. I'll be the dumb ass at the bar."

"I'm counting on you, Joe."

I dropped the connection. Put my head on the wall.

I had to play. And I had to save a man's life I didn't even know.

The guy on stage finished up and I drank up, stumbled out.

I found a Western Union, telegraphed a guy on Loggerhead Key with a thirty-two foot power skiff. A good friend. He'd come cause I'd do the same for him.

I could get this Guiteras on the power skiff, we'd all live happy ever after.

Batista might not be ecstatic, but I wouldn't be able to hear him bawling about it from Key West.

[31]

You sold it, Smartie."

I would've sworn Meyer Lansky was at the foot of my bed.

"You awake, Smartie?"

Jesus. He was. A couple of heavies in shiny suits behind him.

"Meyer? The hell are you doing in here?"

"I called. You didn't answer."

"I'm hung over. Leave."

"You sold it to Batista. We got a deal. I gotta get back to Miami. You hearing me?"

We got a deal? I thought it was my deal. "The hell did you get in here?"

"I told you: you didn't answer the telephone. I gotta go."

"So you come on in?"

"Yeah. Call that Andreu guy. See you around, Smartie."

Jesus. I wasn't sure I wasn't still drunk. I stumbled into the bathroom, pissed, drank a quart or two of water from the spigot.

Slept another five hours.

Woke, called Selma.

She'd checked out. Couldn't say I blamed her.

I ordered two gin Marys and a fried egg sandwich from room service. It got there intact and I was infinitely grateful.

167

Egg sandwich in my belly, gin Mary number two in hand, I challenged the Nacionale's hot water system. I've eaten lobster didn't experience that sort of hot water.

Second gin Mary and many gallons of hot I toweled off, walked out of the bath.

Selma simmered on the big bed. Bare. Available

I walked over, touched her milk white skin.

"Hey, kid."

"Not to seem eager but I've got a flight out in an hour and fifteen, beautiful. You owe me a rumba or two."

I sat on the edge of the bed and touched her. Touched her everywhere I could see. She let me run my hands over her, made it easy for my hands.

Her face became tears somewhere in there. She cried through it all. Cried when she put her head back and fell into her primitive self.

She cried while she dressed. Cried as she left.

Maybe it was me should've been crying.

• • •

Andreu saved me the trouble of telephoning him. Came over to knock on my door. I knew he would. Sooner or later, but I was thinking sooner and I was on it.

The door swung back and he held something flat and small up face-level. "Not a bad likeness."

He turned the palm, showed me a photograph of a guy sitting in a chair. He wasn't happy but it was a comfortable looking chair, and he wasn't beat up.

"What do you say about it? We get some hunting clothes for you, boots, you could be him."

"What's his name?"

"Hudson Pringle."

"Jesus. His folks hated him." I gave him back the photograph. "You got papers and equipment for me?"

168

An envelope from a breast pocket. Papers saying I was Hudson Pringle, adjusted to my physical description. And it all looked pretty used.

"Nice work. The army do that?"

"No. Your friend Meyer Lansky arranged those."

Should've known. Meyer'd arranged every fucking thing else. "This guy a photographer or anything technical?"

"No. Only a writer."

That shouldn't be so hard—pretending to be a writer. Lots of people make lots of dough pretending to do it. Why couldn't I? I could write—could do it somewhat legibly. All I needed was somebody to put the commas and paragraphs and such in the right place.

• • •

The cheap-ass Cuban government, and I use the term in the temporary tense. Had to buy my own outfit. Andreu said I should bill the army.

Fine. I fully intended on stiffing the Nacionale if I could get off this slippery rock unnoticed. I knew the Nacionale was under government—wink-wink—Batista's control. I'd nail the greasy bastard on the tab.

Got me a nice pale tan chino shirt with epaulets. Khaki canvas pants, tall, heavy cordovan boots. I was only a pith helmet shy of a safari. I looked too new but I couldn't fix it.

Andreu could've dropped me off at the rendezvous, but *we* decided a bus would be best. I was to make initial contact in Matanzas. I'd tell a bartender at the certain joint that I was a sausage inspector from Seattle.

"We've interviewed the bartender. He's expecting you."

We were in a new Ford with government plates about two blocks from the hotel, near the University. I looked at Andreu over there wheeling down the *avenida,* using nice words like *interview.*

"The barkeep in Matanzas won't rat me down, will he?"

"No. He's not a liar. He promised us. See, Joe, we have prisons full of liars."

Sounded noble if truth weren't so relative. Yeah, I'd bet they had prisons full of liars.

"What happens then?"

"He calls a man who gave him a hundred American dollars to call a certain number when the sausage inspector arrives. Then he tells you to meet wherever the caller designates."

"This guy's shitting you, I'm dead."

"He's not *shitting* us. Take my word for it, Joe."

The side of his face didn't look at all like a guy who could dance around words like *torture* and never stumble.

"When's a good time?"

"Now. As soon as you can get there."

"I'm not riding a bus anywhere."

"No, I didn't think so. I have a car rented for you."

So, if I'd've been okay on the bus ride, he could've saved a few pesos. Made me wonder about the woodsy outfit—would he have sprung for it if I had balked.

We rode in silence and he slid to the curb in front of the hotel.

I got out, closed the door slowly, firmly. Leaned in the open window, grinned.

Said: "Tell your boss I wasn't fooling about being followed. I see somebody, we're done."

"You have my word. No one but the colonel and me know of this."

I didn't believe that for a second. The man's word was worth nerts to no one. The colonel's either.

"See you, Lieutenant."

"I believe we will meet again, Joe. Good luck."

Sounded like he really meant it. Nice guy for a fascist.

"Hey, Joe."

I stopped.

"Guiteras is under the misconception a small skiff named the *Amalia* is to rescue him."

I turned so he could smile at me and say: "He's mistaken. Watch his face as you tell him this. It should be entertaining."

I watched him slip away in his nice black sedan. Ice picks or vice-grip pliers, seemed I kept doing business with the same cats.

• • •

The casino was doing business already. I could hear its song as I skied across the marbled lobby. Jet up to six, pack all my wares, put the Luger away, wrap a big .45 around me.

A bored looking guy in a monkey suit, even the pillbox on his head, leaned on a podium out front.

"You got a rent car for six-twelve?"

"I look."

He look. He like. He smile.

"Yes. I have. Soon return." He trotted down a ramp.

Not many, a '31 Ford roadster crested the ramp. Yellow as a canary. The ragtop was down, and I wondered if it was worth putting up.

The last few steep feet tested the car's torque and clutch, but it made it. The hop shut it down and it exploded out the tail pipe, blew a smoke ring at me. I dodged it, threw my bag in while the boy jumped out.

He held the door until I got in, closed it gently.

I gave him a buck American. He said, "Good luck." Gave me some smart eyebrows and backed away.

"Thanks. See you in a day or so."

He asked where I was going. I told him. More eyebrows and more *good luck*.

I pushed the starter button. The car complained, blasted another backfire, caught up, and ran.

A wave and I pushed off in the sled, the clutch only slipping some. Chris Columbus made Santo Domingo on a crummy little boat—I could make Matanzas.

171

[32]

I made Matanzas. On a bus.

The Ford lay down on me maybe ten miles from Habana.

A convenient bus showed, I waved him down, gave him five bucks American, and he personally dropped me out front of a rent car place before he hit the bus depot. I wasn't the most popular guy on the bus, so I stood next to the driver to keep from getting shanked.

The rent car joint had a decent Buick hardtop. I took it, paid American. Got sketchy directions from a rent sales guy who I thought might have moonlighted as a bullfighter, seeing his slick hair and penciled-in moustache.

I took the directions toward the ocean—I could smell it coming at me. Got a glimpse in a few seconds. Same clean, blue sea Habana had.

Watching the water I passed my street. Did a couple of rights and a left to get back on directions. The bar wasn't as tough as I was thinking. Not bad for a waterfront joint.

A civilized restaurant area separated from the bar by some high security braided velvet rope.

Border Spanish sufficing, I ordered top rum of the house. What I got was an amber liquid from a wine bottle. It wasn't wine.

Ah. Nobody does cane squeezings like the Cubans. The world ever loses Cuban rum, it'll be a crime. Nectar.

Only a double would do. The heavy man behind the bar, bandito moustache, no bullshit eyes, brought it.

I said, "Man, that's the best rum I ever had. But then I'm just a sausage inspector from Seattle."

The barkeep said: "Seattle? Where's that? California?"

"No. Oregon."

"The food here is most delicious. If you are waiting on someone, it would be an excellent way to pass time." A face saying nothing. A turn. Conversation with a Cuban couple on my right.

I took the excellent rum around the formidable velvet rope, got seated near a window. Early dark gauzed my breathtaking view of the building next door.

Ordered a chicken breast with a grainy tomato-tomatilla-liver sauce. Over saffroned rice. Fried green plantains dusted with confectioner's sugar. And *mofongo*, not because I particularly care for it—I just love saying it.

The maître'd asked the chef, at my request, to suggest wine. I got a slightly sweet French red. Slightly sweet and slightly chilled. A wonderful compliment to the meal. I complimented the chef via the maître'd. The chef sent me a nice piece of nut-encrusted *tres leches* and a startling brandy—slightly chilled.

The moustachioed barkeep brought me another rum, said, "Your wait is over. *Vaya con Dios.*"

We locked eyes. I knew what he was getting at with the last words. I wished him the same.

Paid up in American paper, tossed some benevolent waves of appreciation at the staff, departed the excellent establishment.

A kid, brown as a berry and maybe twelve, sat passenger side in my car. I walked up, put my foot on the running board, his side. I pulled a pack of ready-roll pills, looking off, down the street. Shook one out, nibbled it from the pack. Shook one at the kid.

He took it. I sparked us both.

I spit a piece of tobacco off my tongue. "What's your name?"

"Hijo."

"You think I don't speak Spanish?"

He flicked quick black eyes at me. He was pretty scared but doing well with it.

"You need a ride somewhere, *muchacho?*"

"*Si.*" Looking straight ahead, through the windshield.

"Okay." I walked around, got in the Buick. I fired it up, asked the kid: "Where to, son?"

He grinned. "At the light, turn left. Go long way."

I did as instructed. We ran out of constant habitation, a stop sign occasionally slowing us down.

Nice and dark. Stop sign.

There are situations that in retrospect seem to go in slow motion, but at the time all events seem to happen simultaneously. This was such.

I slowed, an old woman shooed a herd of goats through my headlights, a couple of the goats jumping the beams of dust-speckled light. The kid jumped from the car. My door jerked open and hands pulled me out, began running me across the road, bent over.

I got the .45 out, smashed the butt of the grip into a shin on my right, smashed the barrel into one on the left.

We all three went down but I saw it coming, recovered better. Still holding the big Colt.

The guys made eye contact, read how I was aces up, the only guy with a piece. I looked over at the kid. "Run, dammit."

He stood there.

One of the guys shuffled in my side view.

I went back on them, said, "*Cuidado. Mucho cuidado.* Run kid." The kid stood, began crying. "*El es mi papá.*" Pointing at one of the guys on the ground.

Oh great. I relaxed, dropped the gat to arm's length. I rolled my wrists, one hand palm out, the other holding the gat out. "*¿Por qué?* The hell's going on?"

"They have almost no English." The kid, behind me.

"Why the bum's rush?" I lost the kid to the bad word choice. "Why'd they pull me out of the car?" I made a yanking mime.

Some quick-fire Cuban Spanish. Then: "A government car has been here two times." The dad spoke to the kid. The kid said, "And a truck with soldiers."

Great. "Ask them where they were taking me."

The kid chatted. I got it relayed. They had a vehicle down the road, in a canebreak.

"Where after that?"

More chat. To a packet boat that goes up the river.

Sounded decent. I nodded, put the gat away. Said: "Okay." Put up a wait-a-minute finger. Got my bag.

I tossed the kid my key. "You can drive of course."

"Of course."

"You'll know when I'm coming back?"

He nodded a chopped up head of hair.

"Don't wreck it. And don't get anything sticky on my seat."

The kid grinned. "Sure, *muchacho.*"

The two greasers were vertical. I indicated my wishes with a hand. Foolish me, I followed a couple of swarthy strangers, in a strange country, off into total darkness.

The vehicle was an antique truck with a pig in the bed. One guy got under the wheel; one got in the back with the pig. I got in front. Nobody cried wee-wee-wee cause nobody went home. Went down a road to a side cut that led down to a brackish marsh. A boat stood moored under its own artificial light.

The driver pulled as close as he could, tethered up.

Pairs of wood planks led out across some dank goo for almost a hundred feet. Something like a katydid sparked up a challenge that went to an insane chorus, louder than the industrial revolution. I led the way down the planks.

The packet boat was probably a twenty footer. Eight-nine foot beam on her. Battered bow, diesel putting like a metronome, bubbling from submerged pipes.

I put a leg over the side, sat on the edge of the boat, one foot on the planks, one foot on the boat's deck.

"You know where we're going?"

175

I could see he wanted to play *no habla*. He looked like a walrus in a captain's hat. I pulled the .45 back out, and it made his big salted moustache jump back and forth.

"I asked you did you know where we're going and you said–"

"Yes. I know."

"Good. I stepped in the boat, put the gat on Frick and Frack. "Sorry, guys. No can go, *por favor. Hasta mañana,* babies."

I sat on the engine cowl, cast off the stern rope one handed. Went forward, cast off the bow. Tapped *Capitán Sábado* on the bill of his yachting hat. *"Apúrate."*

The good captain let the current take us off the gangplank before he engaged the screws.

On a plane, on the dark water, the boat was fast, quiet, and nimble. We had the moonlit river to ourselves.

A bottle of scotch came to the top of one of my pockets. I nipped liberally.

"Hey." No hear. *"Hey."* Louder.

The captain turned. I held up the barley-bree.

A smile, a tin cup with some blue speckled porcelain left in a few places. I obliged as full as the cruise allowed.

He raised it in appreciation. I did it back to him. He tasted, got happy. Raised his cup again. "Joe Kennedy."

"To Joe Kennedy."

I lost track of time in the vibration of our vessel, but maybe a half hour a fire flickered to our right. A black man in only pants, and them ragged and above his ankles. He made a sign with his fingers. The captain answered with his own sign.

The Negro spoke over a bony shoulder to somebody we couldn't see.

The captain spun the boat, and I looked over at him. I looked back, and there were several men on the shore now; the Negro was history.

[33]

Pure assumption: the guy in the decent suit of clothes was Antonio Guiteras.

I put up a hand, got six back at me. The captain was in front of me. He didn't see me wave so he waved. Everybody waved again.

Capitáno told me: "Jump when she bump the bank." The boat nosed in at a snail's pace; I went forward, stood on the deck over the bow. Put my travel bag on a shoulder.

Saw it coming, timed my leap.

A heavy clack as the screws reversed, a hard throttle. I had the big Colt out. Hit the ground, cannon on best-dressed.

Only six revolvers of varying lengths were pointed more or less in my direction.

We let the juice settle down, acted like gentlemen. Gentlemen with guns.

Looked like the ball was on my side of the net. "You Guiteras? I'm Pringle."

Nice-clothes was polished, maybe thirty. He'd been vice-prez for a hundred days or so one time and looked every inch of it.

His tan suit was made on him, Egyptian cotton shirt the color of a robin's egg, tie the color of new rust. I'm sure his shoemaker was named Guiseppi or something like that. The skids could've used a polish; the suit could've used a dry-cleaner.

177

"You are not Hudson Pringle."

"Says who?"

The suit jerked his head. "Pepe."

A guy went in the back of his pants. A newspaper. He unfolded one handed, never moved the barrel of his piece off me. Held the open paper out. I looked down, read.

"Ah, shit. Jesus." I relaxed my grip on the gat. "Kill me, please."

"Talk fast."

I was still reading a New York headline about Hudson Pringle being shot in an escape attempt. The Cuban government regretted hell out of it, I'm sure, but right now they were denying hell out of responsibility.

"Brother, there's no way to tell it fast."

"Try." Not a nice guy face.

It didn't move me. I was tired of holding the Colt up. I dropped my arm.

"I know Meyer Lansky. Batista was gonna do me a favor if I gave you a letter, but I figure he's gonna kill us both anyway, so I telegraphed a dark skin island hopper I know, asked him to meet me in Matanzas, and I'd tell him where to pick me and you up and get us to Port a Miami. Quick enough?"

He grinned.

"You Guiteras?"

"Yes. And you are. . . ?"

"Joe Ready. A guy caught up in something way outside a his capabilities and resources. And his neighborhood."

Hands met, shook.

"You seem to be doing quite well. Thank you, but I've got a boat meeting me in Matanzas, too."

"Your deal's hinked. A nice starched lieutenant told me so. The *Amalia's* not coming."

We looked at each other. Guiteras was disappointed but took it stoically. It wasn't the fun Lieutenant Andreu had promised.

He spoke, signaled. Gats went down.

"What do you make of that?"

"You mean this lieutenant telling me about your boat, I'd say they're depending on beating your whereabouts out a me so to take you somewhat alive."

Another smile. Like I was being a shiny student. "How do you get to Matanzas without the army retrieving you?"

"It's what I do. I'm the Artful Dodger."

"Ah. Charles Dickens. Come, friend, let us have coffee and rum, think about extending our futures."

"Amen, brother."

• • •

Our bar was a plank on a stump and a barrel, all under mosquito netting, soft light from kerosene lanterns.

The rum in Matanzas was better, but this stuff wasn't bad. The coffee was class-A—almost sweet on its own. Guiteras, myself, and an older gent sat at the folding table centering the netted space. There were only the three chairs.

No one got introduced. I guess that's revolution.

I pulled out the letter pushed it across to Guiteras. "Mail call."

Guiteras read it, passed it to the old fella beside him. The *viejo* found cheaters—read. Handed the letter back to Guiteras.

They spoke quietly, laughed. About all I caught was something about a *culebra* and an *ave*. I could connect the dots with the laughter.

"Not convinced of Colonel Batista's sincerity?"

The old man said: *"Coronel,"* spat. *"Sargento,"* with plenty of contempt.

"I hear you, uncle. *Estenografo*, eh?"

The old man smiled, poured up some of the righteous rum. He held his glass up. Guiteras and I held up. Clink and a silent toast.

We had little in common genetically, socially, or financially.

The evening moved slow and quiet. We all had our goals and aspirations to embrace. Staying vertical was motivation enough for me.

Maybe Guiteras, the former college professor, wanted to be king of Cuba. Do like Martí, go raise an army, come back, kick some ass. Kick Batista out.

At a break in the silence, I slid in: "Where to after Miami, Tony?"

"California, Mexico, Spain. I can't raise enough money in Florida. The army will go with the popular side. That would be me after I control the east. Then we move on Habana."

"What happens to Batista?"

A shrug. He didn't care. "Probably the same fate that awaits me if the army discovers me."

Some quiet for a bit, the three of us solemn as condemned men.

Then Guiteras said: "He's a fascist who runs a puppet government." Like he was trying to convince me of something. Then quieter: "He kills people with no remorse or afterthought. Those are his ways."

I'd pretty much figured that out, like within the first two minutes of meeting Batista. "What is it *you're* selling, Tony Guiteras?"

He didn't like it. Screw him.

Then some bullshit: "I defend the workers and peasants; I defend their interests."

"What have you done for them so far?"

He smiled, shook his head. "You're having a hard go taking me seriously, aren't you, Joe?"

"For the most part." I held my glass up. "But you serve up decent booze."

"I brought about the eight-hour work day, minimum wage, established a department of labor. I fought for and got peasants the right to the land they tilled."

"That all?"

"I opened the doors of the university to all, rich and poor."

"I've read Marx and Lenin, too. Whadda you think about how Lenin ended up thinking so poorly of his beloved masses? Really ended up hating them."

Guiteras wrapped limber arms around his body, turned right and left in a deep stretch. "I, at times, can empathize with him." He turned back and put his serious eyes on me. He hated me with them for a little. He'd had this conversation with himself before.

The old man stood and staggered out without a word.

In a bit Guiteras asked me: "What is it you've done to improve the world that's so important you feel you can question my politics? As I understand, you're a mobster." His English was perfect.

"Where'd you grow up?"

A smile. "I was born in Philadelphia. Moved here at seven. My mother's a North American. I have grandparents there still." He went quiet, letting me answer. Waiting.

"I'm not a mobster. I know Meyer Lansky because we had mutual interests at one time. Maybe still do."

"And what is it you trade in, Joe? You and Lansky?"

"Human beings. I'm a hired cop. A P.I."

It tossed him. But not for long. "What are you doing in Cuba?"

"Chasing a couple a kidnappers."

Some more thought, then: "Isn't that unusual? Don't you fellows do divorce work? Chase check bouncers?"

"I do kidnaps."

He watched me a while, grinned good. "Still, my friend." Hands came out palms up.

"I'm not promoting myself for sainthood and I wasn't challenging your politics. I just wanted to know is all."

"Wanted to know what, Joe?" Having fun now.

"If you had any politics. I see now you do."

"What're Joe Ready's politics?"

"Survival, baby. It's a jungle out here."

"You're making jokes but, really, don't you choose to go into the jungle?"

"Every day but Tuesdays. I get my hair processed and paint my toenails Tuesdays. When's the cap'n coming back?"

"Whenever we want. He's anchored up river a half mile or so waiting on word to return. Are you ready?"

"Born that way, professor."

[34]

Tony Guiteras sent me off with a name and an address. The data belonged to a fellow traveler in Matanzas. I left Tony with a German machine pistol and two hundred rounds of 9-millimeter hollow metal jackets. We agreed on a time to hook up at a place called Fort Merrill. The name and address in Matanzas would get me a guy who knew where the Fort lived.

I watched Guiteras shrinking into the river fog and wondered if I'd ever see him again. Wondered if either of us would get off this rock alive.

The riverboat dumped me where I'd boarded. Like magic, the kid appeared in my Buick, straining to see over the steering wheel. He did a good job on a 3-point turn, killed the mill.

"He is fine." Patting my fender like it was animate.

"Thanks, kid. Here." I stuck a five at him.

Made his eyes bug. He was scared to touch it.

"Take it and get outta here."

He grabbed the bill, said, "I go you."

"No. You no go me." I poked a finger at my chest. *"Mi pelegro. Largarso."*

He hesitated, then turned and ran. I was alone in the boon-docks.

Me and a bottle of cane hootch sat in the front seat of the Buick, slapped mosquitoes, reviewed our options. Best option I had was go to Matanzas, find my friend Dupree, the friend with the power yacht, get on his bucket and never look back.

No way Batista was letting me out. I'd know he fingered Guiteras. I couldn't be trusted. I was dead as Guiteras. No Pearlie, no Karpis, no Campbell—I should get on the goddammed boat, never look back.

I lay my head back. Couple of hours till daylight yet. I fell off with visions of Dupree's bow pointing toward the Keys. Woke hung over, the sun in my eyes, and pissed off. I knew what I was going to do. I couldn't talk me out of it hard as I tried.

I cursed my foolish self, fired up the Buick, turned it around, headed to Matanzas. This moke that knew Tony Guiteras was the one who could show me where this Fort Merrill was. Guiteras said it was at a place called the Boulder. It was where Guiteras was meeting a fellow insurgent, a guy name of Carlos Aponte, and his rag tags.

Guiteras had eleven guys besides himself; Aponte would have another six or seven with him.

I hated to tell these guys, but the skiff wasn't made to hold that sort of humanity. Somebody wasn't going north.

• • •

The bay at Matanzas smelled of fish. Should have. Looked to be a fishing type settlement. The view coming over the hills that kept the sea at bay was boats, docks, fish houses with tin roofs and more boats. All size boats, all ranges.

This Jesus—no last name given—I was meeting had a fish house on the eastern shore.

Rubbernecking like a rube got me Dupree's skiff. Hard to miss—Chinese-red, lunatic-purple, and some toxic green they hadn't corralled and named yet. Bigger than I remembered.

Maybe most of Guiteras' party could repair to Miami; I'd ask Dupree.

184

Jesus' fish house was no better or worse than most. Rusted corrugated tin, ancient dock of diverse planks.

I tethered the Buick close to a doorless opening, the only one I saw. I could see through and beyond. Only a bay view worth a thousand bucks an acre in LA.

Jesus was inside cleaning fish. Maybe grouper; I wasn't sure. Didn't matter—I hadn't come to buy fish.

"'Lo, Jesus. I understand you understand English pretty good."

I got Jesus' attention, all of it.

"Yes? Who told you?" Concerned eyes.

"The guy told me said to give you this." I flipped a Mexican coin, tiny like a fingernail. Maximillian on one side, some sort of bush on the other. I didn't recognize the bush.

Jesus caught the coin in mid-air, uncoiled his hand, and looked. He watched the coin, flipped it over, watched it some more.

I watched him. Watched his hand, his fingers. One of them, the right index was missing the last phalanx and moved in that odd way an abbreviated finger moves.

He shook his head. "I cannot. I cannot take up the cause. My wife and children starved while I was in the revolution. No."

I stood there standing my ground or something. If I got told to bounce, I'd go get on Dupree's blithe boat, fish my way to Miami.

Some huffing and some serious head wagging, he said: "What do you need?"

"Tony wants to lam out. You dig lam?"

"Yes. I can't help. I no longer own a boat." A cynical laugh. "The revolution took it. Sold to save my dock and my fish house."

He says you know where an old fort on the Rio Canubar is. Deserted place."

"Desolate is a better word. Yes, I know it. You have a car I see. I will show you this place, this rock, and you will go away and leave me be."

"Fine. Let's ride."

Jesus washed his hands, but he still smelled of fish in the close confines of the car.

I tried several times to ignite a conversation. Jesus would have no parts of it. Finally told me he didn't care to talk to me. Told me I needed to heed the way.

The way was pretty chopped up and full of turns but not far from the docks.

It was indeed a dry, inhospitable piece of rock. *Desolate* sold this real estate short. Dismal. Fucking rats wouldn't've lived here.

The Buick took us around and I could see the river. Maybe the end of the same I went upstream on last night. Nice deep water, stone pier that wasn't going anywhere the next two-three hundred years. Jesus told me if I went out of the bay, went left, I'd see the mouth of the river on my left.

Maybe half way back to Matanzas, Jesus' nerve gave out—just like that—at an intersection. I stopped—he got out.

That's the last I saw of him for the most part.

• • •

Dupree was the color of iodine. His hair was redder but that same particular hue. His eyes were as blue as mine. Swore one of my horse-thieving forbears did some island hopping way back.

Who knows? Who cares? Dupree was a man to be counted on. Hard as it got, the big Negro could stand his ground. Punch like a steam piston, shoot like a guy in a Wild West show. He never gave me a front handle—I accused him of being a Fauntleroy or something.

I'll qualify Dupree—I saw him pick up an unfortunate fella in Key West and toss him at four of the fella's pals. Knocked them all down. Then they all got up.

When they got up's when I met Dupree. I don't care for odds like five on one so I jumped in. I kicked one of them so hard he's probably still at the dentist. Kicked another's legs out from under him, turned a table over on him. Dupree and I were back to back when help arrived.

It wasn't our help. We tossed knucks for two good minutes, moving to the door back to back. We made the door and Dupree shot a left hand out, grabbed a pee-wee about five-two, swung him around like a club, yelled, "Open the damn door, mon." Beating the little guy's legs and body on the wall, right and left, the little guy screaming in Dupree's face.

I got the door open and he let the spic go; we ran like hell. Down the block, up a quiet alley, we sat on a couple of barrels and laughed like lunatics.

Been pretty tight friends since. I come to Miami once-twice a year; on occasion he comes to New York or LA and I meet him there. We get drunk, cut up, fight if a fight finds us. We piss on the sidewalk and dare the cops to fuck with us.

That's my baby Dupree.

Then there's his damned boat. Maybe I was calling the wrong guy Captain Saturday. The boat could've passed for the good ship *Lollipop*. He called her the *Obeah Woman*, had it painted on the stern.

I put my Buick on a shell lot and crunched over to the dock. Clunked down the dock to Dupree's ship.

"Permission to board this nancy-painted boat?"

From below: "Hey, Joe, you want I should come topside knock you cold, mon?"

"You wouldn't be the first."

"And I wouldn't be the last." Dupree appeared among his words, wiping greasy hands on a greasy rag.

"Hey, the paint was free. What should I do? Tro it out?"

"You ever hear of tint?"

"Mon, I don't sleep outside so it don't keep me awake. How the hell are you?"

"Good as grits. Yourself?"

"I never complain on Fridays. Get in here and let me show you some whiskey I found."

I leapt down, put out a hand.

Dupree hid my hand in his, pulled me in, gave me one of those manly hug things, slapped my back soundly with his left paw.

He pushed me back, studied.

"Look at you, mon." I'm waiting on a compliment. "You're getting ugly as hell. You luck up and make fifty, you'll be hideous." A big laugh. "Good to see you, Joe."

"You too, Dupree. You mentioned alcohol."

"Yes, I did. Oh, my friend, just wait. I saved this because I know no one who could appreciate this more than you."

He disappeared below. Bumped around some. Emerged with a cloth bag.

"Get those chairs, mon."

I dragged a couple of sun-stressed cane chairs, pushed one at Dupree, pulled the other to a folding table set up on deck.

Dupree pulled the bottle out. *Bushmill's.* The color of garnet. "Thirty-seven years old, my friend. I took it as salvage off a grounded freighter."

"Salvage my ass. You're a goddam pirate. Pour me a handful."

[35]

Idon't do business good hung over. Don't think about business when I'm in that particular condition.

Sometimes you have no options. Sometimes business chases you down, screams in your ear.

That's what they make Bloody Marys for. I'd had exactly two when Lieutenant Andreu showed. I could've used a couple more.

He smiled pretty good like he was proud of himself for locating me. Invited himself on board. That part made Dupree's hackles rise.

I introduced them, investing as little enthusiasm in it as I could. Andreu sat on the motor cowl, a knapsack over a shoulder.

I couldn't see a piece on his belt, figured it for a bagful of hardware. Not a real handy place to keep your gat.

"Your boss ready to keep up his end of the deal?"

Andreu smiled, shook his head, like I'd told a good one. "Joe, Joe." More headshake. No more.

"Lieutenant, would you care for a Bloody Mary?" Dupree being a gentleman.

"No. No, I don't think so. I've got my own." He went in the bag. Came out with a small jar. The liquid in it was more pink than tomato. He unscrewed the cap. "A special ingredient." Reached in, put Jesus' stubby finger, the one with the missing phalanx, on the table. Jesus wasn't attached.

189

Shit got my attention. I could feel the juice warming my neck and face. I could've killed Andreu.

"Where'd you get me?" I'm trying to hold on to the adrenalin.

"The packet. We were watching it." Still proud of himself.

I could only look at him. I had no words. Guiteras was dead, or worse.

"Do I get my guys extradited?" I'm not even here anymore. I'm somewhere else.

"No." Smugness.

"Why?" Time slows down, gets syrupy.

Andreu pulled the knapsack open, let my German burp gun slide out, onto the table next to Jesus' abbreviated finger. "This." He wagged his head, tsk-ed me some. "Arming enemies of the state? Joe, that's a serious offense here."

I took the table over with me, but I got him before he ever saw me coming. Got my left hand involved with a good hank of his greasy hair, pulled his head back as we fell.

Face to face, my Luger under his silly little goatee—that's how we hit the deck. Down there between the motor cowl and the port side if port is the left side.

"Cast off, Dupree. And don't fuck around."

"Who's captain? You now?"

"Please cast off."

"Better."

Strained from Andreu's pie hole: "I've got men watching."

"If they're not in a boat, you're nixed, baby."

I could see in his eyes his boys weren't in a boat.

"You're fucked, Eddie. Be nice and we won't drop you off on Loggerhead Key."

He knew what went on at Loggerhead Key. Insurrection, daddy. Anti-Batistaros.

The lieutenant was nice while Dupree fired off the sixteen-cylinder Rolls Royce mill, cast off, and sped away.

Among the confusion of the engine noise, I said, "I'm gonna stand up. You're not. Got it?"

He didn't seem to get it.

I poked him pretty hard under his chin with my piece. "You got it?"

"Yes. I got it."

"Good." I kept my face in his, my hand in his hair but got my lower section on knees.

"Dupree." Pretty loud.

Noise.

Louder: "Dupree."

"Yes."

"Pull out a piece, put it on this babydoll while I get up."

"You look so cute down there, mon. The both of you all smootchie."

"I'm standing up." And I did. Put the gat under my shirt while I did.

Vertical, I stomped on Lieutenant Andreu's crotch. He screamed some, writhed a lot.

Dupree looked back, surprised but grinning. "Why do you do that, mon?"

"You were him, you got to thinking hard, what would you do?"

"I see, my friend. Yes. I'd jump out in the busy harbor, gain attention, swim like a mad man. Maybe you should jam him once more. Insure his compliance."

Andreu was still in pain, rocking back and forth now, knees up.

"He's good for a few minutes." I'm yelling in Dupree's ear, holding on to the back of his captain's chair. Dupree's letting the big mill eat water. The pipes were submerged but it still sounded like amplified lions.

"Where are we going when we are finished running out of Habana?"

"A telephone in North America."

Some thought. "Marathon?"

"Marathon it is, my captain."

I looked at Andreu. He'd quit writhing and was only looking pathetic and holding his future with both hands.

"But Loggerhead's not outta the question, Eddie. Be nice now."

He nodded.

We got out in international water, I let him get up and limp around and look at me like maybe I was the fascist and he wasn't.

Eight-ten miles out he started getting edgy again. I knew why.

If he were we, we'd be swimming around dodging bullets by now.

After a bit, me watching him, smiling a little here and there, I decided he needed a drink.

I yelled at Dupree to ease off and keep an eye on Eddie. I grabbed the German burper, and went below. Uncorked a decent bottle of scotch I had in my travel bag hidden under some guns and stuff, locked up my hardware and some other guns Dupree'd left lying about, took the hootch topside. Put the bottle on the table in front of Andreu but held on to it so it wouldn't tip.

He watched it, reached over and glommed it. Did a respectable slug. Then one more for good luck. Then one for prosperity or something.

The bottle came back at me. I passed Dupree the bottle, bumped his arm with it.

He looked back, grinned and took the hootch. A tall cup sat in a hole in the whatever-you-call-a-dashboard in a boat. Dupree poured like he owned the bottle. Turned back, a finger hooked around the neck. He grinned, showed me enough gold it could've been his retirement plan, took a slug off the neck.

He passed. I took the bottle, knocked back enough to make my eyes water, passed baby on to Andreu.

The good Lieutenant took, held the bottle up as a toast, drank. Said: "May I stay in Miami, Florida?"

"You mean forever, Eddie?"

"Sure. Sure. I have an aunt and uncle there."

192

But no passport or papers. No money. No class. Damn, Eddie Andreu was gonna make one hell of an American citizen.

I'd've wished him well but for the finger. Sure the kick to the groin was satisfying, but this baby either aced or was present when Jesus got aced, when Guiteras got aced.

I had that feeling again where adrenalin just barely gushes enough to make the ticker flutter to attention, makes the cheekbones check in like a heroin kick. That's the one I hate. The one that scares me. The one where you're calm on the outside but inside it's like some intense weather condition. I could kill you when I feel like that. I have to watch myself.

I took the bottle and gulped some more.

Another hit, I realized I'd been staring at Andreu.

He said: "Please. Please, Joe, don't kill me. Please."

"Why don't you go below, Eddie." Not a question.

"Sure. Sure, Joe." Andreu rose, went through a short door. I closed it behind him

Dupree motioned for my ear.

I put it close.

He said, "I have a shotgun in there."

"Not to worry. I locked it up."

Dupree raised the orange caterpillars living over his blue eyes and dropped them.

I said, "Temptation shall the wicked know."

"What verse is this?"

"I just now made it up."

"I see." Dupree cut the throttle, coasted to nothing.

"Watch this." I withdrew, sat on the motor cowl, laid my Mauser beside me on another cushion.

It took him a while. Long enough Dupree and I'd nearly finished the bottle of scotch, maybe twenty minutes.

Slam the door open with a shoulder, run up the two steps, put the German burper on me.

And click on nothing.

Dupree shot him in the side of the head with a pretty feminine-looking .38 automatic. That close, the shot was through and through, but slowed down enough the slug made a *bloop* noise not far from the boat.

Andreu pitched away from Dupree and started leaking like a fountain on Dupree's deck.

Dupree looked at me. "Tell me, my friend, did I hear a click just before I drilled the man?"

"Could have, baby. The stutter gun was all loaded up with 7.65's."

Dupree wasn't real happy. He knew the German full-auto was 9-millimeter. He'd given it to me; he knew the 7.65's were useless in the gun. "You bastard." But he grinned to the gums.

[36]

Fuck you, Meyer." I'd made it to a phone.

"Watch it, Smartie."

He had some more but I said: "Fuck you."

"It's a foreign country, for outloud crying."

"Come on. The guy'd be goose stepping with the Nazis he didn't have Roosevelt's dick in his mouth."

"Listen, Smartie, you're thirty years old and all balls. Listen to Meyer. Listen." Silence.

"All right." But it wasn't all right.

Lansky'd been in on a deal where I got used and abused. No telling what I missed out on by tackling Andreu—God rest his soul.

"You fucked the guy."

"No, I didn't. I gave his guy the letter, Meyer. That was the deal. So he sends the finger nippers to see me. Nice work. Thanks."

"Smartie, I'm telling you right now, I'm Meyer Lansky and you'll not talk to me in this fashion."

I turned a lot of air loose a couple a times. "Sorry. I tend to get upset over injustices. Most especially when it involves people I've turned out."

"As well any gentleman should, Joey. Just let the juice go down and think about these things I tell you."

"Go ahead."

"Okay. The colonel says sorry but politics trump business deals. So okay, he snuffed a couple a guys. . . ."

195

"He snuffed twenty guys."

"Okay, Joe. It ain't your politic. Leave it lie. Go get what you want outta these fascist bastards before some commie savior waltzes in, gets the girl."

"He tells you he's still jake on our deal?"

"Tells me."

I put few beats between our words. Then I said: "Meyer, if you're setting me up and I manage to jump sideways. . . ."

"That a threat, Smartie? Sounds like, huh?"

"Does kinda, now I think about it."

"One more thing. The colonel wants to know what happened to his lieutenant."

"Tell him don't wait up nights."

"My, my. Lookit Smartie taking care a business. Bye, Smartie. Until then."

"Till then, Meyer."

To this day I don't know Meyer fucked me or not.

• • •

I cradled the phone, walked a couple of blocks, walked out on a pier.

"I gotta go to Cuba, Dupree."

"You're crazy, mon."

"Crazy? You interested in a piece a thirty grand I got riding on this deal?"

"As if it were salvation in a jar I'm interested, my friend."

Habana wasn't a good bottle of hootch away. We made it but were drunk as hell.

The world kept tilting on one end, and I knew I was either gonna vomit or slide off.

"Dupree, I ain't sleepin' on this fuckin' boat again. I got a room at the . . . somewhere. Where? The Presi-damn-denté. No. The Nacionale. Okay. The Nacionale. I'm gettin' a damn taxicab outta here. Where are we?"

"Duarté's dock."

I repeated it as I fumbled with the difference in elevation from boat to pier. Jesus, I was drunk.

No cabs but a guy wouldn't mind making a couple of bucks American was kind enough to offer. Somewhere between Matanzas and Habana raindrops hit the car in big soft blobs like butterflies. Then hailstones like marbles rat-a-tatted on the hood and roof. My driver muttered at his *Madre Maria.* The hail passed and tropical rain drove the car toward Habana. I pulled out a five, lay it between us. The guy nabbed the fin, drove like a seasoned pro.

Took me straight to the Nacionale. I rattled my key at the desk clerk. He nodded; I staggered. Caught a rocket up six floors. My head kept going when the rocket stopped.

The hall moved worse than Dupree's boat. Left side up, then down while the right side went up. Thank God for hard plaster walls. I bounced back and forth.

Got the key in the door. Pushed it open and took a few feeble steps.

The door slammed behind me.

Alvin Karpis and Harry Campbell were smiling like all get out, sitting on the couch in my suite.

I couldn't focus on who, but somebody said, "Nail him, Pearlie."

Something about the size of a freight car hit me behind my right ear.

That's all I remember. Lucky me.

[37]

Jimmy sat for a while in the big quiet of a hospital at ten-something in the evening. Pretty sure Joe was sleeping.

Machines played out the mechanical song of his condition. The beat was slow, the rhythm unsteady.

The door clicked open and the same painted nurse made sure Joe was alive and Jimmy was behaving himself.

She asked if Jimmy wanted a sleeping chair.

He told her he was fine, thanks.

The big nurse said goodnight, called Jimmy *Mr. Ready.* He didn't correct her.

The door shut and Joe said, "She gone?"

"Yeah."

"I was acting awake I'da had to give some sort a sample a some fluid. Hell, way they stick me around here I should be beef jerky." Then a jump sideways: "You get the girl home?"

Meaning the kid from Miami Jimmy'd just brought home from Cuba, their latest case. Joe had already asked this earlier. He'd started doing that a few months back, asking you the same thing a couple or three times. Jimmy let it go, played along, said, "Yeah."

"How hard was that?"

Jimmy shrugged. "After Elian, what's Uncle Fidel gonna say?"

"Somebody kept it outta the news I noticed."

198

"Yeah. There was one local radio affiliate, a Spanish station, couple of newspaper guys. State Department people were jerking each others' joints so nobody'd break ranks on how this Cuban soldier got over to So'wes' Eigth'a Street and back to Cuba with his daughter under his arm unnoticed."

Joe left it there, was quiet.

Jimmy picked the story up, told it in a low steady voice, Joe's mechanical life song setting cadence.

[38]

Joe broke out a couple of bumps of coke for a pick-me-up after the story. Jimmy had questions about Cuba, but didn't ask—too much morning.

The coke had belted his appetite, but the reefer was coming back on. Jimmy switched to beer, let Joe talk him into a sandwich.

A foot and a half of Cuban sandwich got pressed, cut in half and put on the table by the time Jimmy rolled and lit another joint.

The sandwich found Jimmy's appetite. Told Joe the sandwich was fan-fucking-tastic.

Joe said it was all in the bread. Had to feel like concrete in the hand but melt in the mouth when crushed.

Jimmy said the meat was also fan-fucking-tastic.

Joe said he'd roasted the pork himself, had a recipe straight from Habana. Said it like that—Ha*b*ana.

The knock at the door required a roach patrol. Jimmy emptied all the ashtrays in the trash, found a good innocent face. Should've been easier seeing as how he was innocent but for the reefer. And a bump of coke.

The cop, Lieutenant Detective What's-his-name, came in sniffing.

Reefer? Cuban pork? Cocaine?

Joe fired off one of his big green cigars, drifted smoke at the cop, grinned.

"Evening, officer." But had told Jimmy earlier the cop wasn't an officer.

"It's afternoon."

"Yeah? Seems later. You live in a town where coo-coos take potshots at citizens, time crawls, don't it? Your fellas find anything out there in the pines?"

There was a copse of tremendous Australian pines off to one side of the pier. Jimmy hadn't thought about it but it seemed like a good place to hide, take potshots at citizens.

"I think this'll go faster if I ask the questions, sir."

The cop had a problem with Joe.

Joe didn't have a problem with anyone.

The cop asked—Joe told him he didn't. That came after Joe said, "Oh Christ, one a them." Then told the cop how he didn't have to listen to this shit either. How he could make one phone call and the cop in the fancy Peter Max tie would be fetching coffee and doughnuts for the boys in dark suits and skinny ties.

Joe and the cop let the scale adjust.

When it did, the cop said, "I'd rather you didn't, sir. I'm aware of your situation. Could we see if we can find this shooter? I'd like him outta my town. I'm sure you would, too."

Joe agreed, said, "I don't have a clue. I've been here almost a year. None of my people have given me reason to think I should be worried."

The cop said it looked like that situation was history, how things had changed and maybe Joe should talk to *his people* again.

Jimmy was two steps behind the conversation. What *situation?* What *people?*

Joe said, "Somebody takes a few wild shots at the people fishing on the pier, you come see me."

"With all due respect, Mr. Joseph, the shots seemed to have been in your general direction."

"Or the Spanish blood on the other side a the pier. You ask them?"

"They're next." A cop look.

"And I'm first?"

The cop did a good cop sneer, like he was getting tired of Joe's shit. "Of course."

"Of course? You got two wealthy Cubans, you make me first. Lieutenant, you ever hear of illegal drugs?"

"You mean like marijuana? Like has been smoked in here in the last little while? Sure."

"Kids these days. Whatcha gonna do?" Joe pointed at Jimmy. "Wild ass neighbor kid here, but you make me first. Been fighting over getting ripped-off—an LSD deal in the park. Kicked some guy's ass. What's the cat in the leather hat's name, kid?" Throwing it all at Jimmy—bringing up something Jimmy'd told Joe in private—but grinning about it. "And you make me first?"

Jimmy felt himself flush, went hot when the cop put the cop look on him. "Hey, it *was* bad acid."

The reefer, the tension, the thing about *bad acid*, or what, Joe and Jimmy both laughed.

The cop was muscled about halfway up. He said, "Am I missing something?" Like a high school principal.

"You're missing quite a bit, sport. I say we're done here."

"I'd say so too. Good luck, Mr. Joseph. This guy seems like he's got motivation and means."

"But not much aim. Lieutenant, check out your Cubans. It ain't me. I swear it ain't." Joe put out innocent hands.

"I hope so, sir, for your sake." Then: "You might want to watch who you're hanging out with," to Jimmy.

"Yeah, like Cuban drug peddlers." Joe putting a bold smile on it. "See you, Lieutenant. There's the door."

Jimmy'd never seen anyone treat the law like Joe did.

Maybe the lieu hadn't either. He stood motionless, hung on the moment. Turned and used the mentioned door.

"Smug bastard." Joe to the door.

"He's all right. For a cop."

Joe made a noise through slack lips. Poured.

202

Jimmy twisted a jay.

No words for the joint.

Then Joe said: "See, kid? I don't let the cops or anybody run me over. It's not allowed. They wanna be assholes and break the rules first, shame on them."

"What's that from? Copology one-oh-one?"

"No, baby. Life one-oh-one. Welcome to your awakening."

That got to bob around and around like a plastic duck in a carnie's float game.

A sharp knock, Mom saying, *Joe,* through the door.

Jimmy said, "Ah, jeez. She's heard." Meaning the incident at the pier.

"No secrets around this place, huh? You may as well let her in, get it over." Joe stubbed the reefer, stoked up his stogie.

Dot came in, controlled hysteria keeping her in constant motion.

"Jimmy? Are you okay? Joe?"

She grabbed Jimmy, went to wet relief. Turned, grabbed Joe, gave him a hug. Back to Jimmy, wouldn't let him go.

"Please, for God's sake, someone tell me what happened."

"What'd you hear happened, Dot?" Joe all relaxed, Mr. Laid-back.

"That someone was shooting at you and Jimmy." Her face wanted it to be not-true.

"Who told you that?"

"Saul Goldstein. He saw a big commotion, asked the police."

"Was he on the pier?"

"I don't guess so. He told me he was on his patio when the police arrived."

"I thought he fished every Friday." Joe thought it was kinda funny, smiled.

"Joe, stop being trivial. Jimmy, did someone shoot at you and Joe?"

Joe and Jimmy harmonized on a *no.*

"Dot, some kid shot out toward the pier. Just happened Jimmy'd caught the biggest fish in the ocean. The kid shooting couldn't miss it."

Dot was back to near hysteria. "Oh my God." Hand over her mouth. Then both hands covered her face. From behind there, she said, "How close? God, I don't want to know. Yes I do. How close?"

She peeped out.

Joe shrugged. "Like to the other side a the room. Not close at all."

Dot wasn't buying. "Jimmy, how close?"

Jimmy looked at Joe, said, "Not close, Mom. Just some crazy kid being funny. He shot my fish is all. We're fine. Both of us."

Dot shook her head. "I've got to take a tranquilizer and lie down. I can feel a migraine coming on."

She left shaking her head.

Joe looked at Jimmy. "You know, we don't slow down, she ain't gonna let you play with me anymore."

"I'm hip." Jimmy put in a pause, added a grin. "Who was shooting at us, Joe?"

[39]

Next few, life was tolerable. The Lebanese hash was still plentiful and a truckload of Captain Marvel MDA had hit town.

The park was nice when the breeze blew and Jimmy was taking advantage of the cooler weather—on the bench, under a palm tree the sun had stepped out from behind.

The binder and pencil beside him, him watching the ocean. Watching it cream and retreat, almost languid for big water.

Jimmy could sense someone walk up, stand behind the bench. No sound, no smell, just sensed it.

He looked back. The cop—Lieutenant Hernandez.

"Mind if I sit?"

"If I did, would it matter?"

"You've either been watching too much Mod Squad or been hanging around Mr. Joseph too much, Jimmy."

Jimmy let the wind have that. The cop sat.

"He knows who the shooter was." Nice pause, then, "Do you?"

"No."

Some more pauses.

"Just, *no*. No snappy comebacks?"

"Nope."

A short break.

"I bet if I turned you upside down and shook you, I'd find some of that good hashish going around. You wouldn't believe how much trouble a gram or two of that stuff can get a fella into in this state, this county. Hashish? Whoee, powerful stuff to some bumpkin Billie-Bob judge from Wauchula."

Jimmy got tired quick. Maybe he was hanging around Mr. Joseph too much. He went in a pocket, slapped about a gram and a half of hash wrapped in foil on the bench between them. He looked at the cop.

The cop wagged his head. "Put that shit up. I'm not vice. I don't care a damn what you smoke or toke or take. I really don't."

Jimmy put the sheesh back in a pocket.

"Lieutenant, I'll tell you how much I know. I know so much I'd like to know what you and Joe Joseph were talking about, the part about doughnuts and skinny ties, you saying you knew his situation. Okay—what the hell is his *situation?* I'd like to know. I'd like to know who his fucking *people* are." Jimmy noticing how he'd gotten different with cops, cursing and stuff.

Lieutenant Hernandez watched the Atlantic hit the sand.

"I don't know anything about your neighbor other than he's under the—and I'm quoting now—*management* of the FBI. Yeah, Joseph's right, I'm small potatoes. I get nada from the guys in dark suits and skinny ties. Any contact beyond a cursory inquiry, I should let them know."

They were quiet, both watching the sea.

Jimmy was tilted. Joe was looking more and more for real by the moment. The whole world was lifting on one side a little. Slick dude like Jimmy could slide right over the edge he didn't watch it.

"What is it you want from me, Lieutenant?"

"I wouldn't want you to feel like you were ratting out a friend. . . ."

Here we go.

". . .but should this man take you into his confidence about this shooting, I'd like to know."

The notebook lying between them, Jimmy said, "The guy never talks about his past. Not to me anyway. He tells me something, I'll let you know."

The cop didn't believe it any more than Jimmy did.

"Here's something else, all I got, Jimmy. The slugs were .245 Winchester, not a common round, and the shooter wears about a size eleven shoe." A shrug. "Give or take. In sand, it's hard to gauge."

"You find out where he shot from?"

"Yeah. The Australian pines, down by your condos."

"No one saw anything?"

"No one ever does, Jimmy. No one hears anything. We could be a race of deaf-mutes for what noise a cop gets from the public sometimes. A guy pops off a couple of high caliber rounds, no one hears shit."

He stood, stretched a bit.

"See you, Jimmy. If I were you, I'd watch my ass."

"Yeah, you mentioned that before. See you around."

Maybe twenty feet behind Jimmy, the cop said, "I'd be careful about standing too close to your mom, too, if you consider our shooter's aim." A laugh. "Lemme hear from you, Jimmy. You're in way over your head."

Jimmy sat there a bit, picked up the notebook, wrote .245 Winchester in it.

He walked into the surf, stood balls-deep. Had to talk to Joe. Only way to go. He was going to put it on Joe just like he heard it from the cop, see what Joe had to say about it.

• • •

"Yeah, so what?"

So what? "So what the hell's going on? Who are you? What'd you do?"

"Ah. You think I did something. Because the Feds gave me a new name. By the way, my real name *is* Joe Ready, like I told you. Maybe the Feds owe me a favor or two. Maybe I didn't do anything."

Jimmy shook his head. "You're a fucking trip." More head work, a smile. "Damn, you're good."

Jimmy got the ice eyes. "Sit your ass right there, chump."

Joe spent some time in his bedroom, came out with a fistful of paper.

"Read it." He slapped the pages on the counter in front of Jimmy.

Jimmy shuffled through. Some were only yellow. Some were black background, white lettered copies.

Two black ones from J. Edgar Hoover warning a guy named *Ready* to stay out of Bureau business or else. The name Joe'd used in the Lansky story.

One from Melvin Purvis thanking Ready, then one from Purvis warning Ready *the boss* was losing his patience. A nice one from a Clyde Tolson guy that was almost odd, girlish. Almost begging Joe to come to DC, let Clyde show him around.

A couple more on more modern FBI letterhead. One was about a Bobby Greenlease. From the text—a lot of *unfortunates* and *sads*—Bobby must not have made it, but Ready had helped run down the culprits.

Jimmy restacked the pages, watched them a bit.

"So why're you using a phony name?"

"What's your guess, kid?" Joe back to having fun.

"You ever catch Pearlie Friedman?"

"No."

"You know where he is?"

"Yeah."

Jimmy saw it coming, knew he was real close to needing to step back, but said, "I need to hear about him."

"Then so you shall. Let's go way back, baby—LA, late twenties."

[40]

One of Joe's monitors went off, beeping and blinking urgently.

The suddenness of it made Jimmy jump. It registered and put him on his feet.

Joe said, "Relax, Kildare, just one a my meds running low is all. It'll get a night-shifter in a couple a minutes."

It did. A large, young unfriendly woman in pastel medical clothes. Joe made a few jokes. Nobody laughed until she left.

"Hey, kid, you ever read your notes from back then?"

"Yeah."

"Still got them, huh?"

"Yeah."

Some raspy breath, a puny cough. "Why?"

Jimmy shrugged. He didn't know. "Just one of those things you hang on to."

"It all means something, kid. More than just how I had to make a few quick choices, court opportunity."

"You were squaring up with Pearlie on Marian Parker."

Joe grinned, sipped. "That ain't what I'm talking about, kid."

There was a good sized piece of silence.

The machine noise took over again.

Joe cleared his throat, sipped water.

"Tell it, kid. The one about Pearlie and the two psychos."

[41]

Twenty and slinging suds at a pig in LA, thinking I was a pretty big deal still, still that young and uninformed. Still too young to know there ain't no big deals—just good runs.

I came out of a rough neighborhood with a couple of older brothers who didn't mind heavy work. Long as it involved nothing legal they were all over it.

A couple of years of going home with booze in my shoes, I started running from the big payola my misguided brothers kept offering. Ran so hard I ran right into a cophouse, signed up.

Twenty-six wasn't the cleanest year the LA cops ever saw. I held the line, didn't rat out the pad, didn't rat out fellow officers. But I wouldn't take their money, wouldn't join in their field trips. Everyone figured I'd get over it seeing who my brothers were. Seeing who my brothers were, nobody jacked with me either.

I chased smash-and-grabbers; caught a few. Chased illegal greasers; caught very few. Collared drunks; tried to keep them from puking on me. Hit a guy with my stick for hitting a chippie he was escorting—bold bastard hit her with me looking at him. Mostly I directed traffic, wrote meter violations, shook doorknobs. Fun stuff. Not exactly saving the universe or anything.

Seemed evident unless I did something outstanding, I was destined to retire with flat feet, a bad back, and a beat-dog attitude.

Next big case, I was gonna go in street clothes, see what it got me. I still thought a lot of myself—thought I was smarter than all the other cops in all the cophouses in LA.

A kidnap fad seemed to be kicking in. You could say it got imported from Europe or Mexico or South America. Doesn't matter. It's too easy to come up with when you've got a few *haves* and lotsa *have-nots*. Got popular as cheap beer in a college town before you knew it.

A twelve-year old girl named Marian Parker went stolen from school—like most of them are. Someone in chauffeur's duds walks a good story in the front door, walks the kid out.

I took my situation to the family table. I told Mattie and Jess the sad story. It left them unmoved.

I told them I needed a promotion like I never needed anything.

They mumbled, said they'd let me know who it was. They did. Did it in an hour and a half.

Was a guy outta New York set the game, guy name of Pearlie Friedman. He was running with a local moke, Danny Renahan, a punk originally outta Frisco Bay area, or could be Chicago—depended on who you asked.

I really didn't care. I wanted the current version, the LA version, of Renahan.

• • •

The Sarge let me have a few days to tend to some pressing personal business. He eyeballed me good, said, "Don't do nothin' I wouldn't do." Let me off with nothing more than the trite old line. I took it as a positive sign and got to work.

Danny Renahan wasn't so hard to find. He was a carefree boy. Went loud and dangerous where he went. People remembered him. Maybe like a bad case of the cordie they remembered, but they remembered, avoided.

Couple of keeps told me Danny showed up at your rail you'd eventually have to give some kid a couple of nickels to go out to the paystation, call a cop—that kind of guy.

Blithe-baby-boy-Renahan. Found him at a cheap pig out by

the beach. Kinda place has scant, colored neon lights inside, snuggly couples alongside your beach garbage—drunks, junkies and worse you can find it. Neighborhood rummies lined up at the bar.

The place so cheesy it didn't even have a name. Was in a converted beach house, a rickety two-story woodpile. Had a high rear balcony over some rocks a depressed drunk didn't need to see.

It wasn't bad but felt like a fag joint, all the quiet lighting, blacked out walls.

I had a few pops, nined-up in my brown pinstripe, two-tone tips, deep brown fedora—made in Italy. I hoped I didn't get mugged on my way to the can by somebody in khakis and an undershirt.

A loud knock, another. Danny gained entrance.

A couple or more people looked over.

Nobody said: *Hey, Danny.* I didn't cause I didn't know Danny from nobody.

The barkeep slapped the bar, said, "Sir, you need another, that'll be another five." Talking about the five I was gonna pass to him if Danny came. He had five and a current phone number on me already if Danny didn't make it tonight.

I dropped the promised wampum, said, "How 'bout two of your best."

He said, "For you and your friend." Meaning Danny.

"No, baby. Me and you. Then I'm gonna drift."

"I see. Would a good single malt scotch interest you, sir?"

"Like pictures of naked girls would interest the Pope, sweetheart. Only in an ecumenical manner, though."

"Strictly ecumenical. Yes, sir. Then scotch it is." Not bad repartee from a guy in a cut-rate pig.

I drank the nice whiskey, went outside and skulked in an alleyway.

Renahan came out—get this—counting his money. Like he was the only moke on the planet, like it wasn't a dive out by the beach he was leaving.

212

I smacked him flat-palm in the nose and mouth. Knocked him on his ass. He tried to look but I put a foot on his face, felt him up.

Only a small auto—.25 cal—a knife from here to Corvallis, a roll of nickels for punch.

I scattered his pockets, told him to get up.

He cursed me like a master profaner so I hooked the front sight on my service revolver in a nostril.

The crazy bastard was still squawking when I thumbed the hammer back.

He shut up and acknowledged my existence.

"Be a good boy and we'll walk opposite ways in a minute or two. That work with you?"

He nodded pretty good for having a front sight up his nose.

I withdrew it.

"You need to see my badge?"

"Not with that service issue H&R, no, sir."

All polite now.

I wised, figured how to play this.

"You wanna get up, walk away, go on to where you were going before you tripped over me?"

We thought on it. I was nothing more than an obstacle in Renahan's psycho noodle.

"Yeah."

"Two small tidbits. One: where's Pearlie Friedman. Two: who else was in this little game at start up."

Blank face. I hate fucking psychopaths—they eat time.

"You need some more persuading?" I moved the big gat into his face area.

"Un-un. Pearlie lammed. Caught a train the day it popped."

"Yeah? Make me believe." I bumped his nose with the .38's barrel.

"I know it. Packed that ugly pink suitcase a his. Gold corner pieces. Had another bag too. I dropped him at the train depot. Pearlie's history, bub."

I whacked Danny pretty good on top of his head, said, "Don't call me bub. Who else you got?"

"Nobody, brother. Not even me. Just Pearlie pulled it."

I raked his left cheek good with my front sight, slapped him with an open left hand.

"The truth gets you a hundred dollar gold certificate; another lie gets your head in that rain barrel over there."

"Man, I'm clean. I jumped out way before they nabbed the kid."

"That's why I'm trying to give you a break, babydoll. I know you're clean as fresh dishwater. So who's *they*, Danny?"

"Pearlie and Eddie."

Okay. "Who's Eddie?"

"You real on the C-note?"

I whacked him on his head again. "Serious about everything, precious. You best yack and like pronto."

"Eddie Hickman. A fucking nutcase. A sicko."

Coming from who?

"This Hickman, he still around?"

"What's he worth?"

"Baby, I'll hit you again you insist."

"He took off for Oregon."

"You sure on that? I can find you, Danny, so be sure."

"Hell, he's my best pal. He's got friends in Echo. I'm sure. He's history too, copper."

I felt icicles on my nape. "The girl dead?"

"I'm sure." Like, *Of course.*

I played a C-note with my shoe on his face, pushed it into the sidewalk.

"Danny, I ever—and I mean ever—see your ass in LA again, I'll put horse in your pocket, drag you to the cophouse. Walk, baby, while you can."

I kicked him for the probably-dead kid, a good rib shot like they show you at cop school, left him rolling around on the sidewalk sucking air, looking for his dignity and his hundred dollars.

214

[42]

The vestal-at-moment Ready brothers checked; one of them—I don't recall which—came back with:

Yeah, Pearlie blew. The Hickman punk's still around. Try that raunchy pig down by the beach. So-and-so saw him last night there with the guy Danny Renahan you got told about.

Damn. Maybe if I'd dropped svelte Danny one more good shot on his head, I could've shook Hickman out of his ass. Damn me.

Then the good news: *The girl's dad got a ransom note. Did I know that?*

Hell, didn't look like I knew squat from a gnat's ass on the current subject. I was just burning up leave.

Time for me to get serious here. One place left to go. Back to the no-name pig in a wood house on the Pacific.

The plan was a dictate of circumstance, not direction. I had no direction; it was showing.

• • •

There was a parking spot off the crushed shell parking area surrendering to sand and sand spurs. I got sand in my shoe but made the side-entry door, stood on a small landing while a pair of beady eyes looked at me through a slot in the steel-bound door.

215

I passed as riff-raff and the beady eyes let me in. I thanked him for it, pulled my blue hat low on my brow.

The guys could've been brothers—twins even. Fags, no doubt. Come on—they're dressed identically. Fags.

Hickman was a smaller version of Renahan. But a good likeness. I wondered which was the prototype and which was the knock-off.

The keep remembered me, said, "More of the same, sir?"

"Sure, Jeeves. You don't mind my asking, what's a classy rum slinger like yourself doing in a pockmark like this?"

"No, sir, I don't mind your asking. Prohibition, sir." He put two highball glasses in front of me. Poured one tall and one short, took the short one, held it up. "May it end soon, sir."

I amened hell outta that. Told him it seemed a better cut of people were drinking before Prohibition.

He said he could empathize. Said my friend was back.

I said, "Yeah, so am I. Do us again and I've gotta go do my thing."

He did us; I tipped him a five; he shook my hand. "You're a gentleman, sir. I don't get too many in here."

"I bet. Good luck after prohibition, Jeeves."

"Sir, with all respect, I don't need luck. I just need prohibition to end."

"I hear you, baby. It's been a pleasure doing business with another gentleman. I mean the *good luck.*"

"Thank you, sir. And may your friend look even worse tonight than he did last night. Watch his girlfriend though—a sucker puncher."

I grinned, grabbed something from thin air, realized what a greenhorn I really was. Slipped a peek, read the room. Not a chippie in sight tonight. It was a semi-fag joint. Hence the no name, the low light, allowing the bum-rummies to sit at the bar as cover.

I said *thanks* again, drifted. Hid in my usual alley, clever bastard I am.

Not a great plan, but I'd been paying bills chasing purse-snatchers, window smashers, and border jumpers. And you've never seen a human run till you lock on to a hundred pounds of illegal Mex. Goddam. Out sprint you two for one, pace himself down as you tire, stay twenty feet out in front—all day long you wanna try it. I could run a couple of pansies down, right?

Wrong. Renahan sees me. Stabs me with the cold, nothing eyes. Spark of recog. Broke out like he was looking to catch the last lifeboat off the Titanic.

Hickman was the same as the buck-nothing greasers I chased in LA. Went by Renahan in a full sprint, putting ten, fifteen feet on me and Renahan a second.

I couldn't tell if I was gaining on Renahan or not—I knew I was blowing like a locomotive.

Hickman was sixty feet ahead, maybe eighty. He turned as he stopped. I saw the gat coming around: profile, then forty-five degrees as I pulled the big H&R from under my arm.

I wasn't quick enough. Hickman came around firing. I took the second shot in the side meat—burned like a brand.

Danny Renahan had stopped, turned with the baby gat from last night and a grin. Hickman still behind him, still coming around, still firing. I ducked behind a car. Renahan moved sideways to get a shot on me, putting himself between me and Hickman.

Hickman fired, caught Renahan in the back of the head. I stepped clear, fired at Hickman but Renahan's fall put him in my line of fire—he caught the pill in his temple.

He went down slowly. Two to the noggin, he bled badly.

Hickman booked a fast train exiting stage left. I shot at him a couple of times but never felt like I hit his fleet ass.

Then it was me, bleeding but not bad, and Danny. Danny was pretty much bled out.

I told Danny he had any objections to my leaving he should speak now.

Danny held pat and I drifted as quietly as I could with a hand holding my guts in.

A random hospital, my badge, some stitches, and a mile or two of gauze. A doctor with two doses of nose and a shock of unruly black hair said I should sleep over with them.

I said I appreciated the offer but the night was young. The gauze, the sting, and whatever they shot me with had me walking funny, but I made the front door.

Made the car, put my head back for a second, slept till daylight.

[43]

Woke like a guy who had been shot in the side, then slept in a car.

God*damn*, I hurt.

I sat up; looked for enough grit to get out, walk around the hospital lot, loosen up. Puked first.

Got on out, breathed deep. Tried not puking—puking hurt worse than the pain that had made me puke.

Standing helped. Standing was the meow. It didn't hurt much more than, say, an abscessed tooth.

My breath came back; I walked a bit, walked back, leaned on the car some more. Leaned left and right from the waist. That didn't feel too good.

I walked some, leaned some.

No way I was getting in that car till I knew where I was going when I pushed the starter button

Third trip around, I heard footsteps on the gravel behind me.

"You spend the night in your car?" The doc.

"Yeah. The needle got me. You people hand out strong dope."

"Yes, to gunshot victims. Most people seem to need it when they're in that condition. You want some coffee?"

"Doc. I'd kill for some coffee."

"How do you take it?"

"In a cup is fine."

The doc went back in, set me up with a cup for each hand, black and heady but not particularly hot.

I sipped while Doc and I said farewells.

I toasted his tail lights and killed one cup of the joe.

A kid the color of wet leather let me have a morning edition for a quarter and no change. I felt pretty good about myself, my generosity, and just being alive.

Short-lived. The headline hit me like Hickman's slug.

The damn paperboy probably knew more about this game than I did. Should've been reading the paper. Seems like night before last, while I was kicking Danny Renahan's ass, Hickman was dropping part of little Marian Parker off to her dad. Wired her eyes open, wrapped half of her in a blanket, and tossed her out on the street for a measly fifteen-hundred bucks.

I stumbled to the car, drove home.

• • •

Home that year was a two-room apartment in a marginal area of downtown. Two flights up, end of a long narrow hall with a carpet from the Civil War maybe.

The key pushed the door open. I put a hand under my arm, felt the .38.

My brother Jess, the oldest, was at my kitchenette table reading a magazine.

He glanced up like he was the one lived here and I was the one dropping by. "'Lo, Joey. Take a load off." Pushed a chair from under my table with a toe. "You look like hell."

"I got shot a little."

"Yeah?" It got him off his mag.

"Yeah. What's the what-for? Why're you sitting at my table, reading my magazines?"

"Big Joe Parente's in town, wants to see you." A grin, like we were kids and I had to go to the principal's office.

"For what?"

"This Pearlie thing. He hears you stirring things up out there. Hears you shot a guy in the head." Eyebrows up.

"Yeah. A dead guy." Nearly dead or newly dead maybe.

"You want I should take you to see Big Joe?"

He wanted to come along.

"Mattie gonna be there?"

"Yeah. We'll call him when we leave here."

We eyeballed each other some.

"You know something, Jess, or is this just precaution?"

"Precaution." A big grin. "Hey, you're the little brother. You gotta see one a these guinea bosses, we go too, see you get home safe."

He punched my shoulder; I moaned.

Jess said he was sorry, but he laughed like he wasn't.

• • •

It was common info that Big Joe was facing two years at McNeil Island on a bootleg rap.

Looked like Big Joe the Tailor was lamming. I met with him and a set of luggage, a couple of pieces of muscle.

One of them, a baby-faced punk named Lester sitting on a bar covered by a sheet, made me nervous. The other was an ex-pug. Red hair, bent nose, flowered ear.

We were in a carpet joint I'd never visited in Pasadena. Nice place even with sheets tossed across the bars and gambling dinguses.

Big Joe fit his name sideways. Not so much up and down. He had fast eyes mounted in a catfish face. Breathed loudly, his breath whistling in his nose. Smelled like his last few baths came out of a bottle—smelled like a guy on the lam.

221

I got appraised.

Big Joe did nothing with it; Lester snickered like a punk snickers at a young cop.

"Sit down, relax. We talk." A voice like he drank lye for breakfast.

"Mr. Parente, you want me to relax, you need to get rid of the hop-head."

Parente leaned around. "Lester, you scaring the young man?"

My brother Mattie said, "Hey, Lester, what say me and you take a walk, leave Jess and the patty to tell each other's fortune while little brother and the boss chat. What say?"

Lester said nada. Looked pretty hard at me.

"Go for a walk, Lester. We've got a long boat ride." Boss Parente.

Lester hopped off the bar, and he and Mattie used a door.

Parente said, "I think you two could go have a drink on me. Me and the kid are aces. Right, kid?"

I said, *Aces.*

Jess and the pug drifted.

Parente watched me grimace and sit.

"You just go out on your spare time solving crimes like a guy in a comic book, huh?"

It made me grin.

"I'm tired of pounding the pavement, Mr. Parente. I'm looking to impress the brass."

"Good luck. Your brothers don't pound pavement."

His eyebrows were wooly as feather boas. He arched them at me. I could have taken it for amusement but his mouth stood on cruel.

"Yeah, and I don't have to wear a rearview mirror on my hat brim to see who's behind me."

"Yeah, I guess both jobs got good points. You take money?"

Zinged it right over home plate.

"On payday." Stood on that. Pretty good swing for a kid. It looked good all the way to the fence, maybe third row.

Till he snagged it. He said: "Payday like cops get, is it really even worth waiting for?"

The fat man had a point.

He whistled through his nose and I tried to think about it over the noise.

Big Joe yelled some Italian over a shoulder. I don't know much dago, but I knew he was ordering cocktails.

"What're you waiting on, Mr. Parente? One a your boats to take you to Canada?"

A smile from an indifferent mouth. "You're a real thinker, ain't you?"

I shrugged.

"Don't be gettin' no big ideas would shame your brothers. You ain't leavin' till I do, Joey." More grin, a clumsy wink—like he was unfamiliar with being decent.

"Mr. Parente, my brothers set this meeting up. I did something with some *big idea*, I'd pay like any other moke who crossed them. I know who my brothers are and so do you, and we both know blood's only so thick. Let's get honest here. I want these guys took this kid. You wanna make sure your. . . ." I made a stupid face.

"Company would do."

"Make sure your company doesn't end up getting the ticket on this deal." I gave him a beat. "But Pearlie Friedman's in your company." Gave him back some arched caterpillars.

He flapped a dismissive hand. "If you stretch."

"Yeah, the cops or the newspapers probably won't stretch."

Parente grinned like he liked me. I grinned back.

"The crazy boy's headed to Oregon. Word's on a place called Echo. Pearlie lammed. I hear he ran to East Texas. Could be straight dope or not—people I know there ain't seen him yet. Hey, kid, it's free and it's all I got. Go find the bums and God bless. Get outta here."

"I don't have to wait till your boat gets here?"

"Nah, you passed. You was lying, you'da told me how honorable and trustworthy you were when I challenged you. Nah, you told the truth. You're scared a your two brothers." A grin. "You should be. . ." more grin, ". . .I know *I'd* hate to have 'em pissed at *me.*"

Our drinks came and we drank to mankind.

I drifted while the drifting was good, snagged a couple of brothers off the low front wall.

Up there with Parente's heat. A murder of crows.

Jess and Mattie jumped off.

Lester, the red-hot, said, "See you, copper." Flipped me a middle finger.

I walked on, intersected the brothers Ready at Jess's little Packard coupe.

Jess said, "You want, I'll shoot the big-mouthed baby-faced punk off the wall."

"Nah. Let's go to the Meridian, get some mediocre food served over shitty service."

One of them said how the Meridian was a dry joint.

I pointed out how we could stop at Pop Hoopengarten's drugstore, get pints of bond.

Musta sounded good, the uneventful food and service, and the Meridian didn't make me a liar. Mattie and I had some meatloaf with a mustard and catsup blob on top. Jess ordered steak. If it wasn't a piece of an old saddle, then it was cut from a tiger's ass. I accused it of being horsemeat.

Jess said, no, he'd had horse in France, last visit. Wow, he needed to go back to Europe for a few weeks. Maybe Cannes. Maybe Greece—was that considered Europe? Hell, maybe Monaco, do some gambling. Asked me did I want to go to Monaco, do some gambling.

Right. I'm sitting here thinking how I'm pulling down eleven dollars a week.

[44]

That year I had a Studebaker might make it to San Diego should the weather be fairly cool and the traffic friendly.

No way the sled would go up to Echo. Hell, I was afraid to drive it to San Fran, and a long-legged girl I knew had moved there. She was worth the drive but, when I'd go buck-rut nuts, I'd get maybe as far as looking at the cord showing through in my sad-sack worn-out tires.

Guys that know how to put a shank in a neck bone don't have sad-sack tires.

Jess was out of town so Mattie loaned me a little Bugatti roadster. It was like riding in an open icebox but went around a corner like it had magnetic wheels.

I drove it like it was my big brother's, made Portland in about twenty hours, give or take. I found a marginal part of downtown, looked for a joint I could afford.

The Hotel D'Arbor. Nice moniker. Somewhere between dive and just worn out.

Nothing to take pictures of in its day. Now a tired frayed relic of that.

A girl on desk. Cute girl. Blonde bobbed hair, flapper cap and dress. A sparky little kewpie doll with nice cans.

I came out punching. "There's gotta be a story."

She smiled. The smile glowed, lit the lobby.

"What? What story?" Not getting it but knowing it was coming from fun.

"A girl like you. . ." I gestured at the accoutrements, ". . .a place like this?"

"My daddy owns the joint." Mimed my inclusive gesture perfectly.

"Your feather's crooked."

She took off the sock, shook her head. "The damn thing itches like head lice."

My kinda girl—one doesn't mind talking about the cooties.

"I did come in to get a room, but if you'd care to show me your favorite restaurant, I'm open."

A pixie's look across her eyes. "I can't go out with people who stay here."

"Company rule?"

"Daddy rule."

I grinned. I wasn't done yet. "I'm an LA cop on a case. That do anything for Daddy?"

"My, my. We don't get any of your kind in here." A drama face of thought, finger on her cheek, eyes up. "I'm sure Daddy wouldn't mind. I'm gonna put you up on five, in the back."

Oh yeah? "Daddy fat?"

"Is a walrus fat?"

I got a key with *512* stamped on it pushed at me. Smoothed out a borrowed twenty, got change.

"Register, please." She pushed a lined book at me.

I spun it, signed in, said, "Daddy give you a name?"

"A big one. Orfamay. You can laugh. I'm quite used to it."

I didn't laugh. I smiled some though. "Hey, it's not Ernestine or Clementine. Whadda they call you?"

"My brothers call me Orf the Dwarf. My friends call me May."

"I'm Joe Ready, May. What time's good?"

A look at a clock on a wall behind her. "It's six-thirty. How's eight?"

"Eight's perfect. Where?"

"One-oh-one. Right there." A point down the ground floor hall. "And you might want to chew some chicle, eat some cardamom seed or something."

"Daddy don't care for the barley corn?"

"Oh, Daddy cares lots. Mommy's the one." She opened a drawer, held up a pint of Canadian whiskey. "How do you think I know about gum and seeds?"

It made me grin. She was perky as hell.

"See you at eight. May."

"Yeah. See you, Joe Ready. Here." She tossed a box of chicle at me.

I shook out a little, popped it in my mouth.

"Does it work if I chew it while I have another drink?"

A headshake. "See you at eight. And don't stagger."

• • •

I didn't stagger. I acted like a cop. Showed off my badge.

Passed muster, had a shot with Daddy in the office on the way out.

May was right—the man wasn't climbing five sets of verticals. If he lived through it, he'd need the fire rescue squad to get him back on ground floor.

I got some stern fat eyebrows and: "Take care a my baby, fella."

I told him I certainly would while May giggled.

We made the door. I said, *Whoee.*

May slid a hand over my arm. I squeezed it a little, made the hand feel welcome.

"We driving or walking?"

"What kinda car you got, Joe Ready?"

"I'm driving a European speedster. It's my brother's. I *got* a beat Studebaker coupe with Bald Eagle tires all around. I'm really a cop, sweetheart."

She snuggled in. "Let's take your brother's Speedster. But I'd ride in a beat Studebaker with you."

The girl was melting me slowly with words. But I didn't seem to mind.

The little two-seater took us to a roadhouse with decent hash, outstanding music and libation.

The juke joint could've been a car repair garage looking at its cover. Inside it wasn't a garage. Bright clean walls with cheap sconces, but the attempt was honest. A few tables scattered toward a stage that was maybe a foot higher than the linoleum floor. An area in front of the stage was boxed off with a low metal corner—sawdust on the dance floor. All you could ask in a roadhouse.

Turned out to be a light, enjoyable evening. We danced; we ate; we had a few of May's friends drop by our table.

Thank God the little bathtub of a car came with a co-pilot. Must've been a co-pilot. Somebody drove back to the hotel, and I don't recall it being me.

• • •

Daddy maybe was too fat to climb the stairs. Mommy wasn't.

Five-thirty she was at the door. She was banging, shouting. A key was going in the door.

May went out the fifth story window naked as April itself, clothes clutched over her breast.

I grabbed her pillow, pulled it over, punched it, clutched it.

The old woman came in, shouting, waving. Doing some language I didn't know.

I should've been taking this more seriously, my being a cop and all, but I asked her how you said *beer* in her tongue.

The question stalled her till her nose woke her. "I smell her. I smell my girl." Her nose was going like an English pointer's.

She sniffed her way around the bed, put a paw up and froze on the spot where May had slept.

Aha, with a big exclamation point, a good sniff.

"Lady, they sell that stuff by the gallon at Woolworth's. Please. I'm trying to sleep." I showed her how.

"Where is my daughter?"

On the fourth floor roof. "Who?"

"Orfamay."

"Oh. She went home last evening. Said she was gonna get up early and go to confession."

I could've slapped her and got less stupor.

Man, I was thinking strong.

"Please forgive me. Good-bye."

"How do you say beer in your language?"

She told me. May told me again when she came back in——nipples hard as rock candy. I still can't say it.

[45]

A couple hours snuggling, I kissed Orfamay good-bye, told her I'd see her on my way back through. Headed east to Echo, the address Big Joe Parente had blessed me with.

The address belonged to a boarding house with the required veranda. Some fancy trim work hung like spider webs where porch posts met box beam. The balustrade was less ornate but pretty lacy. Unrelated hard, wooden chairs loitered about the veranda. A tired looking checkerboard was on a weathered table. Bottle caps were cast across the board randomly. There were probably twenty of them.

Not a bad place. Old but fresh.

I opened the energetic side of a pair of glassed doors. Same inside as outside: old but fresh and clean

Eddie Hickman had chosen well. I was glad to see him being sensible with his fifteen C-notes, spending them carefully.

A small white sign said *Manager.* The sign was over the first door on my left. I knuckled the door and got a cheerful lady with short, no-nonsense white hair and a round red face.

"I'd like a week's worth you got a vacancy."

"I got. Come in, lemme see who you are, young man."

My interview took place in a small living room, maybe twelve feet square. A lifetime cluttered it, cluttered every inch of wall—

either shelves, bric-a-brac stands, or pictures. A set of Dutch kids next to a black Jesus, a mother elephant chained to a couple of inch-high elephant calves. Then cats, dogs, you name it, all in porcelain.

We sat on hard furniture with sticky wooden arms. I said I was a fella named Joe Ready; she said she was Flo Mumsford but everyone called her Mums.

"Where are you from, young fella?"

"Los Angeles."

"California?"

No—New Hampshire. "Yes, ma'am. I'm a police officer there, but I'd rather we kept that to us."

The happy face left. "No trouble here, right?"

"Oh. Oh no." I laughed like a rube. "No. I've got to identify a moke in jail here. See if he's LA's man on a bank robbery. If he is, then I'll be here for another week while we extradite him. Just paperwork."

Mums beamed. "Your mama must be so proud."

"Sure. Mom's a saint." Who prefers living on a Crow reservation in one of the Dakotas, drinking reservation shine. Blind in one eye from it. She's a saint for sure.

Mums stood, walked over, patted my cheek. "And you're a fine son, Joseph. I'll give you second floor in the back. It's close to the outhouse."

Saturday lunch was forthcoming, and I could meet Mums's boys.

I could hardly wait.

There were some goobers and some lumberjacks, two cowboys with rings on their heads where a hat would sit, a sales guy who didn't look like he was much of a salesman. No Eddie Hickmans, not a one.

The food was superior. I hadn't eaten home cooked that good since I could remember.

I wounded myself. Had to nap off a few helpings after double dessert. Slept okay, but the outhouse door had a coil spring of tungsten steel. It would twang and then slam the door shut harder than they slam the gates of hell behind you.

The molasses pie was working on my dinner mates like it was working on me.

Went down, let the outhouse door slam shut a couple of times in case anyone was still napping.

Then I went out and sat in my car, jockeyed parking until I got across the street, maybe three car lengths back. Watched. Snuggled up on some TNT, bonded stuff from our neighbors to the north. Mumsie wouldn't allow such indiscretions—so she told me. I didn't believe it. Not with the crowd at the double-long table. Not with the salesman in the celluloid collar. Nor me.

A few nips, no Hickman.

A few more, no Hickman.

Another, and there he was on the veranda. On the stair, on the sidewalk.

Short leather aviator's jacket, pegged black pants, and if I wasn't mistaken, a pimento scarf. Fandango boots that would've passed as sleek Mexican boots but for a cuff caught on some rear foxing. The heels were high and the toes were dangerous looking. Greased up hair-do.

We were going to a see if Echo had a fag club, or I'd eat Eddie Hickman's pimento scarf.

I followed on foot. We took a block east, then a couple of short blocks south. A house on a tired street of tired little houses. Bingo, baby

I watched the knock: two-wait-one-wait-three fast ones. A long wait: seven slow ones. Abara-damn-cadabra.

Smoke and music fell out. Hickman fell in.

I walked back, got my car. Put it across the street from fairyland, watched some.

I could go in, watch the show, follow him out, but the middle part just seemed like voyeurism—spying on a room full of queers. I could hang pat in the car. And be bored.

The Canadian whiskey won.

232

• • •

Like three rounds, it won. Third bell, I toweled in.

Hadn't factored the cold. Cold and boredom teamed up are a couple of fat ladies in the car with you.

I walked over, did two-one-three-seven, got abara-cadabared in.

Queensville. Somehow more gay than LA.

Maybe it was I was used to the fags in LA. The club on the beach, once you were thinking about it, yeah, you could see boy-boy, girl-girl, but keeping it subtle.

Not campy. Not country campy like these boys. Boys—no girls.

A middle-aged queen was on a stage of planks and barrels. She wore a Little Bo Peep outfit, staff and all. The face was painted rubber. The eyes were the size of golf balls, blue as eyes ever got.

A voice like a Tennessee dirt road. A vocabulary like a county fair outhouse. I might have blushed.

The barkeep asked me my pleasure, called me *sweetie.*

I told him I was sure he had some decent Canadian back there and spread out another borrowed twenty. He assured me.

Proved it with a rocks glass full, four cubes of real ice. Maybe piped in from the Canadian tundra.

Oh, man. Legal liquor kicks ninety-five percent of moonshine's ass. This stuff was harsh like melted cream cheese. It rolled out its own velvet carpet for the slide to the stomach. Landed with a bang. I liked it—did a double, realized I was acquiring a taste for hootch. Just like good old Ma.

Ma was a half-breed drunk. Pappy was the kindest man God made yet. He'd strap you you needed. But it made him cry more than you when he had to.

Worked in Peeler's hardware emporium downtown. Twenty-eight years service, he got this hammer someone had painted gold at his retirement party. The party was the two Peeler brothers, two other employees who don't register right now, Phyllis Crowe, the bookkeeper, me and Jess and Mattie.

So sad. So, so sad.

We—Jess, Mattie and me—knew Pap was looking for a nice going-out-the-door check.

Nope. Got a gold plated hammer.

Sad, sad.

So sad Jess and Mattie knocked the place over, popped the Peeler brothers with Phyllis Crowe buying in collaterally by simply being there. I'll mention Mattie was at that time married to Marilou Peeler. Pop came outta retirement to run the joint and died two months later.

Sad but not as sad as a sixty year old dragger showing off her cock.

Bo Peep flipped her staff, hooked the hoop skirt with the bow, hiked up.

Had I uppers, I'd have lost them.

The Peep had a salami you could tie a knot in. Swear to God, straight as a taut string like I am, I couldn't not look.

I said *Jesus* a couple a times, turned away in awe.

The barkeep was watching me. I shook my head, grinned.

He said, "Enough to make your straight eyes ogle, huh?"

I grinned, dumped the rest of my double. I sat the glass on the green napkin, tapped the glass for another. "It show?"

"Sweetie, if you ain't a cop, you should go to Hollywood, play one."

Ouch. Another greenhorn strike. I felt like a pink thumb all a sudden.

"We're paid up." The keep shoved the twenty back at me, topped my glass up.

"Excuse me?"

"Our pad. We pay religiously." Some brows, then: "Oh God, tell me you're not state."

"LA, precious."

"Long way from home, sailor."

"Bye, baby. Keep it loose." I dropped the triple.

"I'm known for the opposite. Got a grip like Chinese hand-cuffs."

"I bet." I turned off the stool, slid a fin at him.

"Sweetie, big pretty like you? You ever take a hard left, lemme know."

I pulled my blue felt down with a hand, flicked the same hand over a shoulder at the sweet keep. Hit the door.

Cops.

I pulled out my buzzer, held it up at a couple or ten uniforms flanked by a fleet of cop mobiles.

The badge caught them off. A long man with a short round face nabbed it. His face got redder.

"Los Angeles? Buddy, you're a long way off base."

"Yeah, I am. Got one I'm taking personal."

A suit walked up looking like an Oregon State representative. Suit—big suit, dark serge, maybe blue. Gray hat. He needed to be clued. The long short-faced man withdrew. All I heard was the suit's side—the uniform was quite demure.

It went like: "LA?" . . . "Huh?" . . . "Lemme see the buzzer." . . . "It's right. Whaz his supervisor's name?" . . . "Then ask him."

I got asked. I told.

Some more buzzing outta short-face.

Some quiet while the tax money thought it over.

"His man inside?"

Some stupid time outta the tall uniformed cop. I sighed.

"You know, you could talk directly to me like I was standing here."

The state palooka didn't care for my mox. His dislike made him put little dark bird eyes on me. I was supposed to be scared, I think.

I held the quivers, said, "No, my guy's not inside." Not as long as LA wants him he's not.

235

"He queer?"

Like your bird eyes are queer, baby. "Yeah. But not here."

The eyes pecked at mine.

"You wouldn't mind sorta sticking around till we get this little work done here, would you?" Almost not a question.

"Not a bit. I was hoping you'd ask."

It got a grin. He looked back at a couple of guys in uniforms, grinned some more. "He's a funny guy, boys." Back at me: "How bout you wait at the cophouse for us? Know it?"

I shook my head a little.

"You went out the back door a the place across the street—" add a thumb jerk over a shoulder, "—through the joint it backs up to? You're looking in these guys' front door." Meaning the cops. "One street over. You can't miss it."

"My, my."

"Yeah, *my, my.* See you in the high sheriff's office, kiddo. Hope you got on chain-mail drawers. I hear he's a real ass chewer. Good luck, son."

The gallery thought the heavy state cop was funny. Long short-face giggled like he should've been inside with the rest of the pansies.

I drifted. Could've stuck, watched the fairies get sticked, but I'd seen the act before, in LA. It left me feeling queasy in some way I didn't understand.

• • •

The cophouse was where it was predicted to be.

I went in, told another long guy I was waiting on the boys were raiding the beauty parlor next street over. The guy had a long, sad face. My statement made it slacken up, get maybe three feet long.

He was gonna say *huh.*

"Huh?"

"Tall cop, sandy hair, young face? A guy in a suit?"

More *huh?* face out of him, then, "Who're you?"

"Cop out a LA."

"Yeah?" His face wasn't getting any shorter.

"Yeah. I better clam till the big boy gets back. You know how it is with these things."

He didn't have the foggiest notion how it was. Neither did I.

Someone yelled for Peterson. A chain being pulled across the edge of a board was what the voice sounded like.

My bet was the under-drawers-eating sheriff.

Long tall slid off the stool and disappeared.

Here we go.

Maybe a minute and a half, while I hit a butt, long shanks came out double-time.

Behind him came a guy maybe five-six, thin as jailhouse contrition. Jet hair bear grease wouldn't have tamed, a widow's peak would hurt Valentino's feelings. White shirt, brown and yellow tie—ugly thing. Brown serge suit pants that would have a related coat lying about somewhere. Black cop brogans older than me.

Then the eyes. The good sheriff had some eyes.

From down the hall, my view, it was like two holes poked in nothing. Black as a sliver of obsidian. Sharper though.

I could've been a picture of me, the way he was looking. Like I was, for all intents, inanimate.

"What's his name?"

Jesus. What's wrong with talking to me directly here in Oregon?

I told him even if he'd asked the desk sarge.

"And you're from Los Angeles?" Ended it to rhyme with fleas. The voice was totally incongruent with the package.

"Yes, sir." All I had.

"You wanna expand on that?"

"You mind if we kind a wait for the guy in the suit's over at the playhouse cuffing queens?"

He minded. Told me he minded. Told me to get my ass in his

office like yesterday. Called me son, but I wasn't expecting much of a father-son relationship.

Wishing I'd worn my chain-mail drawers.

• • •

"Whoa." Hands up—hands that could lead music—at me.

I whoaed.

"So this homosexual shot an LA cop?"

"Yeah." Me.

"It kill 'im?"

"No. He's a tough bird."

"This queer—gotta name?"

"We identified him as one Mickey O'Hanahan." A grade school buddy of mine. Just a name off the shelf of unused names.

"A Mick, huh?"

"Sounds like. I never saw him. Just got a description."

"Why you lookin' up here?"

"His boyfriend slipped up and told us."

It made him show me a set of teeth that were so perfect they'd have to spend the night in a glass of seltzer water. "How'd you boys in LA get him to slip up? Hoses?"

"Hop."

The widow's peak dove at the eyebrows. "Say how?"

"The roomie was a high flyer. We locked him down. Third day, a detective comes in, drops a bindle of coke on the floor just outta arm's reach. Next day, the detective goes back. The guy's bleeding from trying to get at the bindle. He was begging to stool up."

"The dick give him the hop?" He didn't want it to be so.

"Why?" I grinned like I enjoyed beating fags with my nightstick.

The real version? The one I saw? The cop gave the head the dope. Why not?

The real version, the junkie lied and the cop got some more

238

coke, scraped his battery connections into it, gave it to the punk. I didn't see that part, but I heard it was ugly.

Sheriff Delano—according to a carved plaque on his Amish simple desk, nothing on it but the nameplate—thought it was good policing. So I told him the real version, the one with battery acid. He liked that one even better.

Liked it so good he broke out the office bottle and a couple of well-used glasses.

We drank to good police work, and I was glad I hadn't worn the iron undies. The chain-mail's rough on the short and curlies when you're sipping imported whiskey out of a greasy glass.

[46]

My new friend, Sheriff Delano, let me view the new batch of pansies. And me all ready to act stupid. Didn't have to act—Hickman was missing in action.

The state boy came in ready to get cute. He noticed how the good high sheriff and I were all buddies now.

After my look see, the suit caught me in front of the jail. Requested a few moments of my time.

"You and Delano take a drunk out in the alley, sap his knees?"

I showed him I could grin. "He does have a weakness for discipline. That what we're talking about here? You investigating him?"

"No. We're talking about a guy name a Hickman kidnapped a girl, sawed her in half. Heard of 'im?"

"Might've."

The beady eyes watched me, pecked at me.

"This ain't New York but they do got telephones up here. I used one. Got a call back." A big nasty grin, then: "Your lieutenant wants to see you like real bad, baby."

"Should I wear my iron underwear?"

The big grin settled down and went to a head wag. "Baby, you're about the cutest rookie I ever saw. You stay in trouble in LA?"

"I got a decent arrest record. That helps."

"Yeah, I heard. Heard this Hickman boy shot you."

No idea how he nabbed that. "A little bit."

The state cop laughed. "Tough cutey." Laughed some more. "Hank Clarenden's the name, baby. And you leave the state with Hickman, you'll wish you hadn't. I know real good where LA is, and I don't take to a fuckin' too good. See you, baby. I'm at a bed'n breakfast called The View. I'll be listening out for your call."

He found a pack of ready rolls in a coat pocket, shook himself one, and walked away.

Enough to make you say *my-my* a couple a times to yourself. Looked like I was working for the State of Oregon—for free. Less than free—I owed Mattie a C-note on top of it all.

My-my.

Seemed like a nice time to wise up, quit acting stupid.

Clarenden had driven off in a fairly new Ford, but another car followed my car. Headlights held a respectable distance, traded off with another sedan, traded back while I drove around trying to wise up, trying to get back to Mums's without an entourage.

The wise-up found *me*. A freight train. Blocking the street, waiting on a hostler.

I walked up to a train car, noted it was belt buckle high to me. Walked back to the little car, measured. The starter button made the engine purr. I wedged myself up, unlatched the fold-forward windshield. Slammed the car forward, ducked sideways.

The Bugatti slid under the train as the hostler engine slammed a freight car into it. The whole shebang shifted a foot to my perpendicular; panic and adrenalin ruled body and mind. I gunned the Bugatti. Its tail end slid away and the iron wheel came behind the car.

The wind in my face got rid of the jitters. A little side mirror showed me two sets of headlights beyond the train. See you boys at Mums's you figure it out.

I hid the car in an alley a couple of blocks away, walked to the boarding house.

Gaslights put some frail shadows around the porch. Two guys were at the checker table. One was the hangdog salesman. The other a heavy bald man with a dome like Everest rising from a cloud of gray hair. The salesman was still in his suit and tie but had on an experienced overcoat. I could smell the mothballs across the porch.

The heavy man wore rough khaki pants, high boots with miles of shoe lacing, and a canvas coat with a fleece collar. I would've guessed him an engineer of some sort. He spoke with a heavy British accent. I'm not good on telling one from the other, but he rolled some of his consonants pretty harshly.

There was a lot more arguing about rules than playing. The big Brit referring to the King's rules, the salesman saying: *Whose king? This is the United-damn-States of America.*

I found a shadow, pulled over a chair, and leaned against the wall. Watched the checker debate.

The wind had died, but it was getting colder, maybe forty or less. I wrapped my overcoat around my legs, turned up the collar, pulled my hat down against the cold.

There was a pint of rye in my pocket but not for long. I pulled it, unbonded the cap, and swigged. I wasn't much on rye.

The salesman was. Smelled it over the mothballs.

"Hey, buddy, you ain't got a spare shot a that rye, do you?"

"Sure." I passed the jug.

The salesman made a face of awe you could put on a cardboard church fan. I could've been over here walking on water. It made me wonder about the peened-aluminum flask on the table when I walked up.

"You'll be sorry, my friend." Owner of the flask. The Brit took a shot from his flask, recapped it.

The salesman looked beat, gulped a good third of my rye. It made his eyes water, and he belched a little one. He put the bottle back to his lips.

I said, *hey*, came off my lean, nabbed the bottle on my way down.

The big man sniggered, slipped a bottle cap checker forward with a big sly pinkie finger while his opponent was coveting my rye.

"Aw, come on, buddy, let's drink it."

Steps on the wooden sidewalk. Hickman and another punk. I took a big gulp of rye, passed it to the sponge to shut him up.

"It's yours, friend. Merry Christmas."

"Thanks, buddy. Thanks."

Hickman and his companion came up the steps. I leaned back, wrapped up against the cold. Dropped my chin.

The boys looked like they'd been running through the woods. Pants legs wet up to their knees, hair disheveled, clothes pricked.

The guy with Hickman was older. Hickman was only nineteen, a punk. This guy was late twenties, blonde pretty boy with some muscle.

We watched them use the door, no one saying scat to nobody.

The Brit did some form of *pshaw*, sniggered again.

The sales guy's tongue was waiting on the last drop of rye. He got the drop, said, "Getting to be more queers here'n regular joes."

"Hey, my friend, you listening to Arnie here? The lady-boys had whiskey, he'd be down there wearing nothing but a tutu." He roared a laugh.

I pushed my hat up. "I hope they're not next door to me."

"Nah. You're second floor. Mums puts the young and the funny in the back on her hall. The dark haired boy's all the way back, in number eighteen, last room on your left."

"See you gents at breakfast."

The salesman was feeling the rye, thanked me like I'd cleared up his mortgage or something.

The big British guy said, *yeah*, but looked at me funny. Like I might be up to something.

I was, but nobody including me had a clue what it was I was up to.

• • •

A view of my options, I chose a sawed-off sixteen gauge Italian pump. A loaner from brother Mattie.

I'd ad lib the rest.

I was getting some good breaths of air, getting ready.

A rap, a "Joe?" from Mums.

"Yes, Mrs. Mumsford?"

"There's a gentleman to see you."

Yeah? I stashed the pump gun, opened the door.

The bird-eyed cop. Looking over Mumsie's shoulder, grinning.

Mums saw my face, wrinkled the skin on her forehead. Looked back at Clarenden.

He smiled warmly, said, "Thank you, Mrs. Mumsford. Joey and I can take it from here. Right, Joey?"

I said *sure* and stepped aside for him.

"Thanks, Mums." And closed the door.

The cop looked around. "Not bad. How's the grub?"

"Good."

"Come on. Don't get un-cute on me now." He sauntered, nosed. A bottle of Scotch was on the dresser. He bought himself one from the neck. Another. Capped the hootch, turned, leaned, back to the dresser. Smiled a big phony one.

"I'm gonna clue you in on a couple a things cause I like your style just a little. Whadda you think I am? An Oregon State cop?"

I shrugged.

"Wanna see my buzzer?"

I wagged head.

"Good, cause I ain't got one."

He let me gnaw on that. It got my attention. "Yeah?"

"Yeah. I'm outta San Francisco. I'm a private dick. You

244

following along?" He flipped clothes back in my suitcase exposing the shotgun. He shook his head a little.

"Yeah, I'm following. Who's paying you?"

"Marian Parker's daddy's a wealthy, well-connected man, baby. Knows people know other people right here in Oregon, at the State Police headquarters even. I gotta piece a paper says I'm a special investigator for the Oregon State Police." He unfolded a sheet of paper.

I read. He was straight or he was a decent forger. Oregon State letterhead.

I fussed with that, had nothing to add. Then I saw his side. I'd bet I was about to hear about it.

"See how I do it? I get paid, use influence, reputation, money. Got big ideas. Then along comes you, stepping on my game. The hog-leg? That your idea of a big idea?" A point at the chopped Beretta.

I stood pat.

"I see. You wanna make more dough'n you'd make in ten years as a cop? All legal?"

Hell yeah. "Sure." I didn't sound excited.

Bird eyes laughed. "*Sure,* he says. Mr. Parker's aware of your efforts. He told me about it in an earlier conversation this evening. Oh, that's right—you thought I called the Oregon State Police. Mr. Parker would like to meet you, show you his appreciation when we're done up here."

I had to ask. "You come here to smoke the guy?"

"Hell no. I said legal—I know I did. We just bundle him up, take him to the marquis at the county jailhouse. Oregon will see him home to LA."

"What kind a money are we talking? Really?"

"I'd say a good solid twenty gees, baby."

"What's my share?"

"Your share? That's your share, sweetheart. Let's go get the goose what lays the golden eggs."

I said, *Let's.*

He said call him Hank.

I said quit calling me Joey.

He said he'd try. What'd I think.

"We know they'll jump out a window, run through the brambles. How bout you knock, I'll catch them when they tumble out."

"Look at you. Thinking all a sudden. Come on. And leave the scattergun. Take that Mauser. That's for close work should you need it. The shotgun, you might shoot me."

"Wouldn't want that."

"No. Wouldn't want it. Stay close to the house."

"I've done this before."

"Sure you have. And got shot for it, baby. Stay close to the house."

[47]

Right up to the end, right up to the knock on Hickman's door, Clarenden was looking good. Looking smart. Looking uptown.

He knocked hard enough I could hear it from the dormant flowerbeds, heard him say *state police*. Nada for maybe half a minute.

The blonde muscle boy comes through the window backwards, screaming bloody-damn-murder. He smacked the ground, then lots of gunfire in the room.

I kicked blondie, hit him on the noggin hard as I could with the Mauser. I was wishing for the scattergun.

The punk on the ground screamed some more while I reached up through the window and dropped some blind lead into the room.

Things got quiet but for blondie moaning.

Someone, Hickman I guess, yelled for Reggie. I pointed my gat at the guy on the ground, thinking it had to be Reggie, put a foot over his mouth.

I saw it coming, ran to the wall, left Reggie on the ground.

One guy, then another, ran by inside the room, both firing out the window.

Reggie jumped up, made it maybe five feet, three or four slugs landed in him. He went down, jerked some in a new silence.

This wasn't so good. No peeps outta Hank, two mokes with rods in the room.

Another run by.

I timed it, shot. Finessed me. Here comes number two from the other way, nearly got me in the head.

Scrambling, a door slamming, a couple more shots in the hall.

I ran around back, went in the door there. Perfect timing if I wanted to see two men disappear out the front door.

"Shit."

Hank Clarenden was slumped against a doorframe a few rooms down. They'd hit him through the door. The door was more full of holes than a drunkard's memory.

He'd made it away from the door without his pistol. A big .45 army model. It lay in the hall.

Someone had slowed down long enough to put two in the top of his head.

I was glad the eyes were closed.

A door peeped open by me, slammed shut. I ran for the front door, losing my overcoat for the sprint.

Went by the checker players, cleared the six or eight steps. Arnie says to my back, "They went left."

I wheeled left, saw two figures maybe two hundred feet ahead. Pumped it and closed in to fifty or eighty feet before they saw me coming.

Both turned and I veered right, behind a car. Pills pinged around me.

Footfalls, I'm out shooting, giving the Mauser plenty of fall. I see sparks fall around the guys. Again they're a couple hundred feet ahead. Again they stop.

I veer left. More shots.

Four magazines and a half a box of cartridges in a pocket, I could do this all night.

Didn't have to. My guys stepped out next time, popped maybe three rounds. A hard quiet, then serious shoe leather. Outta pills?

I put on the sprint. The pistol got cumbersome, got stuck in my pants, safety off.

I'm neck-breathing on them. Eddie Hickman in his bolero jacket and a long thin moke in a gray flannel suit, no hat for either.

Twenty feet, the three of us harmonizing sounded like the *Spirit of St. Louis* taking off.

Eddie put on his sprint, long-tall split left, pulled a gat.

I pulled, shot him in the left buttock. In my peripheral I could see him go down, saw the gat skid across the asphalt to intercept me.

I kicked it like a soccer ball; it spun off into the night.

Another deep reach, I close a little on Eddie. He went hard at it again, made me have to think about fogging him.

Again I'm up within thirty-forty feet of him; he just stopped. I came up with the Mauser ready for his turn-and-shoot trick.

No trick; he just bent over, hands on thighs, spent.

I hit him at a full run, slammed the gat into the side of his head on the way.

Both down, me on top and bigger. I got a scissor grip on Eddie, watched his head down there between my knees.

A few deep catch-up breaths I squeezed Eddie's air off. Couldn't hold it, eased off, got a few more buckets full of air. Squeezed, held it till Eddie did the chicken-dance, passed out.

I cuffed him then sat on the ground, knees up, arms around legs, still breathing hard. I looked back—the other guy was history.

A couple of minutes Eddie stirred and I stood up, worked the cramps out of my legs. My side hurt like hell, but I wasn't bleeding.

Eddie sat up, looked at me. He finally recognized me from LA. You could see his eyes saying, *Oh shit.*

"Get up, punk." I gave him a good nudge with a shoe. He kicked at me.

I put my feet on him cop style for a minute, maybe more, dragged him over to a sleeping gas station. Dragged him around to the john. Big Schlage padlock but screws on the hasp you'd use on a watch.

I used Eddie's face to push through the locked door. We were in. *We* being Eddie.

On the floor, Eddie's coming out of the fog the kicking brought on.

"Go ahead, kill me." Crazy-ass eyes. Challenging me. Serious about it. Getting up on his knees, me in the doorway.

I held the pistol up, put it on him, flicked on the electric light.

"Who shot the guy in the boarding house?"

"Fuck you." I leaned over, put the barrel in his mouth. He started moving his head back and forth, fellating the pistol. A break. "Shoot me, cop. Please." Mouth back to the gat.

I stuck the gat under my arm, grabbed his face and bent him back, put his head in the toilet, grabbed his belt, lifted his body up, stood him upside down.

When he quit kicking, I pulled the chain, washed his hair for him.

He finally got some air, used it all for a wet cough. I threw him to the side. He lay there, coughed dramatically in spasms.

I said, "Who was the other guy? Pearlie Friedman?"

Eddie rolled over, squinted at the overhead light. "You know, why're you asking me, asshole?"

"Eddie, you wanna do some more toilet acrobatics?"

"Fuck you."

I grabbed his hair, pulled him up, got a grip on his belt at the small of his back. I picked him up as high as I could, dropped him on the tile. Did it again. Then again.

He screamed some; moaned some; asked me to stop some.

"Watch your manners. Was it Friedman?"

"Yeah. This is where we were to meet. Originally. Then the yellow Jew lammed out, left me holding the nickel. It ain't fair, I'm telling you. Come on, copper, kill me. Please."

I didn't. I dragged him out, put him in the boot of an Oldsmobile parked under the gas joint's overhang.

Snooped around, found a length of wire. Wired the boot handle to the bumper for insurance.

I called Sheriff Delano from a pay station on a pole but got the Sarge on the desk. The sheriff? He was at Mums Mumsford's boarding House.

Bless him. "Call him or get someone to go over there, one. You got a guy that's both your murderer and a kidnapper locked in the trunk of an Olds at the Sinclair gas station on the Portland Highway."

"Say what?"

"You know the Sinclair station?"

"Un-huh."

"You know an Oldsmobile when you see one?"

"Yeah."

"Then come get the guy helped kill the dead guy at Mum's. Tell Delano I said happy Christmas."

I pronged the phone, walked back to my brother's car, left a nice suit and a double-barreled Beretta hogleg behind. Never saw Orfamay Quest again either. I hauled it south, deciding to spend a day in a motor court when I was back in good old California.

[48]

A day went to four. I had sixty bucks left when I'd finished in Oregon—started with Mattie's hundred and twenty of my own.

So what I went home broke? I could possibly be a wealthy man back in LA. But a dead man's promise seemed cold and remote as the deep green Pacific behind the motor court.

LA came over the crest of a hill about dusk on a Monday.

I went home, let out some musty air, gathered up my cop stuff, put it in a tote sack.

Up behind some second hand saucers was a joint I'd found in a car on Sunset. Turned out the car belonged to the DA's golden boy. I kept the smoke; had to cut the lawyer loose.

I broke the reefer out, smoked it down, slept in my own bed from seven in the evening until nine the next morning.

Mattie's house was almost on the way to the cop station—like Pasadena is on the way to LA from Santa Monica. I went anyway, swapped cars in Mattie's absence.

I was glad. I didn't have the heart to tell him about his Beretta.

The cophouse was far closer than I wished, but I made up my mind on the ride despite.

I parked out front in the slots for big brass, went in, looked at old Sarge.

He jerked his head at the lieu's office—as predicted by Hank Clarenden.

The lieu was ex-army, son-in-law to some muck with the city or county one. Not far from a Sheriff Delano. Lieutenant Corder got *his* kicks beating up on the serfs. He didn't want details. He wanted results. He wanted good answers.

The rest of the station looked and smelled like all cophouses. The lieu's office was a visit to a museum. African masks, a warthog head, a tiger's head, camel saddle, figurines of race cars, an American flag, a big Fifth Army shield next to a picture of Washington crossing some iced up river, foot foolishly on the bow seat. An Oriental carpet so old it could be rolled up, put on the curb, and no one in this neighborhood would want it. Silk flowers from who-knows-where. A small totem pole. A bamboo desk, a teak and leather chair big enough for Corder and his brother had he a brother.

I knocked, got an order to enter.

I entered.

Corder slowly lay down the long black pen he'd been making doodles with, his eyes only on me.

Yeah, Delano's soul mate. There was a thin moustache and the hair wasn't as dark, no widow's peak. But the eyes were the same.

A finger came up at me. "You're suspended, son."

I was maybe seven years younger than him.

A spin, I showed him the tote sack full a cop duds. "Can I just quit?"

A long sad stare. Then he surprised me. "Word is you could be in for a piece of cash. I think it'd only be fair you were to pass some back to old friends." Still no smile, no emotion.

"I remember any, I'll do it."

"Good," like he was counting thousand notes. "Mr. Parker wants you to come by." A desk opened. "Here's the address and telephone number. I was you, I'd go by in person."

I was you, I'd stab myself.

An address in the best area. Close to my brothers. Bankers and killers. Movie moguls, stars, and starlets. Ball players who were as absentee as the transient wealthy. Oil-soaked Texans and Okies. Gangsters and senators. Old money and new money—no in between. That's what LA'll always be.

• • •

Someone in a chauffeur's uniform tended a couple of iron gates. The gates took advantage of a break in a tall cement and coral wall that ran a hundred feet each way from the gate. His pants were a little short, his peaked hat a little big; he said nada or nuts. He waited on me since it was my go.

"Joe Ready. I believe Mr. Parker is expecting me."

A real smile. "Yes, sir, buddy. He is indeed. Could I shake your hand?"

I put a slightly befuddled hand out the window. He shook hell out of it. "You're a big deal around this hacienda, buddy. Park her wherever. I'll ring the house."

Big deal? I'd bungled the whole sad mess from jump street.

I put my Studebaker on a patterned brick drive and hoped it wouldn't drip too much oil.

Out of the car, on the bricks, I aimed for a set of doors that maybe were once on the Vatican. Ten feet tall. Each slab a good six feet wide. Inlays of different woods, ivory, what could have been gold, and some black stone.

I was looking forward to pounding the iron ring in a brass lion's mouth, the lion nearly life-size.

No chance. One of the doors swung in while I was mid-reach.

A youngish fellow in a stiff shirt and tailed suit gestured me in. Clipped English: "Please, Mr. Ready, won't you come in. Delighted to see you, sir, if I may say so."

"Thanks."

A parquetry foyer had a couple of doors off it, a hall by a wide lazy stair. I wasn't sure anything I could see sitting around hadn't come over on the Pinta or the Niña. I would've been scared to sit on it.

The butler led me down the long hall. We'd climbed off the parquet to bounce on cream carpet with a foam rubber pad.

We skirted a kitchen stolen from a big hotel restaurant. A group of domestics became parade spectators. Lots of smiles, some *hellos*, some *welcomes*, one *bless you, sir.*

Out a door, down a set of steps that married into more brick—rambling walks that dodged and darted around a lot of green stuff.

A man in a morning suit and a woman in a high-collared dress sat in slatted aluminum chairs at a stone table.

Another chair was at ready. There was a coffee urn on a granite slab. Fancy pastry leaned in perfect order across a wide platter. Jellies and sugared fruits. Dates, currants, stuff I'd never seen before. A piece of iced cream cheese big as Mattie's Bugatti.

Both man and woman rose as the butler and I approached.

They smiled but fresh sorrow left the smiles leaden.

The butler came out with: "Master Joseph Ready, sir and madam."

I'd never been announced before. It didn't feel as glamorous as you'd think. I nodded, said, "Hello."

Parker came forward, offered a hand but no names. I guess I already knew who they were.

"We're so glad you could join us. I hope we're not interrupting your church service."

It was ten o'clock, give or take, Sunday morning. "No." I took the hand, watched the circles under his eyes.

He was a broad-faced man, maybe forty, copper hair unashamedly combed over a shining freckled scalp. There was a stickpin in his tie that could have been a pearl or a chicken egg.

His nails were polished as was his manner.

He retrieved his hand, put it out flat, palm up. "My wife."

"How do you do, Mrs. Parker?" Wishing I'd said *nice to meet you* instead.

"Very well, Mr. Ready. And you?"

"I'm well, too. Thank you."

My, weren't we formal?

Mrs. Parker went where I suspected most late-breakfast affairs in this neighborhood usually don't go: "How's your gunshot wound healing?"

"It's fine. It wasn't that serious."

"You're being modest, young man. Please have a seat." Mrs. Parker sat.

The butler withdrew; I came around to the vacant chair. Parker and I sat.

He said a blessing, pretty stock. No mention of Marian.

Parker ate heartily. Mrs. Parker and I sort of picked.

I'm sure it was her current disposition as well as her usual habit, being very thin.

I picked because I didn't know what to do with food that went much beyond meat and potatoes. I watched Parker, tried to mimic while we talked weather, the citrus crop, the stock market.

After a few bites, Mrs. Parker excused herself. She had to attend to some household agenda I didn't really catch.

The butler brought a cut glass decanter out like he'd been hiding behind a bush, waiting for her to go.

It sat on a tray with a small ice bucket, two glasses, and two expensive looking panatelas on a smaller tray with a gold lighter.

The butler bought me and Parker one, held the lighter to our cigars. I'm sure the cigars were good—I didn't know enough about stogies at the time to be much of a judge.

Parker wanted the whole story.

I gave it.

The part about Hank Clarenden closed his eyes, his head barely going left and right.

Finished, all he wanted was: *Who is Pearlie Friedman?*

I gave all I had. He nodded.

"You know Hickman's blaming everything on a man named Cramer?"

"Yeah."

"You think Cramer's this Friedman fellow?"

"Probably. I think he's more scared of Friedman than he is the hangman."

We finished the scotch. Parker poured us another.

"You've possibly got an idea where this other man went?"

I nodded.

"Are you going to tell the police?"

"Why, Mr. Parker? Hickman'll deny knowing Friedman; Friedman surely won't spill. All else is just gangster talk, street talk. You know where I got the info; you know who my brothers are."

Parker drained his glass, poured himself a small one, nailed it.

"I told Hank I'd give you twenty thousand. Any man gets shot helping a man who can afford it deserves that much. Where do you bank, Joe?"

My underwear drawer. "I don't."

"You do now. Tomorrow morning, you come by my office, I'll have a bankbook for you. You know where my office is?"

"Yes. Listen, Mr. Parker, I didn't come by here. . . ."

An interrupting hand. "I don't care a damn why you came. Tomorrow morning you're twenty thousand dollars richer. You agree to go find this Pearlie Friedman, there'll be another twenty in the account."

"What am I supposed to do when I find him, sir?"

A long cold stare. "I don't care. Whatever you deem just. I don't want to know, either. Set him up; kill him; I don't care. Just let him know why it's happening. Tell him it's for Marian Parker."

Silent tears came. I stood, placed a hand on his shoulder. He reached up, patted my hand.

Call it the handshake, call it whatever you want—Parker and I had a deal.

I left him in the silence. It was his silence. I didn't dare touch it.

257

[49]

2:17 A.M.
Jimmy may have dozed. Wasn't sure.

Soft soles running. Another set, this time accompanied by the sound of a cart's neoprene tires hissing on the linoleum.

Someone shouted something from chemistry class that Jimmy recognized but couldn't have repeated.

A heavier set of hard soles. Maybe the doctor.

"They lost another one. Shit, kid, my luck might be better in a hotel room in Vegas."

"You're gonna bitch so much, why don't you go ahead and die so you can chill out?"

"Screw off, kid. This is my wake. Hit me." Joe bumped his water glass.

Jimmy splashed water in it, added a taste of scotch. Then another. It was Joe's wake.

The hall was quiet again. A few minutes a few people walked by speaking low. The staff. Someone in the group laughed. The gaggle joined in, passed on down the hall and out of ear range.

"Go ahead, kid, finish it."

Jimmy sat, watched a neon line race across a screen, dissipate as another followed it. He didn't like this part of the story.

He and Joe had not spoken of it since it went down, not once since it happened. Didn't speak at all for nearly a year after.

Then Dot passed and Joe showed up at the funeral, asked Jimmy did he want to go to Australia with him, work on a kidnap case. Out of the blue, just like that. Then thirty-odd years of looking for stolen people. From Spokane to Bahrain. Made piles of dough, had a ball, played some dirty tricks on some deserving people. All those years and Joe never mentioned the story until now.

There was a reason. That was Joe's style. He'd never taught Jimmy anything directly—always a parable or an on-the-job training session. Let Jimmy sort it out later.

Jimmy didn't get it yet—why Joe wanted the story told—but he would. And it would be a good one.

"Let's wait on daylight, Joe."

"Jimmy, tell the story, baby."

"You ready?" Setting it up, being Joe's straight, knowing Joe's stock answer.

"Born that way, kid."

[50]

Man, that's gruesome. They sawed her in half?"

"Alive. Wired her dead eyes open for her daddy to see, get the measly grand and a half."

Jimmy made a shuddering noise. "How old's Pearlie now?"

Joe thought. "Maybe seventy-two, -three. He's four-five years older'n me. How about a gin Mary?"

"Only if you got celery."

"Oh, I got celery. Got a bottle a gin I think's sacred or something. Made by friars on some hill somewhere. Maybe they made it with out-of-date Holy water, huh?"

"What's gin made of?"

"Gin's moonshine flavored with evergreen berries. Pretty much corn. Some other grains, but mostly good old corn mash. Then you toss in your juniper berries and that particular secret ingredient and you got gin. Gin's rot gut, kid, all of it."

"Make mine a tall. I'm gonna go try and break somebody's heart."

Joe looked at Jimmy straight-faced. Then grinned.

"I'll make you one worth crying in. Whose heart you breakin', you don't mind my asking?"

"I don't know, but his shoe size'll be an eleven, give or take."

• • •

The general, the Saul guy, a guy named Edgar something who smoked cigars smelled like you were burning dog shit. Two more Jimmy'd not met. Yet.

Checking out all the old sacks. Looking at feet like Cinderella's prince, looking for a size eleven-twelve, maybe a ten even, somewhere in there.

How he was gonna tell, these guys were all hanging out in the clubhouse, or whatever you called it, and the floor was laid out in twelve inch Mexican tile. Jimmy'd measured. The tile was about eleven and a half. Had a half-inch grout joint. Then Jimmy'd measured his own size ten sneaker. Exactly a foot long

The floor was like the foot sizer in a shoe store—that black steel thing with sliding gizmos on it. Anybody had a foot tile size or longer was suspect.

All but Edgar and one of the unknowns were candidates. Big-footed guys. The general's maybe a thirteen or better. Huge old guy.

Jimmy'd pretty much counted the general out. He was who he said. The guy was a fucking comic strip general. Big chin, vacant eyes, large mouth, little or nothing to say that mattered.

Saul's feet were smaller, maybe a ten like Jimmy's so not out of the running.

Third guy, the new guy, hit it perfect near as Jimmy could tell.

"Hello. How are you gentlemen?" Nice and polite.

"Very well, Jimmy, how are you?" The general.

"Fine, General. Thanks."

"Hello, Jimmy. You look well with some sun." Saul being nice and polite too.

"Hey, son." All Edgar had—too busy stoking up a dog turd.

Nobody budged. Jimmy held.

The small guy stepped up. He was bald as pavement and had ears so sharp he looked a little trollish. Strangest thing: the guy's eyebrows were almost gone. Jeez, his eyelashes, too.

"Jed Bodine, Bodine Plastics." A smile like Jimmy should be saying, *Well, of course.* "And you're Dot Cotton's boy. College boy, ain't you?"

Jimmy saw it. Saw he was a mean little cracker out of Alabama or some dismal place like that. Didn't care much for college boys. You could tell by his tight little voice.

"And a writer I hear." The other new dude, a big goober with an accent.

"A writer?" A nasty little laugh, a look over a short shoulder at his big goober friend. "Hey, Fritzie, they any money in writin'?"

The big goober said, "If you're endorsing checks, I'd say yes."

Lots of laughter on Jimmy's tab.

The goober wasn't a goober. The accent had a touch of some sort of Teutonic in it. Seemed smarter than he looked. Big, skinny, gray-haired dude. Concentration camp commandant eyes.

Jimmy said: "I'll remember that. I've gotta do something to bring in the checks, don't I?"

"Indeed. I'm Fritz Holtzclaw. Nice to finally meet our resident author. What's this newest piece attacking, Jimmy?"

"Some interesting stories I've heard."

"What sort of stories, Jimmy?" The guy staying on it like it mattered.

Saul blew it, bless his goofy heart. "I think Dot said that Joe Joseph fella was giving him stories. Yeah, Jimmy?"

"Yes. Some stuff from the thirties. Like how life was back then." A nice smile.

Jed Bodine said, "I'll buy it. I'll buy it just to put on my shelf, say I knew somebody could write a book. Hell, most a my friends not only don't read, they cain't read."

Some more laughter. Easy room.

How about a little business?

"Where's everybody from. General, you start."

"Young fella, you better pick somebody else. He finishes it'll be next election." Bodine.

"You start, Mr. Bodine."

"Jed, boy. Hell, don't make me no older'n I am. It's Jed."
Some easy laughter.

"I'm from a place called Cottondale, Florida. 'Bout eighty miles northwest a Tallahassee. Fam'ly had three hunerd eighty acres a purty good dirt. I sold it to some Germans and took my money to Tallahassee. Bought me a plastic extrusion outfit. Die cutters, engineer, the whole pie."

Edgar was next in line. "Detroit. Woulda done thirty-three years on the line wasn't for that stupid damn war."

Edgar wasn't talking Viet Nam so watch out—the general would have issues.

"Hold on, fellow. I tend to disagree. There'd be a helluva lot a goose stepping going on in Europe if we hadn't gotten involved." The general.

"Yeah, sure. Like the French or the Gerries wouldn't cut our guts out they had the chance. Italy, too."

"England's still a staunch ally."

"Sure, weigh their short asses off against China or Russia, either one. We just spun the cylinder, bud. This thing in Asia? Another spin, rich guys becoming princes. Shit, General, we've condensed it to its purest form."

The general was lost. "What's condensed?"

"War, man. *War's good for the country,* used to be our slogan. Then some guys saw the gain, cornered it. Nowadays you plunder the victor by selling him bombs, General. Then he can go bomb the other guy back to his cave." A grin, a puff on the dog turd.

Jimmy all the sudden liked Edgar.

"Well." The general was pretty put off. His big long cheeks flushed down to his long chin. "That's somewhat unpatriotic, Edgar. Even for you."

"With all due respect, fuck you, General. And your wars. 'Cause I don't like war don't make me no traitor. I fought my ass off over there."

"Then I'd have to call you a patriot, sir." The general trying to not look like a prick.

263

"Didn't have shit to do with patriotism. It was fear. I was Jimmy-here's age. I was scared to goddam death."

Nobody had a thing to say.

Fritzie's turn. "I grew up in the States but went to South Africa before the war. While I was still young." The accent eased up as he spoke more. "I was in Johannesburg for many years." A big smile under serious eyes. "Here I am, retired from the diamond trade." Hands out, then: "From New York to South Africa to here. I'm afraid it's quite boring."

Jimmy said, *Oh he didn't know about that.*

Fritz said, "Let me assure you, young man, it was a very uneventful career. Never so much as a speeding ticket. Saulie, your turn."

"Israel. Since her inception. I invested in her. I did okay. Like my friend Fritz says, *now I'm here.*"

"Saul is originally from the U.S. also. Don't let him kid you."

"Sure. Many years ago. I'd been out of the country for several years before Israel. Drifting, looking for myself."

"You find you?" Jed Bodine.

Ha-ha's.

"See you, guys." Jimmy put a wave on it.

"Hey, we gonna end up in a book?" Saul.

"Never know."

Fritz said, "Yes. The price of living near an author." Some cold blue eyes. "I'd watch that Joseph fellow."

The round table consensus seemed to support Fritz.

"Yeah? Why's that?"

"No one knows anything about him. If you were to ask, he'd lie to you."

"Why do you say that?"

Fritz looked off; the general got funny.

"Hey, guys, don't leave me out here in the cold."

Fritz seemed to be the thinker for the quintet. He nodded at General Big-jaw.

The general cleared his throat. "It, uh, seems as Mr. Joseph doesn't exist much beyond moving here. I, uh, had some associates in Washington do some research. "

Jimmy said, "DC?"

The general stumbled over it.

Fritz didn't. He looked at Jimmy. Right at him, knowing Jimmy's being a smart ass.

He smiled at Jimmy, Jimmy's friend now. "Maybe young Mr. Cotton knows Joe Joseph better than we."

Perhaps, old chum. "Know nothing beyond some old folk stories he's told me." Jimmy shrugged. "I wouldn't make too much out of it. He's a law abiding citizen as far as I've seen."

Good old Saul, Mom's buddy, jumped in. "Hey, Jimmy's right. The guy *seems* okay. Give him a break."

"What? Till he does something?" Bodine.

"What?" Saul doing it good, eyebrows up, palms up. "What's he gonna do? Start a gambling hall in his condo?"

Edgar said he wished.

The general didn't think it was a bad idea either.

Jimmy gave them a group shrug. "Mr. Joseph's cool. He's got a pad looks like Hugh Hefner lives there. Got a round bed with black satin sheets."

No one was impressed but Edgar and Saul.

Edgar said: "No shit?"

Saul said something in Yiddish that sounded like what Edgar'd said.

Looked like Joe'd just made a couple of friends.

"No shit. See you boys."

Some waves, some salutations at the back of Jimmy's head. Some glass door, some sidewalk. Some breath.

Jimmy had it. Had Pearlie Friedman.

Had him cold.

[51]

"Who's Fritz Hooseclaw?"

"Holtzclaw. South African dude. He says South African."

"So who is he?"

"He's Pearlie Friedman.

"Wait. Wait. This Fritz fella is Pearlie Friedman?"

"Yeah. That's what I been telling you."

Joe leaned back on his bar stool.

At the breakfast bar, no gin involved. Yet.

"Why?"

"Why what? Because he *is.*" Jimmy was pumped. He elected a finger. "One—his foot. Got a perfect twelve. Hangs over a one foot tile perfect."

Joe grinned. "The dope from the cop about the footprint?"

"Sure. And you said you'd heard Pearlie was in South Africa."

"Among other places, kid." Some thought. "I don't know."

They sat, Jimmy getting pissed.

Maybe two minutes went by. No nothing.

Joe said, "I got some Heineken off the boat. I bet you've never had a Heineken wasn't skunky."

"You're not gonna tell me, are you?"

Joe retrieved a couple of green bottles, found his church key with the Rockette on the handle. Pop and pop.

"No."

"Just *no?*"

"Yeah, just no." A beer held aloft. "I don't wanna bore you, kid."

That might make some sense later, but now it didn't mean shit.

"I'll find out." Jimmy expecting Joe to argue him out of it.

"Don't put all your eggs in one little basket, Jimmy Cotton. You got a list or something, use it. Check mokes off when you're sure on them. When you check him off, forget about him, move on to the next one. That's how it's done, baby."

That's all Jimmy got. No use pushing.

Sideways jump: "How do I open a locked door?"

Joe looked up, beamed. Got off his stool, got a bottle from over the fridge.

He pulled two cut snifters from the same cabinet.

Two the tall way.

Joe sniffed. Ah-ed.

"Kid, you keep breaking your own record for the smartest thing you ever asked me." He held the glass up. "Three hundred forty year-old armagnac. Here's to your education, baby." The glass came up.

The cold finger ran up Jimmy's spine, but the armagnac killed it.

He said: "How do you pop a lock?"

Joe savored. Said, "It's called a rake. I'll get you one works off a batteries."

So what do you say when a conversation goes where this one'd gone?

Maybe: "How about another shot of that juice?"

Joe grinned. "Goes down sweet, don't it?"

• • •

A power rake.

Looked like an electric toothbrush with muscle. Had some little rods sticking out of it. The rods moved like mothers you turned it on.

Did his mom's lock twice, no snags. She was gone.

Did Joe's. He was gone, too.

Locked it. Raked it.

Tried the slider and nearly yanked off one of the magic wands. Okay, so rakes don't like slider locks.

Loose plan: watch Fritz Holtzclaw till he leaves; go in his pad, check him out.

Check what out? See if he left any notes to himself admitting he was Pearlie Friedman?

Maybe just check him out would have to work for right now.

Jimmy sat up in the Australian pines with his chamber pipe, two grams of gold Lebanese hashish, a half sack of decent Jamo collie, three tall Schlitz beers.

Bowls full of collie with flecks of hash stirred in kicked Jimmy's ass up around his shoulders somewhere. The beers didn't do squat to help out.

He was bored, slapping at insects and ready to go. He'd sat on the damp ground till he felt like he could take a hairbrush to his ass it itched so bad.

And here were Fritz and Saul, double-knitted out the ass, the both. Saul juking like a kid, the Fritz doing it cool in his lime green slacks.

Jimmy visually accompanied them to Fritz's Mercedes, an old four-door diesel deal about fifty feet long. The boys smoked off for the evening's reveling.

Time to revel himself. Time to use some new power rake skills.

Fritz, second floor of his mom's building but, uh-oh, one of the adjusted brunettes from his mom's party—the one with the husky voice—out in front, doing something with a big plaid bow on her front door. Stepping back for a look, not happy with what she was getting.

She huffed out some, *Hey, dear,* at Jimmy. He said hey back, kept moving. Went down to Saul's on the ground floor, next building over from Mom's. Why not? He was running with the bad guy. Did that make him a target? His size ten foot didn't count him out, did it?

Raked his lock, pushed open his door.

"Hello?" A question. "Saul?" Nada. "It's me Jimmy Cotton. You home?"

Maybe not. Jimmy eased the door shut until it clicked too loudly in the viscous silence.

It wasn't Joe Ready's place.

Plainer than his mom's place. The whole condo one bland color. Cheap, fifties deco crap. Thin, oval wood shapes. Tables with different levels. Chairs in green and brown vinyl. Bare terrazzo floors—you could have washed the place out with a garden hose. Harvest-gold bar top, avocado appliances. Brown patterned resilient flooring in the kitchen.

Jimmy prowled around in Saul's business at a desk. Some checking account sheets. Some IRS crap, didn't mean shit to Jimmy.

A pilgrim couple salt-and-pepper set in a small cabinet with some other nonsense. Seemed funny a Jewish guy would own pilgrims. Brooms and mops in a taller cabinet.

Plain white dishes, plain stainless tableware.

Double bed with a pink-and-black Afghan, more terrazzo on the floor. More blah everywhere.

Saul might not kill you but he could bore you to death.

The walk-in was full of double knit and wool. Old wrinkled shoes, maybe five pair. Two felt hats and a straw that was almost like a cowboy hat but flat brimmed.

Not much else. A suit bag. A suede suitcase. A lever action rifle with a good-sized scope.

Not much at all. Take a close look.

Two-forty-five Winchester. Oh shit.

So the lock clicks in the other room and Jimmy spends the next two hours under the lower row of Saul's clothes while a Cuban girl half-ass cleans the condo and then screws Saul when he comes back.

While Saul was washing his sins away in the shower, Jimmy hauled ass.

[52]

So now this Saul Goldstein guy's Pearlie. You need to make up your mind, kid." Joe thought it was all too funny.

"It's him. He's got the gun."

"You're saying this milquetoast old Jew is Pearlie Friedman?"

"Yeah."

A head wag. "I could see the Fritz guy. This Saul fella? I ain't seeing it."

"You're fucking with me, aren't you?"

"Yeah."

"Come on, Joe."

"*Come on,* my ass. You work it out. You got my rake. You got my stories. You want I should hold your hand while you go ask them which one's Pearlie?"

"I'll tell you about Saul and his house girl."

"Sweet Melinda? They call her the goddess of gloom. Everybody here's fucking her. So what?"

"What if this gets dangerous?"

"*Gets?* It already is dangerous, baby. Remember somebody shooting your pompano? You got a gun yet?"

"Permit—and hell no I don't *got a gun yet.* Jesus, Joe."

Joe got up, laid his cigar in the beanbag ashtray. Went inside. Reappeared with a couple of Heinekens.

He sat, got comfortable, busted the caps off the beers. Slumped some more. Looked at Jimmy through an upturned bottle, Jimmy seeing the cool cold eyes through green glass. He pushed a beer at Jimmy.

"Then get out, kid. Walk off."

No *go home to mama* in it. Flat. A statement.

Still pissed Jimmy off.

"You don't think I can handle it?"

A shrug. "It ain't *can.*"

Jimmy could feel the flush continuing. He felt like Joe was fucking with his head. Being hip to it didn't seem to deter the feeling. Like Joe was challenging him.

Jimmy chugged the Heinie in like three gulps, stood with his eyes watery.

Joe's eyes still on Jimmy behind the shades.

Joe reached in a front pants pocket, came up with a wicked little bone-handled automatic, shoved it at Jimmy.

"Stick that in your pocket."

Jimmy looked at the pistol, looked back at Joe.

"You know how to use it, don't you, kid?" A head wag. "Oh Jesus. You never shot a gun, have you?"

"No." Jimmy noticed he'd quit acting like he knew shit he didn't since he'd met Joe.

"Hell's bells." Joe rose, "Come on."

"Where to?"

"In the kitchen to get some beers corralled in a cooler. Take them out to the glades, empty 'em and break 'em with your new piece. Come on. And be cautious. That thing's loaded."

• • •

Joe brought a High Standard .22, also an automatic. With that one, from fifty paces, Jimmy could bust a green bottle first shot. The little silver bone handle .25 was worthless. At five-six paces Jimmy could hit most of the bottles, sometimes. Worthless.

Joe said it was a lady's gun—at twenty feet it'd bounce off you anyway.

Jimmy asked about the .22.

"Assassin's gun. Takes to threading you need a muffler on it, but for a handgun it's quiet already. It'll kill a man at fifty feet you're a good shot. Within twenty feet it's deadly. But your pro? He'll use it just like it is. Walk up with it in a newspaper, a map, like he's gonna ask you a question. Pops you two in the eye, goes back to the suburbs somewhere, cuts his grass like he was a regular person. I'll clean it and you can have it you want it."

Jimmy wanted. "I'll clean it."

"That ain't the cleaning I'm talking, kid."

Joe told Jimmy he had another ten-round clip and a holster that went inside your pants. "Don't get caught wearing one a those things. They'll burn you up."

Wow. Jimmy owned a gun. A gat. A piece. Peace creep with a piece. *You say you want a revolution.*

Embarrassingly empowering.

"You ready to go?" The beer was gone, the bottles now shards.

"Sure, kid. Hey, I know a rib joint in blacktown'll make your tongue slap your brains out. Got cane sweetened ice tea tastes like the nectar of the gods."

"You ever regret killing that Harold dude, Pearlie's partner. Know who I mean?"

"Yeah, I know who you mean. Sure I have. Gone both ways at one time, baby. Got drunk and used it for a good reason to put a bullet in my brain." Stalled at the door to his big Caddy. Over the car's top: "Got drunk and used it for a reason *not* to put a bullet in my brain. Let's go get some pig ribs."

Joe opened his door.

Jimmy said, "You think I'm a coward because Kent State scared hell out of me? Because I ran?"

Joe grinned pretty good. "The second the shooting started, you run right then? Break out for wherever?"

272

"Hell no. I got my ass down, tried to see where the shooting was coming from. Which way was out of there, who was shooting at who."

"That's what I figured. See you at the rib joint." And he got in the Cadillac, fired it off.

Jimmy shook his head, looked across the pitiful ass glades. No straight answers out of Joe. The guy spoke in parables like a gangster Jesus.

But, goddam, Jimmy was so unbored he could barely tolerate himself.

The alcohol and the daily adrenaline rushes were wearing well on his psyche. Maybe his karma was drifting a bit, but it wasn't so far gone he couldn't swim out and get it. Maybe.

Hell, it had even gotten to where the cold prickles up his back didn't bug him. Much.

[53]

The mosquitoes had found Jimmy in the Australian pine copse. Cigarettes, reefer—they came through the smoke like B-52's. Big black mothers that would squish when you slapped one.

An hour and change sitting in the bushes; not a clue what he was doing.

Saul's condo was forty feet across some St. Augustine lawn that was almost black in the dark. Jimmy would see him moving around in there.

Hey, here came Fritz across the black grass. Knocked on Saul's slider. A shoebox under an arm, a bottle of hootch in the hand attached to the other arm.

Saul appeared, slid the working panel of glass aside.

Fritz went in. Jimmy could see him hand over the bottle.

A few, Saul came back in frame with a couple of tall ones, gave one over to Fritz. Pulled the drapes over the slider.

Shit.

Fuck it. Jimmy stood, smashed the butt, stepped from the tree cover.

He walked over to the concrete planter that surrounded Saul's patio, put up a foot, untied his sneaker, fumbled with it. Peeped like a guy named Tom through Saul's kitchen window.

Saul and Fritz were at the breakfast bar. Tall drinks on the laminated counter.

Fritz drank deep, mimed humility but moved his lips in appreciation. Slid the shoebox at Saul.

Jimmy put the other foot on the planter, untied that shoe, watched Saul open the shoebox and pull out a pistol, an odd hammerless revolver. Saul hefted it, threw down on some imaginary nemesis. He fiddled; the cylinder flopped open. A wrist movement snapped it shut. He placed the gun back in the box. Replaced the lid.

Saul stood, fished out some folded bills, counted out a few to Fritz.

Fritz recounted, hid the cash in a shirt pocket. He held his drink up in anticipation.

Saul bumped his glass into Fritz's and they sealed the deal with a drink.

Jimmy got the rush under control, noted he was only leaning on a planter, peeking in a window so far as the rest of the world could see.

He turned, walked back to the trees.

The dark shelter wrapped Jimmy. A voice said, "We've got laws against what you were doing just now." Jimmy's feet were ready, set. He recognized the voice—the county cop Hernandez. It didn't settle his pulse though. Only barely kept him from hoofing out.

"Jesus, man."

Some quiet. It fit loosely in the darkness. Jimmy could make the cop's silhouette out was about all.

Some more quiet since there was plenty of room for it.

Then: "The hell are you doing, Cotton?"

Jimmy didn't know so he didn't comment.

The silhouette said: "You're out past the breakers and drifting fast, kid."

He couldn't be ten years older than Jimmy. Calling Jimmy *kid*. Jimmy hadn't mentioned the word *pig* yet, but he was thinking about it.

Prudence ruled. Said, "I was tying my shoes." Even in the dark it sounded lame.

"Sure you were. And I just beamed my ass down from the Enterprise. So now you've found a couple other guys—I'm talking besides Joe *Joseph*—whadda you say's going on here in this happy, groovy little community your mommy's bought into?"

"Fuck you. *Lieutenant.*" Trying to make it sound as shitty as possible. Still thinking: *pig*. Fuck it. "Your mommy make you think your dick's short so you gotta carry a piece and keep your authority in a badge wallet?"

Hernandez's silhouette chuckled. "Fair enough. We'll leave moms out of it. Seriously, kid, what's this guy dragging you into? Honest to God, I don't see you as overly motivated by anything. No slight intended."

None taken. Sorta. "I'm not sure what you're talking about."

"Sure you aren't."

A car pulled by somewhere, sweeping headlights across the cop. He had on Levis, espadrilles, and a black tee shirt with something written on it in day-glo.

The outfit said *off-duty* to Jimmy. It said *personal*.

The lights wicked away.

Quiet.

"These people play with guns, Jimmy."

"Who?"

The snicker. "Funny boy. Here you go. Another freebie on your new playmates. Fritz Holtzclaw? He's facing prison in South Africa if they could get him back there. Wanna know why?" A beat. "Sure you do. Selling arms to guerillas. That wasn't go-rillas, Jimmy. *Gue-rillas.* Guys who'll eat your innards after they kill your white ass."

The current was cold and swift right here.

"Come on, man, I know you got something to say. Something cute Joseph taught you while you guys were drinking and getting high."

Telling Jimmy he'd been watching.

276

Jimmy shrugged. "So bust us."

The nose laugh. Some fumbling. A match. The smell of pot. Good pot. Sativa. Flowers.

The ember lighted Hernandez's face. Lips working on the joint. Finished, he held it out to a reluctant Jimmy.

Jimmy sat tight.

Around the hit: "Come on—you sat here—smoked two already." Again telling Jimmy he'd been watching.

Jimmy took the reefer, hit it.

Wow and a half. Tasted better than it smelled. Maybe double wow.

Jimmy and the cop passed the joint back and forth in the dark. The one studying the other's face when he toked.

Done, the cop thumped the doob off in a showy arc of sparks.

"Jimmy, you're a pretty cool guy. That Kent State shit—musta been hell. Don't get edgy and bored, do something dumb. Okay?"

Jimmy was stoned as a gourd, nothing to say.

The snickering. "You fuck up, call me. I'll see what I can do for you. Here."

The cop passed Jimmy a fat joint. And went into the darkness.

$$\bullet \ \bullet \ \bullet$$

"Good shit, kid." Joe licked a finger, soaked a troubling run line on the reefer. "No doubt, cops get the best dope. Got lots of evidence to select from."

"So what about Fritz, Joe?"

"What about Fritz? The guy sells guns. So what?"

"Call your friend. Find out who he is."

A good grin. "Hold on." Joe slid off the stool. Kept a hand on the breakfast bar for balance—obviously fucked up tonight.

He returned with a couple of pieces of paper and a torn

envelope. Tossed it across the bar to Jimmy, slid back on the stool, nabbed his scotch rocks, drank. All one motion. Smooth tonight—dressy black straw pork pie.

Jimmy read—plain typewriter paper, no letterhead. Fritz Holtzclaw. AKA: Franz Voltz, Sidney Vander Plat, Boris Kelper. The Feds weren't sure who he was. American born maybe. Unavailable for a 1950's court date under the Boris Kelper version. Country of origin unknown. The charge? Possession of stolen guns. Gone until he bobbed up in South Africa. Sold hardware to whoever had the cash. There was a paragraph dedicated to an incident where good old Fritzie took a counter-offer on a shipment, set up the original buyers. Forty-three people executed and dumped in a marsh. Made a nice photo.

What made him rich in Africa ran him out—politics. The volatile sort. Lit down in Miami, then West Palm Beach. Palm Shores Condominiums. The Feds were eyeballing him but laying off. No real proof of who he was, probably.

Jimmy put the pages down, adjusted the little pistol in his waistband. Cleared his throat. Showed Joe some uplifted brows.

Joe went deadpan, said, "Remember a guy in the story I was telling you about the Lindbergh kidnap; remember Pale Anderson?"

"Yeah. Eddie Spaghetti's errand boy."

"Right." No more.

Jimmy watched Joe. "Fritz is Pale Anderson?"

"Yeah. All grown up."

"And Saul's Pearlie Friedman all grown up."

"Sure, kid. Whatcha gonna do about it?"

[54]

Whatcha gonna do about it?
Righteous question. A toughy. Maybe the Sphinx knew the answer. But the sphinx wasn't talking. Neither was Joe. Challenging Jimmy without the challenge. The opposite—daring Jimmy to walk off.

The cop. Asking Jimmy did he know what he'd walked into. Saying Jimmy was being pulled in, duped.

Maybe so. Or maybe Jimmy was just writing down some stories a guy was telling. *Whatcha gonna do about it?* Why should Jimmy do anything about it?

The thing between Joe and Saul/Pearlie was ancient history. Wasn't anything to Jimmy beyond cursory curiosity. Jimmy didn't know if any of it was subject to some statute of limitations. Or if Pearlie Friedman had ever even been charged with anything. The cop didn't know who Pearlie was. Seemingly he didn't—he hadn't mentioned.

Screw it. He was just writing down some stories.

He brought that and a big ass shark tooth back from the surf, went in his mom's patio door. No Mom.

Maybe grab a soda, grab the spiral notebook, nab the shady bench at the park, work on the stories some.

Jimmy opened the desk drawer. Hmm. Maybe by the bed. Nope.

Okay. When did he have it last? After the Parker story. At Joe's.

Jimmy went around the hedge, knocked. No Joe. Then Joe in a silk robe thing, cigarette, the same black pork pie as last night and slippers. At ten in the morning.

He slid the door back but stood fast in the opening.

"Hey, kid. What's happening?"

"Not much. I leave my notebook over here?"

"Nah. Look wherever you got stoned last." A grin on it. "Look, Jimmy, I'm . . . entertaining here." A head jerk at the bedroom.

"Oh. Shit. Sorry. See you later, Joe."

"See you, kid."

The door slid shut. Jimmy watched Joe disappear through the hall doorway.

Turned, went back home, to his room. Turned it upside down. No notebook.

The caffeine in a Dr. Pepper got his brain revved. He'd come back from Joe's, made some notes in the margins, put the book and the mechanical pencil right there, in that drawer.

Look in the drawer for time number ten or twelve. Still no notebook. But the pencil right there.

A juice rush warmed his face, made his hands feel funny. Made his ears tingle.

No way. No way Pearlie broke in here and took it. Unless maybe he had a good power rake like Jimmy did.

• • •

Jimmy gnawed at his fingernails—got one to bleed—till Dot came in.

"Hi." Like she was surprised.

"Hi, Mom. Seen my notebook?"

"Nope." Mom real quiet. Funny acting. "I'm going to shower and get ready for a lunch date."

"Yeah? With who?" A date?

"Oh, with Joe. Next door." Not looking at Jimmy. Getting busy putting dishes in the dishwasher.

Okay. "Where were you?" Rats gnawing quietly at the back of Jimmy's brain.

"With a friend. My but you're in a curious mood this morning."

"You, too."

It got Mom's attention. She blushed, went through the hall to her room, closed the door.

No way. A long, lead breath. Please, no.

Fuck it.

Off the stool, out the slider, banging on Joe's.

Joe, still in robe and slippers, Bloody Mary going, hat going.

Opens the slider, says: "You're just in time, baby." Held up the hemic beverage.

"Are you fucking my mom?"

Joe took a long drink, sighed. "Yeah, kid."

Boom. Just like that. *Yeah, kid.*

This wouldn't stop there. "How long's this been going on?" Sounding like a parent.

"Does it really matter, kid? Do you really want details? Your mom's a healthy middle-aged woman with the same urges. . . ."

That was enough. Jimmy put a hand up, palm at Joe.

He just kinda walked off, across the lawn, across the air. He was spinning so fast, felt so light, he could have walked across the water.

He tried.

It didn't happen so he stood in the ocean, knee-deep, gentle swells chilling his balls.

Christ. Where'd this part fit? Joe and Dot. Balling. Oh, God, what a horrible visual. Jimmy slapped the water.

How about just swimming out, try and make Spain.

He stood there a long time. Till the tidal current had undercut his feet, and he was ankle deep in the sand below.

Still nowhere to put it, he walked up to the cloistering copse of Australian pines. Flopped down, leaned on a tree.

The roach from the cop joint was tucked behind the cellophane of his Kools. He made a Jefferson Airplane from a strip of match cover, smoked it until the cardboard made him cough.

Some better. Not much though.

Jimmy knew a fat girl with flowers in her hair who still had a few grams of the Lebanese hash. Maybe she'd be at the park playing marginal guitar and singing off-key.

He stood, brushed sand off the seat of his pants, took one step. Froze.

Flies were going in and out Fritz Holtzclaw's mouth. Pale Anderson's mouth. Holy shit. And right where the cop had been standing last night. Holy shit.

Holy fucking shit.

Jimmy ran through the length of the tree cover, away from Palm Shores. Slowed when the trees ended. Walked fast across the park.

Down a wooden stair. To a drum playing trash can on the beach. Puked his last three months of life up. Puked until the heaves set in, bitter bile on his tongue, eyes watering, tears mingling with saliva and snot and goo. All stringing down his chin in fine strands.

Jimmy stumbled to the outdoor shower station by the park pavilion. Shirt and all, under the cold jets of water.

A couple of kids, a boy and a girl who could be related, stared at Jimmy, Jimmy washing out his mouth, spitting, blowing stuff out of his nose.

The boy was wet when Jimmy walked up, but the girl stood outside the circle of water, one palm enjoying the spray. They simultaneously sprang away, giving Jimmy a couple of looks over sunburned shoulders.

All the mucus expressed, Jimmy shook off like a dog. Breathed deep a couple of breaths.

Call the cops? Answer questions about peeking in on Fritz and Saul?

Pearlie.

Whatever.

Pale Anderson, Boris Kelper.

Jesus Christ. Who the fuck's on first?

Go see the cops and what if snoopy-ass Hernandez was watching Jimmy, watched him go in the trees, watched him run out?

Fuck. No choice. Straight to Joe's slider, but skirting the Australian pines. No one in the trees with Fritz. Yet.

Pound and no Joe. Pound harder. Loud enough Joe emerged sleepy and disgruntled looking.

He slid the door. "Tell me we ain't gotta fight over this thing." He blinked his eyes open, stretched his arms in a plain white tee shirt. Plaid Bermudas hung below. "Come in." Stepped aside. "The fuck happened to you? You fall off the pier?"

Jimmy dashed in. Sat at the bar. Said: "I need a drink. Something strong."

Joe got the decanter with the armagnac. Got the two matching snifters. Poured three fingers in each.

Jimmy nailed his. Sat the goblet down, eyes still having enough left in the tear ducts to water up a little. "Hit me."

Joe watched. Poured.

Half the glass. Jimmy nailed it.

He would have puked if there was anything left inside him besides his nuts.

"Fritz, Pale Anderson—he's dead in the trees." A head jerk.

A moment of quiet. Then: "You kill him?"

"Hell no I didn't kill him. Almost stepped on him, flies in his mouth."

"Flies already found him, huh?"

Already? "Whadda I do?"

"What? You didn't kill him. You see who did?"

"No."

"Then it ain't none a your business."

"But I saw him give Saul—Pearlie—a gun last night."

"While peeping in a window. Jeez, kid, you trying to get Dot bounced out a here?"

Jimmy put out questioning hands.

"Somebody'll find him. You know what I'm wondering?"

"Yeah. Why'd Pearlie kill him. I think I know. My notebook's gone. Anderson got a mention. Maybe Pearlie felt like it was gettin' too crowded."

Joe had no expression. "Plus Pale sold him the gun he's gonna do me and you with."

"Yeah, I thought of that, too." Another one: "Why'd Pearlie put him right outside his own back door?"

"Goddam, kid, Pearlie's seventy-something. How far's he gonna run with a rug over a shoulder?"

Jimmy chewed the inside of a cheek, "I gotta go back, see if he got the notebook for sure."

"Don't do it, kid."

Didn't really sound like Joe meant it.

[55]

Some guy taking a shit found Fritz Holtzclaw—Pale Anderson—about two o'clock.

Looked like everybody who lived at the Shores was watching. Cop cars on the St. Augustine. A meat wagon full of Fritz was stuck in a sandy spot, a lot of cops rocking it in near unison.

Lieutenant Hernandez was there—shirt and tie, no joints. Looking across the crowd at Jimmy, creeping Jimmy out.

Some guys with sandwich bags and tongs didn't seem to be having much luck.

Jimmy shouldered out of the crowd, kicked his clogs behind the sea wall, hit the beach.

The curl was cool on his hot feet. He splashed at some baitfish with his toes. Too fast for him.

So was Hernandez.

His voice said, "Jimmy. Hey, Jimmy."

Jimmy stopped, turned. Hernandez was cutting an intersect to Jimmy's path. He'd left his shoes somewhere too.

As he approached, he loosened the tie, popped his top button, tugged at the tie some more. He could have been some guy worked in an architect's office but for the big revolver high on his hip.

He fell in, said, "Let's walk."

And talk, Jimmy was betting.

285

Didn't take long. "That could have been you lying out there, flies shitting on your lips."

"So you don't think I killed him?"

"Oh hell no. You're on the victim team. You're one of the kill-ees, not kill-ers."

"Thanks."

"Just how I see it, brother. Why'd Joseph kill him? He know about Joseph's past?"

Jimmy grinned but mostly inside. The cop didn't know shit about Pearlie Friedman. Didn't seem like for all his sneaking around he'd seen much more than Fritz going in Pearlie's last night if that.

"Hadn't heard one way or another."

A hundred feet, Hernandez stopped. Faced Jimmy when Jimmy stopped.

"I'm no lawyer but if this Holtzclaw guy's death ends up connected to whatever it is you're withholding. . . ." He let it fall. "Maybe you should go ahead and get yourself a lawyer lined up." A cop grin. "Cause I'm going to pick you up eventually. See you."

Jimmy watched the cop's white back go as they had come. At the park, he climbed the stair and used the boardwalk.

Jimmy walked another fifty-sixty miles down the beach, then back. No one home at Dot's.

He had a couple of chicken potpies and watched "The Beverly Hillbillies." Cleaned up his mess, grabbed the rake.

Jimmy laid a crooked path, doubling back on himself to see if his favorite cop was following. Didn't seem that way. Hung out in the laundry room a while just to be sure.

Then back in the trees, steering wide of the spot Fritz was using this afternoon. He could see Pearlie in there at the kitchen sink, puttering. Dried his hands, cut the TV, locked the slider, dropped a broom handle in the channel.

The front door closed, keys jingled. Silence. Jimmy couldn't

Please return the items by the
due date(s) listed below, to
any Memphis Public Library
location. For renewals:
Automated line: 452-2047
Central Branch: 415-2702
Online: www.memphislibrary.org

Date due: 2/22/2022,23:59
Item ID: 0115284143001
Title: If I disappear [large prin
t] : a novel
Author: Brazier, Eliza Jane,

By using the Memphis Public Libra
ries, you saved: $34.99

Date due: 2/22/2022,23:59
Item ID: 0115273210902
Title: The devil's odds : a myste
ry
Author: Burton, Milton T.

By using the Memphis Public Libra
ries, you saved: $25.99

Date due: 2/22/2022,23:59
Item ID: 0115281867362
Title: The vanishing season
Author: Schaffhausen, Joanna,

By using the Memphis Public Libra
ries, you saved: $24.99

2/22/2022,23:59

see around the corner but Pearlie was gone. He didn't use his car; Jimmy needed to jam.

The rake was out when he rapped on the door. No answer.

Jimmy inserted the rake.

The door opened on the next condo over.

Jimmy almost snapped the picks off yanking the rake out.

He was knocking when the neighbor noticed him.

It was a chubby blond Jimmy thought he'd met but couldn't remember her name.

"Hi, doll. How's all?"

Jimmy could smell the perfume from where he stood—a good twenty feet away.

"Great. You?"

"Perfect, doll. Saulie's not there. He's at Fred and Alta's party. You going?" Hungry old hen.

"Maybe. Hey, I'll see you." And back around the corner of the building.

A look. Blondie was swishing a large tush down the sidewalk.

She turned a corner and Jimmy raked his way in.

Damn, he was getting good at this breaking and entering.

Jimmy pressed the door shut like it was a moth's wing. No click. Rake in the pants? Nope—little .25 cal pistol there. He held on to the rake.

A low lamp was on in the living room, the only light.

Not a thing new in the living room. Not on the breakfast bar. Not on the dining table.

Jimmy hit the kitchen light and wouldn't have seen it but the way the spiral wire peeked out around a box of Chex made it jump out. The notebook.

Shit, what a rush.

Cut the light; grab the notebook.

Out the slider? No, Pearlie'd put the stick in there. Front door opens. Spin.

"I figured you'd show."

There's Pearlie Friedman. Not looking shit like goofy Saul. The hammerless pistol pointed at Jimmy's chest.

"Mitts up, punk." A pistol gesture.

Jimmy put his hands up, got relieved of his new pistol. He was rushing like hell.

The rush went south, settled in Jimmy's knees, putting a little rubber in them. Pearlie told him to sit and Jimmy was ready. He slid on a bench on the wall side of the table.

"First I thought it'd be Ready. Then I figured he'd use you. It's how he operates."

Pearlie held the piece down, drew the slider drapes by hand.

"You're a smart boy, sonny. So smart you let Ready get you killed."

"You gonna put me out there where they found Fritz?"

"Why not? Only a moron would dump two stiffs on his own back lawn, right? See, I'm afraid to talk to the cops about it, but I saw Ready coming out of the trees last night. Tonight too, after you're out there."

Jimmy didn't have squat to add.

"I'm gonna see how smart you are, Jimmy. I give you ten grand, you forget about those stories?"

Jimmy acted like he had to think about it, like his new artistic streak might be worth dying for. "Sure." It was only a game he and Saul were playing anyway.

"One more thing. Call Ready. Tell him to come down here." Pearlie's eyes were flashes of gray. He pushed a phone at Jimmy. "Call him."

Jimmy said, "I don't know his number. Never called him."

Pearlie grabbed the phone, spun the rotor, stood, put the pistol to Jimmy's head, and spun one last number. "Don't fuck up, baby."

A few quiet purrs, Joe answered with a simple *hello.*

"I need you at Saul's."

Some quiet. "He got a gun to your head?"

"You could say that."

288

"I'll see you in a flash." And was gone.

Please call the cops, Joe. Please.

A knock not thirty seconds later.

Pearlie backed to the door, stood behind it, and tripped the lock.

Joe came in like he did it everyday at least once. Waltzed by Pearlie, said, "'Lo, Pearlie." Slid in beside Jimmy.

Pearlie's waving the pistol at Joe.

"Get up, asshole. I gotta feel you up. Get up."

"Sure, Pearlie. Take it easy." Hands up preaching innocence. They came down to slide Joe off the bench. One of them slid Jimmy a pistol. Joe stood, hands at half-mast.

Pearlie felt him, found a trim Luger-looking pistol under Joe's shirt.

Pearlie gleamed. "Perfect. You two crazies break in here, got heat, I blast you both. I like it. How about you mokes? You like?"

Pearlie hit Joe across the face with his gun barrel. "Sit down, asshole. You shot me once." Hit Joe across the back of the head when he turned to sit.

Joe slumped, holding his face.

He pulled his hand down. There was a little blood on it.

"Come on, Pearlie. You'd never sell that to anyone. Once the G-boys find out who you are, you're screwed. Give it up—we all walk away. You don't hurt the kid, I leave you alone."

Pearlie laughed. It was too happy. "Leave me alone? You've ruined my fucking life, Ready. You screwed me with Lansky and the mob. You've chased me around for forty years."

"I knew you were in Israel. I just couldn't find your miserable ass."

Jesus. Joe baiting the prick.

"Might'a ended up like Cuba for you, asshole."

"Where'd you go? Early fifties? Israel?"

"Nah. Did Tripoli for a bit, black market gig. Made dough. Went to Egypt, then Israel. Thinking you had to be dead."

Pearlie uncorked a bottle of J&B, slugged from the neck.

"I come here, you show up. Bastard. Like a recurring nightmare. Then fucking Pale Anderson shows up. Like I needed some more bad advertisement. The only moke can pin a chill on me shows up out a the blue." A slug of J&B, a gesture with the bottle. "You know that, Ready? You know Pale saw me smoke a deputy in Missouri? Sure you did. You fucking know everything."

Jimmy thought: *Oh, shit.*

Pearlie cocked his head. Shook it. "You son of a bitch. You brought him."

Joe shrugged like it didn't matter much. "I told him I'd spill his cover he didn't show. Told him I needed him to nail you. So I lied. Kill me."

Pearlie went red-faced. "Don't push it. We'll get there. Pale, the dumb bastard. He tried to tell me. Waltzed around it till I started looking at you. Thinking: *Yeah, it's him.* I jumped Pale, made him tell me he knew you. Told me he could sell me a piece to take care a you."

"So you used Pale's piece and killed him."

"Hell no. I popped him with a throwaway piece. It's out there in the ocean. Off the end a the pier. All because you gotta stick the kid's notebook in my face."

"Wow. Lookit Pearlie being smart, kid. Been a dumb ass all his life. All he had going was that cockroach survival thing. The king of lamming out." Joe grinned at Jimmy, grinned at Pearlie. "You'll fuck this up, too, Pearlie. Wait and see don't you fuck it up." More grin. "Marian Parker."

"What?"

"Who. The girl you left with Renahan and Hickman."

"How's that my cross?"

"You knew what'd happen you leave a twelve-year-old with those two psychos. It is your cross, Pearlie."

Pearlie was getting it. Getting what it was all about and couldn't believe it. "Over a twelve-year-old girl, you ruin my life?"

"You're a fucking weasel, Pearlie."

Jimmy's eyes jumping from Joe to Pearlie, back, forth. An aura of unreality came like a warm cloud. It fell from the ceiling, made the room unbearable.

Pearlie raised the pistol. "Say bye, asshole."

"Shoot him, kid. For Christ sake, shoot him."

Jimmy raised the gun Joe'd passed him. It was the High Standard. He hit the safety as it cleared the table.

Pearlie saw it, swung his pistol on Jimmy, pulled the trigger. The hammerless revolver clicked; the .22 cracked twice in the abyss.

One pill hit Pearlie in the center of his neck. The other went through his left eye. The revolver clicked again. Pearlie flexed at the knees then collapsed from the waist when his knees hit the floor. He went head first into the linoleum. Blood came quickly, ran across the hard slick floor.

The noise died. No one moved. Then Pearlie gave it one last animal thrash, his feet looking for purchase. He bulldozed on his face for a few inches and it was over.

Joe reached over, took the pistol from Jimmy's hand, flicked the safety. He stood, grabbed up the pistols Pearlie had collected. He waited at the door and Jimmy didn't know how much time had passed.

His eyes came off Pearlie. He looked at his hand, looked at Joe.

"You fucking bastard. You fucker. You set me up. *You* took the goddam notebook. What'd you do, break in and fuck his gun up?"

"Let's go, kid."

"Fuck you." Jimmy stood, ready to knock Joe out. "Just like you always do. Set it up. Sneak around. Manipulate. Get somebody else to do the dirty work. You feel smart? Smartie."

"Look, kid, this started out, all I offered you was something more than vicarious. That's what you said you needed. Hey, there it is, your something more than vicarious, leaking on the floor. I'm leaving. You better come on."

[56]

The gentle boxed light over Joe's bed flickered. A couple of machines went wild over the power glitch.

The light went away. A diesel generator fired up in the dark. The lights came to. Flickered. A big boom. Dark.

Sunlight was fighting for its life off to the east, making the sky a subtle pallet of blues and violets. Jimmy slid his hard chair over by Joe. Said, "You cool?"

"I'm cool." A hand came over, rested on Jimmy's shoulder. "Finish it, kid. I'm tired."

• • •

Next day, Joe's gone. His stuff's there but he's gone. A few more days a moving outfit shows. Packs Joe's belongings out.

Dot was stoic so she knew something. Jimmy didn't ask. He just waited on the cop, Hernandez, to drop by. Practiced not confessing to cold-blooded murder.

Nothing happened. Lots of cops when they—whoever *they* were—found Pearlie. The paper noted both Pearlie and Pale Anderson were found within forty feet of each other, and Special Agent So-and-so of the FBI would pass on information as it came in. Yeah—the Feds nabbed the case. No Hernandez for nearly four months.

Nothing but Dot flying off every couple of months or so, being mysterious about it. Jimmy never asked. Didn't want to know. Didn't want to see Joe.

Didn't want to see the cop.

One out of two ain't bad.

The cop showed on one of his mom's weekenders.

Walked up on Jimmy burning one on the patio.

"You joined the force you'd smoke better dope."

A blue spiral notebook hit the metal tabletop, shook the umbrella.

Jimmy recognized it but he didn't touch it.

After a bit, Hernandez pointed at it. "You know, if the Feds weren't such pricks they'd have that in one of their deep file cabinets. They'd maybe have you, too, if I was as big a prick as you think I am." Hernandez sat, gave Jimmy some room.

Then: "The guy in the corner unit, Saul. He was Pearlie Friedman, huh?"

Jimmy wasn't ready for this, but here it was. "Seems like."

"This was an old grudge, you believe what Joseph—excuse me—Ready told you."

"Yeah. Seems like."

"Who was the guy in the trees?"

Fuck it. "Pale Anderson."

Hernandez thought about it. "The gopher in the Lindbergh tale. Okay. Where's he fit?"

"Bit player. A chump."

"Like you?"

"Yeah. Like me."

"You know, the Feds clamped this thing down tighter than a spinster's knees. Dared me to come talk to you." Some quiet. "Your buddy Ready made you golden."

"Yeah, but here you are, huh?"

"The Feds got short attention spans and a tight travel budget. They've been gone." Brief pause, then: "Who killed Anderson? Ready?"

"Friedman."

"You hear him say that?"

"Yeah. He did it. Tossed the gun off the pier."

The cop said that's what he'da done, too; then he was quiet for a while.

He pulled out one of his nice joints, used Jimmy's matches on it.

A few tokes, he passed it. Jimmy took it. Hit it.

The cop said, "It scared shit out of you, didn't it? Even more than Kent State."

Jimmy toked, nodded, exhaled, "Yeah."

The doob went down in silence.

They sat.

Hernandez rose suddenly. "I'll see you. If you're unlucky, that is." He took a few steps. Stopped. Didn't look back.

"He trick you into killing Friedman?"

"Reading the stories, it would seem that way."

Hernandez shook his dark mop. He turned. Had a decent smile.

"I had it all wrong, didn't I? That shit about *kill-ers* and *kill-ees.*"

"Seems like."

[57]

The lights flickered back but not like they were excited about it.

None of Joe's machines made a peep, all purring quietly.

The sun was dancing behind the cypress trees in the window like it had won the lotto.

Jimmy reached up, laid his hand on Joe's hand.

"Love you, baby."

In a bit they came and gathered up Joe Ready's skin and bones, took them where you take such non-essentials.

Jimmy sat in the room with the rest of Joe for a long time. Thinking. And there it was.

Watch the pea; don't watch the cups. For thirty years Jimmy saw what went down as an old grudge between Joe and Pearlie, with Jimmy playing patsy. Un-un.

Pearlie played patsy. Joe had used him.

Was never anybody *throwing in* with anybody. Joe had chosen Jimmy. Outta everybody in the world had appointed Jimmy his successor. Boxed Jimmy in, left him little say in it.

Why? Maybe he'd seen some defining something in Jimmy that said Jimmy could be good at Joe's game. Maybe he just liked Jimmy. Maybe Jimmy had just been available. It really didn't matter. Joe saw it as an honor and made Jimmy tell the story through so Jimmy would get it.

Jimmy smiled, shook his head. To no one but Joe, he said, "You coulda just told me, Joe." He sat for a bit with his newfound honor. Smiled a lot.

When he felt like he could walk around in a lesser world, he got up and used the door, used the hall, used the elevator.

The lobby doors, big glass twins, conceded the morning and Jimmy walked out into it. It was raining the day Joe Ready was born. It was raining now.